BRIAN CALLISON was born in Manchester in 1934. He was educated at the High School of Dundee before entering the merchant navy in 1950 as midshipman with the Blue Funnel Line, sailing mainly on cargo liners to the Far East and Australia. On leaving the sea he studied at Dundee College of Art. He has held several administrative posts, including managing director of a construction company and general manager of a large entertainment centre.

He also served several years in the territorial army with the 51st Highland Division Provost Company, Royal Military Police, and now maintains an active connection with the sea as Head of Unit, Royal Naval Auxiliary Service.

His first phenomenally successful novel *A Flock of Ships* was published in 1970 and has already been translated into nine foreign languages. This was followed by ten more novels, of which *The Sextant* is the most recent. No less an authority than Alistair MacLean has said, 'there can be no better adventure writer in the country today.'

BRIAN CALLISON

The Sextant

FONTANA/Collins

First published by William Collins Sons & Co. Ltd 1981
First issued in Fontana Paperbacks 1982

Copyright © Brian Callison 1981

Made and printed in Great Britain by
William Collins Sons & Co. Ltd, Glasgow

To my wife, Phyllis,
who reminds me – in the nicest possible way –
of one of the characters in this novel.

CHAPTER ONE

I let myself into the flat using the key they always kept for me between voyages. The way Charlie and Fran were with me, it was almost like having a home of my own. In fact, the way Charlie was, it was almost like having a wife of my own, come to that.

Fran was ironing a bedspread in the kitchen when I walked through. Draped over the board, it afforded an uncharacteristic anonymity to whatever, if anything, she was wearing from the navel down. From the rounded line of her hips upwards there wasn't any doubt at all.

She looked up and gave me a little smile as I entered; a naked, golden half-Venus rising from a sea of blue candlewick. With a Hoover steam iron in her hand.

'Did you get it?' she asked curiously. Unnecessarily too, I suppose, considering it was hooked awkwardly under my arm.

I put the box on the kitchen table and walked over to the window, staring down into the street. Alexandra Parade presents little scenic charm even on one of Glasgow's sunnier days. In the rain it looks drab. In November rain it looks sort of gloomy Gothic, struggling to stay afloat above a tideline of rising damp. I still gazed stolidly out of the window; the Parade's melancholia was more appropriate to my mood of that moment than Fran's voluptuous immodesty.

Lord, but she was statuesque in her domestic abandonment all the same. And it had seemed a long voyage, my last one. Long and lonely, and bleakly celibate. Perhaps the dignity of being master of my own ship had finally elevated me above the carnal necessities common to certain of my less monastic complement – or maybe I hadn't fancied the charms of the nineteen-eighties ladies of Lagos, Douala and Takoradi any more this time than I had those of their mothers as a wide-eyed first-trip apprentice, way back in fifty-three.

Or had it been nineteen fifty-two? And might they not have been their grandmothers . . . ?

I couldn't help being acutely conscious of the box, still sitting on the table in its brown paper wrapping with the Strathclyde Police Authority stamp on it. And so was Fran. That didn't surprise me any more than her state of homespun *deshabillé*, mind you; she might have substituted tumbling raven hair and magnetic cleavage for the slightly battered aspect of the archetypal male newspaper reporter, but she retained the same undeviating ability to sense a story – my nymph of the steam iron would reach for her shorthand notebook at the merest hint of mystery.

And that was precisely what that innocuous box did hold – a mystery. It was one so intensely personal, so unsettling in the way it blew forty-year-old cobwebs from long-forgotten grief, that I hadn't yet begun to grasp the scope of the questions it raised; the full import of its inexplicable resurrection . . .

I heard the board creak behind me as she began to iron again. I guessed the curiosity was killing her and loved her all the more for her perception. We'd been together for a long time, Fran and Charlie and I. An unconventional – no, dammit – a downright Bohemian relationship between two men and a beautiful woman – but this was one of the reasons for its durability. It was a tender understanding.

An old man was walking on the opposite pavement. He had a fat black and white dog with him and I couldn't decide whether he was taking it for a walk, or it was taking him . . . but there was a bond between them too, which transcended

6

leather linking collar to gnarled hand; a tongue-lolling happiness at ground level easing to the quiet pleasure of having a true friend as shown in the old man's tolerance. I wondered if closer observation wouldn't reveal an anticipatory sadness there as well, though. Old men die; fat black and white dogs die; some not-so-old master mariners die – a great many do in time of war . . . There wasn't a war right now, but there had been. Once. What had seemed, until that moment, a very long time ago . . .

'It's a sextant!' I said, staring down at the panting, skittering tug-dog with enormous concentration.

Behind me the creaking of the ironing board ceased momentarily.

'Oh?' she encouraged softly. She didn't have to frame the next question, but even if she had put it into words I couldn't have answered. There aren't any solutions; not to impossible riddles. Rain blew in under the crumbling stone lintel, spattering the glass, and the old man and the fat dog fuzzed briefly into a thousand distorted reflections. I frowned, parrying her unspoken plea with clumsy patronage.

'A sextant's a navigating instrument. Every seaman officer has his own. It's an optical method of measuring heavenly bodies . . .'

The particularly heavenly body astern of me was gentle in her censure. 'And for calculating distances off; vertical danger angles; horizontal angles in lieu of a station pointer . . . You'd be surprised at the irrelevant information journalists retain even after we've filed our copy, John. And it wasn't all that long ago that I covered a branch meeting of the Nautical Institute. They were very helpful. Everyone wanted to demonstrate how to hold it.'

'I'll bet!' I thought, never sure whether she was subtly baiting me or if she really did possess a naiveté in proportion to her sexuality. I muttered 'Sorry' and went back to agonising over the box on the table.

The fat dog towed its attendant charge from port to starboard and out of sight. It wasn't four o'clock yet but already Glasgow was darkening under another winter night. The window panes were rapidly changing from transparency to mirror, reflecting the higher light intensity from within the room. Fran had started ironing again and I could detect her fullness clearly now; moving rhythmically from side to side, a rain-sparkling image of every man's secret aspiration. Yet she found no welcome from my disordered mind. Sextant. Sex . . . I swung round, not meaning to be harsh, but Fran was Fran and she couldn't resist it.

She arched her head, shook her hair until it tumbled wantonly over her brown shoulders, and sucked in her diaphragm to a taut plane of lasciviousness. Her mouth offered a cheeky invitation. 'Ready now, sailor?' she challenged huskily.

God, but I loved her. For her beauty and her outrageousness and her dedication to fleshy pleasure. And for her spiritual closeness to me. To us both; because there was Charlie as well.

'Put some bloody clothes on,' was all I actually said. 'An' stop tarting about like a brothel queen.'

She pouted. 'But I like pretending to be a brothel queen. I would have *been* one if I hadn't got a job with the *Northern Citizen* instead.'

'*And* you'd've been very, very good at it,' I retorted; struggling to lift myself out of the maelstrom of doubt that the box had cast me into. 'But Charlie will be home in a few minutes, and I've got something else on my mind, believe it or not -- so cover yourself up like a good reporter and let me think.'

She relaxed her pose fractionally. It didn't help in the slightest.

'Charlie doesn't mind. Charlie can watch if he wants.'

I sniffed, long past being shocked by anything Fran

suggested. 'Charlie won't want to. Charlie'll just get bored, you know what Charlie's like.'

She frowned suddenly. There was a disappointment there, as if she'd just been reminded of her greatest failure. 'No I don't,' she answered enigmatically. 'I *don't* know what Charlie's like . . .'

Her voice trailed off as I began carefully to remove the brown paper wrapping from the parcel. I knew her second strongest drive had taken charge.

She came out from behind the ironing board and stood beside me, gazing down. I detected the warmth of her proximity, and the fresh-scrubbed scent of her skin. I stopped unwrapping.

'Clothes!' I muttered, more as a plea than an order. 'A dressing gown or something?'

'Yes, John,' she said meekly; a little girl suddenly; anxious not to delay the great revelation any longer than necessary. I waited until she padded back from the bedroom, all legs and tousled hair and wide expectant eyes, and sighed inwardly as I finally opened the package. The carelessly tied wrap she'd shrugged into had done more to heighten her sensuality than all her previous nudity.

But as I've said before – Fran was quite simply, quite ingenuously Fran. And that was why both Charlie and I loved her. In our different ways.

It was a polished rosewood box, slightly battered and darkening around the edges under its patina of age, but beautifully made with a care and craftsmanship underlining the standards of the era from which it had come. When I lifted the enclosed copy of the Strathclyde Police receipt it revealed the brass name plate recessed into the instrument case lid. It, too, had been inset with pride, and the precision of long-dead hands.

I gazed down at it for a long moment, and so did Fran. There was an unfamiliar tightness in my throat, while I could

9

hear her quiet breathing. She didn't understand yet – God, neither did I, for that matter – but she seemed to sense, somehow, that I was undergoing one of the most traumatic experiences of my forty-five-year-long life.

She could never have guessed at the real truth, though. That she was watching me open a grave I'd imagined had been covered for nearly four decades. Yet that was precisely what I was doing, as I slowly lifted that time-dignified lid . . .

It lay there, gleaming softly under the light, its triangular frame and the black ivory handle on the underside held securely by the worn chamois-covered locating blocks. The index bar with its brass microscope still remained neatly up and down in a proper seamanlike manner, while the brass telescope sat trimly in its collar. It was a vernier sextant, which again betrayed its age – not for the older generations of navigators were the advantages of micrometer indexes – and both clamp and tangent screws revealed evidence of wear around their milled edges.

I swallowed with ever-increasing difficulty. I was staring at the erosion caused by the fingers of a very personal ghost.

Yet I knew I couldn't possibly be *doing* such a thing.

Because there are certain lost men who can never, ever return from the dead. And neither can the possessions which they once held so dear.

I began to cry. Right there in that bloody tenement kitchen fronting Glasgow's Alexandra Parade – I, Captain John Herschell, a rugged, seen-it-all deep sea sailorman who'd never revealed his true feelings since he was seven years old. I heard Fran whisper in a voice full of wonderment, 'It . . . it's beautiful, John. You must be very proud to own it.'

And that was the moment when I began to cry.

*

She still had her arms round me when Charlie came in. He whistled and clumped pointedly all the way from the front door, but Fran was above that sort of discretion. I wasn't, though Oh, I didn't mind him seeing us together like that – as I've already said, convention had long been abandoned between us – but I was damned if I'd let him catch me with a trembling upper lip.

I was sniffing, and easing Fran's leech-like embrace, and trying half-heartedly to replace the wrap over silky, swelling parts of her that simply refused to stay covered when he bumbled through to the kitchen. For a long second our eyes met, and there was understanding there; then he grinned.

'Hallo, sailor. Long trip, was it?'

'It seemed as if it was.'

He grinned again while Fran stuck her tongue out towards him through the strands of hair collapsing delightfully across her face. 'It looks like it did. I'll go out again if you like.'

'Cheerio, Charlie!' Fran said encouragingly. I slapped her sharply on the bottom and she giggled.

'Hello, Charlie,' I nodded, smiling too now. I hadn't forgotten the box, and the riddles it presented, but somehow my embarrassing tears had assuaged the first hurt. I felt better, especially as we were all together again. I took his proffered hand and shook it warmly.

'Had a busy day, Charlie?'

He shrugged. 'Female corpse in the Clyde off Stobcross Quay; a wee milk laddie slashed and robbed over in Cardonald; a parrot that can recite the whole of Tam o' Shanter in the Royston Road and a couple of rapes ... pretty quiet.'

Charlie was a newspaperman, too. Also with the *Citizen*. But he wasn't any more typical of the journalistic image than his soft-scented colleague beside me. I gazed at him, thinking how little he'd changed since we'd been boys together and I was a uniform-proud mini-sailor while he'd been a case-room gopher down in the old *Daily Mail*. He was still handsome as ever. His blond hair and his six-foot-two frame, the slightly flattened boxer's nose and the shoulders that had bored into many an international rugger scrum on the hacked Murrayfield turf – they were the things Charlie had which caused many a wistful lady's eye to stray, and assess, and linger an adventurous moment.

Fran's irrepressible appetite had been whetted for rather more than a moment when their journalistic paths finally converged in the reporters' room of the *Northern Citizen*; while my own inter-voyage returns to what was then Charlie's flat offered an inducement to add an element of the sexually outrageous. That was how it all began – how the three of us came to be as one in a second-floor tenement on Alexandra Parade, and how we all lived happily, closely and in complete accord. Only it had slowly dawned on Fran that the thing she wanted most out of her relationship – the free use of Charlie's undeniably well-constructed body at any time of the day or night; along with his washing machine and deep fat fryer and Hoover steam iron of course – was being constantly denied her despite everything she could do in the way of the erotic and libidinous to display her charms. Her fondly anticipated *ménage à trois* dwindled to a *ménage à* two and a half . . . her enthusiastic entry into the world of liberated sex was somehow, with an engaging lack of animosity that only Charlie could have contrived, converted to a truly bizarre consortship.

Because it was only after she'd moved in with him, and become hopelessly captivated by his roguish charm, that she was finally forced to concede that on a physical plane she had not only lost the battle of the sexes, but also the war. That she would never make it with Charlie as a ready-use lover.

I don't mean Charlie was gay, or even a homosexual who didn't hunt the action . . . no! It was more complex than that; rooted from birth in some physiological shortcoming which, surprisingly, never appeared to concern Charlie one bit. Maybe it was even something in his favour – at least it allowed him to bumble through life without experiencing the frustrations of more conventional mortals in pursuit of carnal satisfaction.

Of course I'd known he was like that for years. And don't get me wrong – I loved Charlie Sullivan, but only as the brother I'd never had. Everything I needed to satisfy my concupiscent demands was amply supplied by the insatiable enthusiasm of Fran. And because of the way he was, Charlie didn't feel one twinge of jealousy. It was a tender, crazy, incredibly understanding affair . . .

I needed their understanding now. As my smile faded and I looked down at the table I was miserably aware that I needed their understanding and their help as I'd never needed them before. Charlie stepped over and we all gazed silently at that old brass sextant lying in its rosewood box.

'It's nice,' Charlie mused eventually; perceptively cautious. 'Is it the stolen property your police letter was about?'

I muttered, 'Sort of . . .' and took a deep breath. Gently, ever so gently I lifted the sextant out of its housing and held it in hands that shook just a little.

Someone had cleaned it fairly recently. Yet it couldn't possibly have *been* cleaned in the past forty years; but nevertheless there was a warm gleam to the brass telescope, while the screws were still bright against a black metal frame dulled only by the passage of weeks; certainly not decades. I blinked into the mirrored index glass, and my reflected eye winked back at me. It was bright, carefully polished bright, when it should by now have been dark and pitted and . . . dead. Only the dark edges where the salt-damp had begun to penetrate and corrode the silvered obverse side betrayed a hint of antiquity to mark the half-mirrored horizon glass below. But that, too, was the legacy of time and not of lifeless indifference.

Charlie was frowning blankly. 'Sort of? But they returned it to you. It *is* yours, isn't it, Johnny?'

I couldn't stop myself.

'NO!'

Fran lunged forward impulsively, closing the box lid with a *snap*. The inset brass plate gleamed up at us just as brightly as the instrument it identified.

'But your name's on it, John. There!'

The inscribed legend twinkled under my eyes in the ensuing silence; flowing, scripted characters cut long before electric power came to the hand of the engraver:

JONATHAN HERSCHELL
Scotia Steamship Company
Glasgow

My name. The original title of *my* employer's shipping line.

In fact there was only one link still missing to prove me, beyond any logical doubt, the true owner of that venerable instrument.

I would also have had to be DEAD!

*

. . . recovered as part of the proceeds of a robbery, and believed to belong to you. We would be pleased if you would call and identify the aforementioned item . . .

Several weeks old, the letter had been waiting for me at the flat when I'd arrived that morning, still bemused by the legions of Glasgow commuters who'd all, it seemed, decided to travel by rail at the precise moment that I'd left my ship berthed in Leith docks – and most of them in the same compartment as me.

Mind you, I shouldn't have been so resentful. I was simply a commuter too, nowadays; I just commuted a little bit further to my place of work than they did – like to the west coast of Africa and back. Or perhaps I was more akin to the engine driver. Except that my locomotive weighed fifteen thousand tons and the permanent way was a lot less stable.

I nearly phoned the Strathclyde Police H.Q. to tell them

they'd made a mistake. The letter said 'Sextant' and, as I'd personally stowed my own Hughes instrument in my cabin before leaving the ship, it suggested someone in the C.I.D. had put two and two together and come up with an answer of five. Yet I was still intrigued. His sextant is a natural extension of any seaman navigator; virtually a part of him. Even today, in a maritime world of Decca and Loran and satellite precision fixing, the sextants are as much a necessity as they were aboard the Indiamen of old. No well-run merchantman will make an ocean passage without each and every one of her deck officers reporting to the bridge before midday, sextant in hand in preparation for 'sights'. So, unless that recovered instrument now functioned merely as an ornament on a curio-collector's wall, some seaman must have missed it dearly. Yet if he did, why hadn't it been reported as stolen and subsequently claimed by its rightful owner?

Which raised the second and the most irresistible riddle of all – what could possibly have indicated to the police that it might belong to *me*? Clydeside serves as home for countless sea-going or retired mariners; why should any Strathclyde detective select my name and go to considerable trouble to trace my address, in order to have me identify an item of stolen property which could have no conceivable connection with me in the first place?

I'd struck lucky in my time of arrival. It was Fran's day off and the shriek of welcome she greeted me with underlined the fact that she wanted me almost as desperately as I needed her. But that bloody letter unsettled me – I had to clear the enigma from my mind – so after repelling her initial assault with a strength of purpose which must have made her suspicious that maybe there was a little of Charlie in my metabolism after all, I'd left her pouting prettily to iron in the nude while I tried to hunt a taxi in the Glasgow rain.

And embarked upon a course which was rapidly to carry me towards a mental crisis.

A young detective finally ushered me into one of the C.I.D. interview rooms. At least he seemed young; or maybe I wasn't any more. Either way I got off on the wrong foot, right at the start.

'Detective Sergeant McQueen, Mister Herschell,' he introduced himself.

'Constable!' I acknowledged, shaking the proffered hand. He looked at me a bit hard.

'Sergeant McQueen, sir. I'm a detective *sergeant*.'

'*Captain* Herschell. I'm a captain. Sergeant.'

It took a moment longer for him to smile. It wasn't all that full of humour even then, but I was still glad to see it – he was also a very big policeman, and I'd only forgotten briefly that I wasn't a God in my maritime Heaven any longer.

'Aye?' he'd said, in a manner which inferred that I was merely one routine pain in the neck out of a thousand routine, and probably much more serious cases the Glasgow force had on their files at that moment. That was when he'd leaned down beside his desk and lifted the box, placing it before me.

'Recovered as one item from the proceeds of several robberies which took place some months ago – it's already been dealt with in the Sheriff Court. You can take it away once you've identified it, sir. Just as long as you give me a receipt!'

Even then I didn't sense the proximity of the spectre about to touch my shoulder. I simply gave the rosewood box a cursory glance, noting its age, then lifted the lid and briefly admired the sextant itself before closing the box again. I was still mystified and a little irritated.

'I'm hoping nobody went to Barlinnie on the strength of this allegedly belonging to me, Sergeant. If you'd bothered to call me as a corroborating witness, I'd have had to deny ever having seen it before. It's not mine. Definitely not.'

I caught a glimmer of surprise, but McQueen was

obviously well-practised in the policeman's art of remaining outwardly unmoved. He shrugged.

'No need. The accused admitted having stolen it. In fact he pleaded guilty on all charges. A nasty wee man. We got him cold . . . and as far as calling you to court – the case was heard near four months ago now. We were given to understand you were on the Indian coast at that time . . .'

'African,' I corrected. 'You just said you were given to understand. *Who* gave you to understand, Sergeant? And why should you want to find me? What on earth made you think that sextant was mine in the first place?'

He leaned back and eyed me speculatively for a long moment. It occurred to me then that he was slightly uneasy about something, but if he was he covered it well.

'Are you stating, Captain, that this instrument does *not* belong to you?'

'I am, but you haven't answered my question yet – what led you to believe that it ever did?'

It was his turn to get his own back for the *constable* jibe. And to reveal that he did have a sense of humour after all, even if it was a bit sardonic.

'It's a knack we develop in the police force, Captain. There's wee details that we notice about things; details that us detectives call "clues". So when we find something that has a name and address on it . . . well, we policemen sometimes say to ourselves – that gentleman whose *name's* marked on it could well be the owner of the property.'

Pointedly he pushed the sextant box closer towards me on the desk. I hadn't even noticed the brass plate set into the lid. I did that time.

JONATHAN HERSCHELL
Scotia Steamship Company
Glasgow

I didn't have his ability to remain inscrutable. The incomprehension on my face must have given him a great deal of satisfaction.

'It's not a common name – Herschell,' he continued blandly. 'We checked with Scotia Steamships – or Scotia Container Lines as they are now – and they confirmed they don't have any other Herschells on the books; Jonathans or otherwise.'

Detective Sergeant McQueen permitted himself the trace of a smile, but it wasn't unkind; maybe he was already reading the expression in my eyes. 'Captains or otherwise. And that was how, to answer your question, we obtained your private address.'

The rest of his explanation muted to a background fuzz as I stared at the box sitting there innocuously in that sterile, impersonal police station in the middle of Glasgow; and found myself coming face to face with the impossible. Perhaps it was the shock; perhaps there's a period of anaesthesia to dull everyone's mind before the full import of something overwhelmingly strange sinks in. I know I asked questions, vague, unconsidered ones, and only dimly retained their replies. A fragment of one of McQueen's answers stuck in my mind; something about it having been stolen from a village. Called Laichy?

Maybe I should have listened a little closer at the time, because Detective Sergeant McQueen of the Strathclyde Constabulary had already proved himself right on one point – I *was* the owner of that handsome and frightening box after all.

Only it still didn't mean that was *my* name engraved on it. Merely that I had fallen heir to it.

When Captain Jonathan Herschell, my father, died so violently forty years before.

*

'Your *father*!' Charlie exclaimed. 'Same name, Jonathan Herschell?'

I bit my lip. 'Same company – Scotia Steamships. I followed him into it when I was old enough to go to sea. It was my mother's last wish before she died too.'

Fran gave a little cry and clung to my arm. 'I'm sorry, darling. And so glad as well. It must make you very happy – to find your father's sextant after all these years.'

I dragged my arm away and stared at them blindly.

'Christ, but you don't understand, do you? McQueen said it was stolen from some village . . . Laichy or somewhere. But my father was a sea captain; that sextant was his eyes, his brain, his most valuable possession. There's no conceivable possibility that he would have given it away.'

'Perhaps after his death then, Johnny? Could it have been . . . well . . . sold, or something?'

Charlie was making heavy going of it and my heart went out to him. He still finished what he was going to say, though. 'I'm sorry – I mean your mum, Johnny. Could she have sold it? Maybe even given it to someone she knew in Laichy?'

'You knew my mother when we were kids, Charlie. You know fine we never had any relatives living more than half a dozen closes away, and that she was a wee Glasgow woman who'd never even been outside the city, far less having contact with someone living in a place that *I've* never even heard of. And she'd never have sold it . . .'

My voice trailed off. I didn't want to justify my certainty; I didn't want to aggravate the pain of memory any more despite their concern for me. Mary Herschell, my mother, had died of a broken heart eight years after my father's death, because she'd never learned how to stop loving him in all that time, nor to cease staring from the tenement window twice a day with her eyes briefly sparkling with hope when the postman approached, then clouding over when he passed by. Not even when that war had finally ended, and the missing had been confirmed as truly gone, and most of the other widows had accepted loneliness or some other man's affection. But I knew how she'd clung to unreality, and how his pitifully few belongings – those which hadn't been with him aboard his ship when he died – had stayed in the drawers, and the old uniform had hung in the wardrobe in silent mockery until after her own sad passing. I knew she would never, ever have given away his sextant.

I forced myself to continue. I owed them that much.

'My father was master of a Scotia ship called *Highlander* when the Second World War began. In nineteen-forty-one the *Highlander* was steaming off the west coast of Scotland when she was torpedoed . . . my father died with her. It's a matter of record.'

When Fran's hand tenderly touched my arm I didn't draw away.

'Then one of his crew – one of the survivors – must have brought your father's sextant ashore, John. There has to be a logical explanation.'

I looked at her and shook my head fiercely, feeling the pain that I thought had faded before I was ten years old.

'That's the impossibility – there *were* no survivors, Fran! I've always understood that *Highlander*'s operator only got one fragmented message out . . . she must have sunk almost immediately. And with the instrument in it, that box could never have drifted ashore as flotsam; it's too heavy.'

Her eyes and Charlie's were widening with the same disbelief I'd felt when I first came face to face with the macabre in physical, polished-brass reality. Like me, they too would eventually be forced to acknowledge the impossible. Because it had happened; there was no alternative. I still found myself denying it though . . .

'My father's sextant can't be sitting on this table tonight, because it has to be lying with him, fifty fathoms deep somewhere off the west coast. With him, and *Highlander*, and a lot of other drowned sailormen. Yet it *IS* here, dammit! The records prove it can't be. But it is!'

I knew then that I had to solve the insoluble. To discover the truth.

I owed that, too. To Captain Jonathan Herschell. And a host of other gallant ghosts.

CHAPTER TWO

── *1941* ──

The North Atlantic. In a rage of winter.

They'd described it to Fourth Officer Findlay – the older seamen had. And he'd often wondered about the look in their eyes as they did, for they always wore the same expression; a sort of distant hardness which matched closely their demeanour when they talked of the convoys and the U-boats, and rather less often of the occasions when they'd been forced to watch fellow seafarers retching their lives away in fuel oil welling so thick around a sinking merchantman that it was like staring over a glistening Persian carpet.

He'd actually crossed the Atlantic himself, had Fourth Officer Findlay, but only once as an apprentice before the war when the faces around him could still smile without strain and the only real enemy had been the weather. Even that had showed a tolerance for his baptism, because the winds had never risen above forty knots; the winter ice had merely evinced itself as a pretty white fuzzle, rather pleasing to the eye, which formed around signal halyards and rigging and wireless aerials, and the waves had never assumed greater proportions than those of serrated streets of houses moving majestically in company with his ship.

So he'd never really understood the reason for those grimly reflective expressions when the older men talked about the storms. Certainly he'd never been able to appreciate why they were always bracketed with such horrors as he already knew after a year and a half of the trauma offered by the threat from mine or bomb or torpedo. Not until seven o'clock on the evening of the 13th of January, 1941, anyway. For that was the moment when Fourth Officer Iain Findlay finally began to understand.

It was the time when the Motor Vessel *Highlander* lost what little protection had been afforded her by the lee of the long Hebridean islands and prepared to turn her flared bows to meet the North Atlantic at the height of its monstrous ill-temper. And when a young man's eyes really did lose their last trace of boyish naiveté regarding the power of the sea.

Oh, he'd been told about it often enough, yet he'd never even begun to visualise it as it really was. Could anybody who hasn't actually experienced such a thing for themselves? Could you, for instance, imagine clinging to an open bridge wing which is rolling through an arc of maybe eighty degrees or more, and struggling to face outboard to port against a wind so intense that, even deflected by ballooning canvas dodgers, it still buffets you continuously with a force of a crazily-wielded cushion, so that you have to brace skew-legged just to withstand its assault? And which makes your slit-eyed attempt at vision a mocking agony as cold-induced tears stream horizontally back along numbed cheek bones. And all to the accompaniment of a roaring background tumult which adds yet another dimension of shock to senses already addled by the scale of such violence. Could any man who'd only lived through an ordinary dark night even begin to conjure an image of a blackness so black it's like suffocating in the mud of the River Styx, yet through which you can still observe the terror about you, because the night waves of a true Atlantic storm are illuminated by their own dementia; a rearing, mountainous wasteland of disintegrating peaks and eerie streaking foam and luminescent drifts of whirling spray?

Dimly he heard the wheelhouse door slide open and slam shut again on its rollers. A bulky shape moved deftly towards him, hesitating as *Highlander* wallowed to starboard, running in short experienced steps as the deck came upright again; Chief Officer McLeod turning the momentum of the North Atlantic to his own advantage. A creaming beam sea exploded against the ship's hull directly below Findlay's perch and he ducked as near solid water whipped inboard, rattling the dodgers like frustrated machinegun fire. When he blinked erect McLeod was alongside him, clinging firmly to the rail.

'The Old Man's goin' tae bring her into it soon as he gets a lull,' the Mate shouted. 'You'd be well advised to hang on, laddie.'

'Aye, aye, sir,' Findlay yelled back. He didn't add anything but it struck him his hands were already like white claws gripping the awning stanchion. McLeod's warning was a kindness wasted. A second monstrous wave reared high against the blackness and fell roaring and rumbling across the forr'ad well deck, detonating in a line of vertical rage against the coamings on one and two hatches. The ship fell away further and further to starboard until Findlay found himself looking down through the wheelhouse windows, directly into the sea on the other side of *Highlander*.

'Christ!' he said involuntarily. Then the ship came upright again and he felt embarrassed and angry with himself because he hadn't wanted to let the Mate see how scared he was.

'She'll ride easier wi' it on the bow,' McLeod grumbled. He must have sensed the boy's apprehension, because he grinned savagely through the darkness. 'At least it'll keep the bluidy Jerries down deep.'

'Every cloud . . .' Findlay spluttered back. He didn't really believe it, though; no more than the Mate himself did. The VII-C U-boats were primarily surface warships with a capacity to dive for tactical reasons; the men who commanded them were dedicated professionals, rugged as the allied seamen they hunted. Bad weather for the submarine was a camouflage; a battleground offering cover where the low rapacious silhouette was lost against the maelstrom scene of the horizon.

Had Fourth Officer Findlay's eyes been able to penetrate the darkness a little better at seven o'clock on that appalling evening, then he might have observed just such a shape lying some three miles away and forward of *Highlander*'s port beam. If, for that matter, *Highlander* had continued to plough the rolling course which had already taken her up inside the Minches, then neither the British freighter nor the German U-boat would even have been aware of each other's proximity. But the Motor Vessel *Highlander* was bound for Iceland, not for the North Pole, and so at one minute past seven precisely her master, Captain Jonathan Herschell, began to bring her bows round towards the north west and her destination.

She was turning to port.

It also meant she was now steaming a closing course with a specialist war machine designated U-236.

'Iceland!' Fourth Officer Iain Findlay reflected bitterly; seeing nothing ahead but blackness and a madness of spindrift. 'Who the hell wants to go to bloody Iceland anyway?'

*

The majority of the forty-two other British seamen who made up *Highlander*'s complement along with Fourth Officer Findlay had also asked themselves that question; 'Who the hell wants to go to bloody Iceland?' It seemed inconceivable to them that anybody should, unless he was a trawlerman of course. Or an Icelander.

But war creates a curious shock-wave of circumstance which influences the actions of men and causes them to enter into tasks upon which they would otherwise be unlikely to engage. It was very probable that the same crew would have been in *Highlander* had the world been fortunate enough to remain at peace, but rather less likely that they would have been pounding towards the higher latitudes some twenty-odd miles east nor' east of the Butt of Lewis on that particular night. They were all professional merchant seamen signed on articles with a company called Scotia Steamships of Glasgow, and normally that would have meant their route lay to the south and east, for Scotia Steamships in happier times had sent their vessels mainly on the Oriental trade in search of profit.

A state of hostilities did exist, however, and consequently it was decreed that the Ministry of War Transport and the Naval Control of Shipping Organisation would dictate not only to where an allied merchantman should voyage, but also by which route. Had the pursuit of profit remained the only criterion which influenced their movements, then most ships would have remained passively in harbour for the duration as, by 1941, being sunk was a highly likely prospect, and an expensive one as well.

The Motor Vessel *Highlander* was going to unfamiliar Iceland because nine months previously a German soldier – quite a number of German soldiers, in fact – had entered Denmark in pursuit of Hitler's master plan for the conquest of the world. Iceland was then a dependency of Denmark, which meant that the British, who had anyway long foreseen a tactical need to use Iceland as a base from which to protect their Atlantic convoys, were conveniently presented with an excuse to despatch a force to garrison and hold that vital island. Consequently, for military garrisons require considerable logistic support, ships like *Highlander* had to be diverted from their normal tasks in order to sustain yet another sorely pressed supply line.

And so forty-three men who might otherwise have been heading towards the warmer climes of Singapore or Hong Kong abruptly found themselves high off the west coast of Scotland in winter. That factor might well have explained the hardness in their eyes which Fourth Officer Findlay had already noted and pondered upon. If the prospect of finding one's ship blown from under one in the North Atlantic was relatively high, then the expectation of one's continuing survival in such a case was proportionately low. Even the gratitude one might feel towards God for allowing one to flounder aboard a liferaft can be somewhat short-lived when one discovers one is being cocooned within a suffocating shell of ice within minutes; or that a rescue ship has just passed close-by without noticing because a grey, shivering wretch on a grey tossing Carley float in a grey, all-too-vast sea is no more conspicuous than an individual grain of sand in the desert.

But at least one had the consolation of knowing that the Naval Control of Shipping Organisation was on one's side, and that they would direct one by the safest, if not necessarily the most direct route to one's destination. When they learned from a convoy inward-bound to the Clyde that several sightings had been made of U-boat activity in the area off Barra Head, they immediately instructed Captain Jonathan Herschell to sail *Highlander* north about the Hebrides even though it wasted valuable time and fuel. So *Highlander* had sailed from Gourock as a fast independent without escort, with a cargo of toilet paper and typewriters and woollen jerseys and ammunition and cases of bully beef and the countless other items a garrison needs to fight with.

Regrettably for Captain Herschell, to say nothing of Fourth Officer Findlay and Mister McLeod, war at sea is not merely an exercise in probability calculated from the operations plot of a shore-based NCSO, it is also a game of chance. No Naval Intelligence officer could reasonably have anticipated that the VII-C class submarine now less than three miles ahead of, and rapidly closing with the blind freighter was there because her commander had felt it opportune to seek the lee of the Minches on that particularly dark night so as to effect emergency repairs to his wireless aerials.

Even then the laws of probability were still in favour of the Motor Vessel *Highlander* passing U-236 in blissful ignorance of her proximity. The sea conditions were such that few submarine captains would consider a snap shot at a freighter wallowing fifty feet above at one moment, then fifty feet below his firing platform the next, as offering a worthwhile expenditure of precious ammunition. Even the war game of chance had to be played within sensible limits.

Except that . . . well, U-236 was about to leave station for her base in St Nazaire on the following day. And *Gott* was still *mit uns* in the *Kriegsmarine* U-boat arm in January of 1941. While in anybody's navy a torpedo fired in hope had to be better than a torpedo returned in vain.

. . . but no Naval Intelligence officer could ever have imagined a chain of circumstances like *that* would arise. When he routed *Highlander* the safe way. Up inside the long Hebridean chain.

*

The wheelhouse door rumbled open again with a crash and the Captain stuck his head out, raising his voice across the shriek of the wind. 'Mister McLeod!'

'Sir!'

Herschell watched through narrowed eyes as McLeod left the Fourth Mate's side and balanced warily on his way to join him. It was less difficult to move now that they were heading into the storm, the crazed rolling had reverted to a more acceptable porpoise motion as *Highlander* thrust mightily with the water flaring from either side of the bow in great streaked fans which lifted to the wind, curling upwards and aft to drench the bridge, monkey island, even the funnel itself with constant spray. There was still danger to the over-confident though; every so often she would breast the top of a particularly big one and swoop maybe sixty feet down into the trough, digging deep this time with tons of roaring, avalanching sea consuming the foc'slehead and flooding astern to waterfall over the break of the well deck. When she did that the whole ship seemed to stop dead for a moment, arrested in her leviathan passage; and any man too careless could find himself catapulted savagely forward with the impact of a traffic accident. There were those in the merchant fleet who claimed you should always walk with slightly-flexed legs aboard a ship in war; the upward shock of the deck during a torpedo detonation had been known to telescope ankles, even drive thigh bones into abdominal cavities; but you couldn't walk like neanderthal man during an Atlantic blow. You just braced yourself until your muscles ached and made no allowance for the additional horrors threatened by your enemy.

'I'm going below for a shave,' the Captain said, rubbing his chin absently. He hadn't left the bridge since they'd sailed from the Clyde; he didn't intend to again until they were safely alongside the berth at Reykjavik. 'We'll keep to a zigzag pattern, Mister McLeod. She's heading three two zero at the moment; I've set the timer for eight minutes. Then run on two niner five for a further six and I'll be back up by then.'

He found himself staring ahead through the streaming windows. Or not so much through them as at them; all he could make out was his own reflection gazing back, eerie green from the glow of the binnacle. Another devil mask hovered in company with his, framed under the inverted arc of a sou'wester; Able Seaman Hotchkiss, helmsman of the watch. *Highlander* took another giant wave and the foc'sle reared thunderously; green water surging and shuddering astern to explode against the forward end of the centrecastle deck. She fell away to starboard and Hotchkiss growled 'Shit!', hauling her three spokes to port to bring her back into it. A ton of near-solid Atlantic rattled the armoured glass shielding them.

'We'll no' need to steer a delib'rate zigzag to fox the

Germans,' McLeod remarked pointedly, loud enough for Hotchkiss to hear. 'Not if this bluidy weather keeps up.'

The yellow sou'wester maintained a dignified aloofness; Hotchkiss had been steering ships as long as Bill McLeod had been navigating them. The next comment would be an unnecessary 'Watch your head!'. Hotchkiss had also sailed with McLeod in the Company's ships for years; it was a friendly enmity.

The ship rammed another brick wall and fell ten degrees off with the vibrations shaking her from stem to stern. 'Watch your head, man!' the Mate snapped automatically. Hotchkiss's green reflection bore the trace of a smile.

'Bring her down to half speed if it gets any worse,' the Captain said. 'We're only on revs for ten knots now and the Chief's already been on the phone – complains the screws are spending so much time out of the water we should be an aeroplane.'

'Tam Graham'd find cause for fault on a summer's day cruise in Loch Leven.'

'Aye, well, I'd better see about that shave of mine,' Herschell muttered, turning away unwillingly. He hated leaving the bridge, even for a few minutes, but it would be a long night; he needed the psychological boost to freshen himself for the strain to come. And better to be absent while McLeod still had the watch than to delay until the eight to twelve men came up. The Chief Officer seemed to read his unease.

'You'll be wanting to be back here before the Dutchman takes over?'

'Until we know him better, Mister McLeod. Tried him a while.'

He stood for a moment longer, thinking about his new Third Officer. They'd sent him an unexpected replacement for McIvor who'd just left to sail as Mate in their sister ship *Lowlander* – a youngster who'd escaped from Holland before the German occupation and volunteered to join the British

Merchant Navy until they found a free Netherlands vessel to take him. It promised to be a lonely voyage for him; in a ship called *Highlander*, with a largely Scottish crew and flying the house flag of a Glasgow Owner.

'Aye, this war makes strange bedfellows,' McLeod mused. 'Van der Kroon, is it? The laddie doesnae speak much English, you know. Could be a drawback if there's an emergency.'

'Jan van der Kroon, Mister McLeod. And that's why I want to be here when he takes the watch.'

He slid the door back and a gust immediately pounced into the wheelhouse, snapping their oilskins; riffling and snatching the clipped messages fixed to the bulkhead; bellying the light-trap curtains across the chart room door. The kapok-stuffed lifejackets hanging beside them in instant readiness swung as a permanent reminder of the other threat.

'I'll bring young Findlay and the apprentice laddie inside if it's all right by you,' the Mate called after him. 'They'll no' see bugger-all in this, anyroad.'

'We'll hope it's a two-way drawback if Jerrie's out there,' Herschell retorted casually.

But it wasn't. The Zeiss night-coated lenses of binoculars issued to lookouts on German submarines running on the surface were quite capable of detecting the slightest change in the ocean's texture. While the disturbance caused by the bows of a big freighter smashing white water high on either side was visible even on the darkest of all dark nights.

U-236 was less than two miles on *Highlander*'s port bow by then.

The odds on the improbable occurring were rapidly shortening.

*

Jimmy Beattie was *Highlander*'s four-to-eight standby man. Only being standby man, in Jimmy's case, meant huddling in the lee of the poop housing and staring astern to where the wake disintegrated into a swirling riot of turbulence reaching nearly to his feet one moment as the bow four hundred feet away rose to the crest of a purler, then soaring skywards like a bluidy H. G. Wells moon rocket the next as the ship clambered over the top and crashed madly into the trough.

Oh, and being sick! Just huddling there frozen to the marrow; feeling the screws thresh and shake the deck like they were in a giant's dice cup, and being sick as the sea dog which he definitely wasn't. In fact if it hadnae been for the war, Jimmy Beattie's closest link with the sea would've been as a day tripper on the Rothesay paddle steamer – and *that* only once a year because you wasnae nothin' in the Gorbals unless you was a well-travelled man. But then the war had started and Jimmie hadn't reckoned much on being a fighter pilot. The idea of spending his life living in a hole in the bluidy ground as a sod'ger didn't appeal one wee bit; while the Royal Navy were aye out on the sea looking for a fight. So Jimmie's mum had said, 'How d'you no' join the Merchant Navy before they send the polis tae call you up, Jimmie? They wouldnae expect you tae fight a German wi'out a gun, and the money's better than bein' just a private in the Black Watch like your dad was in the last war. Before he deserted, onyway.'

So Jimmie had gone straight down to Sauchiehall Street one step ahead of the draft board, and signed on with the Scotia Steamships as a non-combatant merchant seaman – and it seemed they German bastards hadn't never stopped shooting at him and dropping bombs on him, and strewing bluidy great mines ahead of him and firin' torpedoes directly at his bunk ever since.

He hadn't stopped being sea sick, either.

It was amazing – the tricks a man's mind could play. Especially seeing very Ordinary Seaman Beattie J. had only been in the Merchant Navy for just over twenty-four hours. Give or take a convulsion or two.

*

The evening meal was over and cleared away in *Highlander*'s saloon by a quarter past seven. The tables had been left empty with only the wooden fiddles in place; you didn't set for breakfast prior to a night of wind force eleven, not if you wanted any crockery left whole by morning. Most of the off-watch deck and engineer officers had dispersed to their cabins or to the tiny lounge on the promenade deck; few of them would sleep during that night, certainly none would do more than remove shoes and uniform jackets and stretch out in the hope of respite from the violent movement and the uneasy anticipation that maybe, just maybe, tonight *could* be the night.

Unlikely, though. A force eleven was always more bearable aboard a ship in war. If you were a religious man it wasn't hard to persuade yourself that God hadn't simply sent it as a punishment but as a sign of His benign protection. And the North Atlantic was as appropriate a cathedral in which to gain religion as any, even if you weren't aware of conscious supplication. A prayer, a keen eye and a lifejacket: the best shipmates you could ever wish for. And luck, of course. The devil's own luck, if need be.

At seven-fifteen most of the ratings were aft, nursing great steaming mugs of tea in the seamen's or greasers' messes. Unless they were on duty like Hotchkiss at the wheel, that was, or Fireman Cullen and Greaser Eadie presently arguing with not entirely respectful heat on the engine room control platform against Second Engineer McKechnie's blind insistence that 'It wis Rangers; no, they pansy Celtic shoogle-heids wis favourite f'r The Cup!'

Or like Jimmie Beattie, of course. Just above them on the poop, feedin' the seagulls . . .

The more introspective among *Highlander*'s complement tended to keep to themselves. Chief Graham, for instance, had never been a man for socialising even in peacetime. Now he spent more and more time in solitary brooding over the folly of his fellow creatures, and listening with pursed lips to the suddenly-accelerated rumble transmitted from astern as one or both of *Highlander*'s propellers came clear of the braking density of the water. He was not a happy man, Chief Engineer Graham, yet it was self-inflicted martyrdom. At the age of sixty-eight he had long been offered the opportunity of retirement, and with one World War and three sinkings behind him no one would have grudged his going. Yet he still clung bitterly to the life he knew rather than face an even more depressing isolation on the beach. Friendless at sea because of his dourness, he dreaded dying in a total vacuum without even the existence of his ship to console him.

Second Radio Officer Stronach was alone at seven-fifteen that evening because he was on watch in the radio room on the after end of the boat deck, starboard side, while the Chief Sparks had disappeared somewhere with his draughts board under one arm and an earnest obsession boding ill for any victim foolish enough to agree to a contest. Stronach heaved a sigh of relief when Chief Operator Trent departed – playing draughts against his senior was like tackling Russian roulette with a fully loaded revolver. If you lost the game Trent's face became suffused with rage because of your utter stupidity. If you won it then . . . well, it just became suffused!

Stronach had wedged himself into the operator's chair as best he could and idly thumbed through a two-week-old copy of the *Scottish Daily Mail*. He tried not to think about the last time he'd been off the south coast of Iceland; and about the raft which they'd sighted containing four cadaverous remnants from some anonymous disaster.

It had been summer then, and the master he sailed under hadn't become hardened to the brutality of maritime conflict. When they stopped and attempted to heave the decomposing corpses inboard in a cargo net for identification, the bodies slipped seawards through the mesh in hideous dissolution at the moment of their recovery. Second Radio Officer Stronach

34

differed from most others aboard *Highlander* because of that experience; he didn't pray that the torpedo wouldn't arrive, like some of his shipmates did, for he was a fatalist – but he *did* ask that if or when it came, it would strike directly below the point where he happened to be. Stronach accepted he might be called upon to die for King and Country, and faced the possibility bravely; but he had a screaming fear of the prospect of helplessly rotting away to slime for them as well.

Second Mate Devlin had never seen a liferaft full of spongy deadmen, but he *had* watched a torpedoed Norwegian tanker burn on a beautiful day when the sea was like glass and a chap felt he could almost walk to safety across the mirror surface. Actually there hadn't been a sign of fire as two columns of water climbed gracefully into the still blue sky; one hit below her funnel aft and the other just at the break of her foc'sle. All she appeared to do at first was sigh wearily and lie gently over, so that the other ships in the convoy could see her lifeboats breaking loose and crashing into free-fall. Then she stopped listing because she was a tanker and tankers didn't usually sink until their lighter-than-water cargoes dissipated. Yet suddenly there were tiny men leaving her in what one might have considered unseemly haste considering the optimum conditions for survival – matchstick figures all hunched and bulky with orange lifejackets, swarming down ropes from her counter, even jumping stiff-legged from the height of her midships bridge deck with a frenetic urgency that any man who hadn't actually sailed aboard a benzine tanker might have found hard to understand. Then flames had flickered impishly around the two blackened breaches in her hull; tiny flames, just like the men, and not at all frightening considering all forty-odd bobbing heads were a good hundred yards from her by then and still swimming with remarkable determination . . . until there was a WHOOSH which shocked the whole convoy and caused the ships steaming in stolid line astern of the casualty suddenly to

35

put helms hard a starboard. The little flames exploded into a darkly red pyre as their two fingers reached towards each other and met; and forty seamen cremated at the base of a maggot of pitch-smoke before the whole tanker blew up in a series of detonations which sent blast waves racing across the once placid surface only to be sucked backwards and upwards into the delicate blue sky along with white hot steel plates and gobbets of blazing fuel and joints of crisping human meat . . .

. . . Second Officer Devlin desperately wanted to sleep a little before he took over the middle watch on *Highlander*'s bridge at midnight, but he knew he wouldn't. Every time he'd closed his eyes since then aboard a ship at sea, he'd relived the images impressed during that pretty autumn afternoon to awaken sweating and stare-eyed with the nightmare of it. It was a state called fear which afflicted Second Officer James Devlin, or perhaps – considering he *was* still aboard *Highlander* on that wild evening – a state called, simply, courage. Because you can't produce the second without experiencing the first. There are no brave men who haven't first tasted the sourness of their own inward terror, yet continued despite it.

Bosun McColl, on the other hand, was more typical of those who sailed the merchant ships in war – it was a job to him, and while he was aware of the hazard he didn't think too deeply about it. Seven-fifteen in the evening found McColl – who hailed from Bolton, Lancashire, despite his Celtic name – eating a raw onion with crunching gusto, oblivious to the motion as *Highlander* rocked, rolled and porpoised towards Iceland. It was a daily weakness on McColl's part; his onion substitute for the usually indifferent pudding prescribed for the rest of the crowd. An interested observer would also have noted a further phenomenon induced by the Bosun's onion, and that was the reluctance displayed by his stout-hearted fellow sailormen to heave-to downwind of their senior petty officer during the hours immediately following chow time. On that particularly turbulent night it was additionally noticeable that, as even the strongest stomachs tend to be somewhat fragile on occasions, the usual social barriers existing between deck and engine room personnel were temporarily overcome when several seamen suddenly decided to depart the messroom where Bosun McColl munched so enjoyably and offer personal felicitations to their opposite numbers residing comfortably, and odourlessly, in the greasers' recreation space immediately below the poop deck accommodation.

The engine room ratings' mess was, therefore, exceptionally crowded aboard the Motor Vessel *Highlander* in the hour before the eight o'clock change of watch. Even the settee running athwartships across the forward end of the cramped space was lined with men squashed intimately together in refuge from a vegetable. While several of them were aware of the shudders transmitted through the half-inch steel plating separating them from the after well deck itself, as each sneak sea collapsed inboard over the bulwarks and smashed thunderously against their protective shield, not one gave a second thought to the possibility that something considerably more penetrating than a North Atlantic wave might impact within inches of the back of his head.

Those same white seas intermittently sweeping the after well deck were causing rather more concern to Second Cook Johnstone and Officer's Steward Archie Sangster. Having completed their duties in the midships galley for the evening they now hesitated uncomfortably at the brow of the centre castle deck ladder, preparing to make a dash for the poop accommodation as soon as they sensed a break in the incoming water. And 'sensed' was an appropriate term. With *Highlander* blacked-out, no lighting was permitted on any open deck, which meant no illumination either for the wave crests sighing outboard or for the steeple-chase-straggle of

37

ring bolts and winches and angled steel deck plates promising a broken ankle to the unwary even in daylight. The wire storm lines rigged fore-and-aft before the ship left the lee of the Hebrides extended little security if you tripped en route, to say nothing of being run over by a hundred bloody tons of Atlantic while you were betwixt and between. The prospect for retaining your grip was about as hopeful as standing your ground before a high-speed steam-roller.

High above the catering staff and the weather, Third Officer Jan van der Kroon was also concerned with safety; his preoccupation, however, being more related to semantics than the forces of nature. Wedged firmly in his bunk, he was utilising his last half hour before preparing to relieve Mister McLeod in frowning study of a battered edition of Anglo–Dutch terminology. Regrettably it was as old as it was tattered, and devoid of the more practical phrases helpful to any not-very-fluent foreigner about to assume control of a British ship under threat from storm and explosive. Translations designed to cope with such dire emergencies as *Excuse me, but please can you advise me on where I might purchase fresh oil for my bicycle lamp?* did lose a little of their relevance in the middle of the North Atlantic in the middle of a war.

At fourteen minutes after seven Captain Jonathan Herschell, briefly divested of his oilskins, was deep in contemplation, in his case of his own square-jawed features presented in the mirror above his cabin washbasin. He saw a tired, middle-aged master mariner with the crow's foot lines of strain creasing the eyes, yet one who still maintained an erect and reassuring dignity despite the pressures of war at sea. He smiled a little ruefully at himself and, as he did so, caught sight of the photograph lying carefully secured against the motion in the folds of his berth. It was of a small neat woman holding hands with a very young boy. The boy's eyes seemed full of wonder at the camera, while his rosy features held an unsettling unfamiliarity despite the fact that the

Captain was gazing at a picture of his only son. Herschell stopped smiling as he reached for his shaving brush. The nature of his calling demanded that he could only be a remote husband and father; forced by long absences to deny his family the company afforded by more conventional bread-winners. Little Johnny was six years old already, yet Herschell had barely spent six months of those formative years with the child – and not one day more in all that time with his beloved Mary, come to that. It was the constant tragedy of every seaman that the greater their fondness for their dear ones, the greater their guilt regarding the means by which they provided for them. For the Captain the pain of each separation was made bearable only by the knowledge that each voyage also heralded a reunion.

Even now the unnatural strains were beginning to tell in his relationship with his child. Oh, Mary still threw her arms around him, not caring at all what the grey-faced Glasgow station crowds would make of such unseemly display, and would cling tight to his leathery hand while the tramcar rattled and clattered on the last home-bound leg to Anniesland, chattering like a wee sparrow about all the irrelevant things which only covered for the dreaded question, 'When are you going back?' – but the boy, Johnny, sat there on the seat in front, holding his father's sea bag and rosewood sextant case, staring distantly out of the window and occasionally turning round at the scolding of his mother to 'Let your daddy see how big you've grown'. Yet when their eyes did meet, there was already a blankness in the gaze of the younger Herschell and maybe even a trace of resentment. When you're six years old, it's hard to understand why your father loves something called 'a ship' more than he loves you.

Despite that, Jonathan Herschell still hoped that his son, too, might become a sailor. It was his dearest wish, but he also prayed that the boy would never be called upon to fight anything more vicious than the seas themselves, should he ever come to command his own ship. He knew he would be a proud father indeed on that great day so far ahead when, God willing, peace must surely reign once again over a brave new world.

At seven-fifteen precisely, just as Captain Herschell was reflecting wistfully on thoughts of peace and goodwill between men, one of two torpedoes fired in hope from U-boat 236 struck the Motor Vessel *Highlander* port side aft, just abreast of number six hold. As Herschell's ship was rolling heavily towards the submarine in that split second the point of impact was considerably higher than the level indicated by her normal Winter North Atlantic War Load Line.

Above the Plimsoll marks or not, the explosion still lifted *Highlander*'s stern momentarily clear of the water. It blew the hatch covers clean off five and six; it partly severed her mainmast causing it to sway drunkenly on screeching steel saw-teeth; it snapped her port propeller shaft causing her to veer instantly in a crazed semi-circle under the thrust of her still-revolving starboard screw . . .

. . . by the time Second Engineer McKechnie had closed the throttles of both engines, nearly half her crew were already dead. The other half were numbly trying to grasp what had happened to them. And the Motor Vessel *Highlander* was already lying beam-on and gyrating through hysterical ninety-degree arcs in the troughs of seas sweeping almost to the level of her boat deck.

It was sixteen minutes past seven on the evening of the 13th January, 1941.

CHAPTER THREE

JONATHAN HERSCHELL
Scotia Steamship Company
Glasgow

Breakfast in the flat next morning had been a subdued affair. Each of us kept staring uneasily at the sextant box sitting in cryptic provocation on the sideboard. My eyes surely betrayed the pain I felt at the implications of its return . . . for if the sextant had survived so incredibly, then what other legacies might also surface from the bottom of the sea? What more ghastly things might now be abroad as well?

Would the old *Highlander* herself even reappear in the light of day, bursting and foaming and gouting foetid water from within her rusted hull? Could her captain – my father – still be standing there on her mouldering bridge surrounded by sightless, bone-bleached officers . . . a crew of eternally voyaging zombies. A *corpse* of long-dead sailormen?

I shuddered and dragged myself into the present; my gruesome fantasies were no more than wavering recollections from a night of nightmares. Oh, we'd made love, but it had been a sad and distant affair with Charlie muttering in fretful lonelinesses through his sleep in the next room, and Fran's hair wet with the tears of her disappointment splayed across my chest. But her arms had never stopped holding me, not once through all my drifting, ghoulish dreams.

Now it was time to face the reality. To attempt to rationalise the inconceivable.

Charlie shoved his plate away half-finished and stood up.

'I'll be doing a follow-up on the slashed milk laddie today, Johnny. I'll drop in and see D.S. McQueen at the same time. Where'll you be about five this evening?'

'Where d'you want me to be?'

'Scuddie's Bar? I'm due McQueen a drink anyway.'

'We'll both come,' Fran said. 'McQueen's nice. And I've always fancied a policeman.'

'You mean you've never *had* one?' Charlie asked with exaggerated incredulity. I had to grin too; the phantoms of the night were dissipating fast now, surrendering to the prospect of action. I'd already decided what I was going to do, and that was to go back to where it all began; to start at the source of the mystery.

'I'm going to look through the Company records. Find out precisely what did happen to *Highlander* . . . as far as they knew at the time.'

'Aye,' Charlie nodded approvingly. 'You might have made a newspaperman if you hadn't been a sailor.'

'I'm quite happy to make a newspaper lady,' I smiled, squeezing Fran's hand and trying to tell her, without using words, that it would all be different tonight.

Charlie bent down and gave her a brotherly peck on the cheek. Inevitably her gown slipped from one rounded shoulder and her skin caught the light; golden satin with freckles.

'There's times,' Charlie said with not-entirely-jocular wistfulness, 'that I wish I was straight.'

She watched his six-foot-two frame recede from sight, and I could almost hear her breathing *Amen to that*! I squeezed her hand again and muttered, 'Go and get dressed. I'll treat us both to a taxi into town.'

Personally I was glad that Charlie wasn't into women. Even now I felt that if he had been I'd have spent most of my nights on leave in a room in the Albany Hotel.

Or maybe not. When the wrap slipped clear of her

shoulders as she kissed me after Charlie had gone, I knew there was more wantonness clinging to me than any single man could ever satisfy.

We were inseparable. No power on earth could come between the three of us. Or so I thought, then.

But I'd forgotten about a dead man's sextant. For a time.

*

'She was torpedoed,' Davidson said, frowning over his spectacles. 'Off the west coast, Captain. Nineteen-forty: forty-one?'

'Forty-one,' I nodded. 'But I want to establish the facts, Arthur. Date; time; her last known position . . . everything you've got on her loss.'

It was still raining and the light filtering through the windows of Scotia Container Line's George Street office reflected no colour at all from the silvered hair ringing the Chief Clerk's temples. He'd been with the Company man and boy and was now getting scared of retirement. He must have already been in his mid-twenties then. He looked at me; it was as though he could read my mind.

'I remember him, Captain Herschell. Your father. He was a fine man; a proper seaman. Like they all were in those days . . . and brave, too. We lost twenty-one ships in the two World Wars, you know? But they still kept going back. Aye, and back for more.'

I said, 'Maybe we of this generation won't get any second chances if there's another one. But my father didn't either, come to that. He *didn't*, did he, Arthur?'

He didn't seem to hear me. There was a sparkle of almost wistful recollection behind the steel-rimmed glasses.

'They used to come into the office – when we were in Sauchiehall Street, that was. And they'd ask if we had another ship ready for them seeing their last one had been blown from under them . . . yet they were still red-eyed and sometimes even shiny-black engrained with the fuel oil.

43

But they had that terrible anger about them, Captain. A fear and a sadness and that driving anger all at the same time.'

'*Highlander*?' I reminded him gently. 'How much can you tell me about her?'

'In the cellars,' he muttered, rising stiffly and beckoning. 'We keep all our dead ships in the cellars here. They're easier to forget that way.'

I'd hesitated as I followed him down through the high-vaulted entrance hall with its mahogany panelling and terrazzo floor, and the glass cases covering beautifully detailed models of straight-funnelled merchantmen long dissected by the breakers' torch. The splendour of a bygone age in miniature, where even the scaled likenesses gleamed with the proud craftsmanship of the men who had built them.

They didn't make models in the yards today. Not of ordinary, slab-sided bonus-constructed freighters. Models didn't show a profit; they weren't economically viable; the real ships themselves were hardly viable now, despite our brave new computerised, electronic maritime world.

There was a great white-marble panel set into the wall above the commissionaire's desk. It had a bronze border cast in bas-relief, depicting grim-jawed men in kapok lifejackets and sou'westers staring steadfastly out towards some unspecified threat. There were broken masts and stylised wave-crests rearing over them, with parts of foundering hulls and jagged spars and flotsam all around.

The angular Roman letters across its top were set in black.

In memory of those gallant men of the
SCOTIA STEAMSHIP COMPANY
who gave their lives for their country
in two World Wars.

There were four columns of names inscribed below. A lot of names; a multiplication of weeping widows and fatherless children. My eyes found the one I was searching for with familiar ease, but the pang I'd invariably felt when I stood there previously was sharper, somehow.

JONATHAN HERSCHELL.
Master: M.V. *Highlander*. January, 1941.

The cellar itself held the hushed unease of the crypt. It accommodated its ghosts in gloomy regimentation . . . line upon line of them; each with its meticulously catalogued remains interred within a leather-bound coffin, revealing the name by which it had once lived, and the manner of its death. For ships do live; and ultimately die: some with dignity in their graceful surrender to the erosion of years; some by accident; many with the screams of the breaker's machines rending their once proud bodies to mountains of steel; and very, very many -- when the world becomes angry and full of hate -- by the hands of the assassin; succumbing to the bomb, the mine or the torpedo . . .

Lowlander: By stranding off Zanzibar: July 1896. *Borderer*: By weather North Atlantic: December 1909. *Shetlander*: By collision off Shanghai: May 1912. *Lowlander* again, the second in that ill-fated line: By enemy action: February 1915 . . .

Highlander.

'By enemy action, Captain. On the thirteenth of January, nineteen-forty-one . . .'

Arthur handed the worn red box file to me and I caught the flash of his glasses against the stark overhead lights. 'She was our third *Highlander*, you know. The first was much smaller, of course; built during the eighteen-seventies of some two thousand tons gross . . .'

I wasn't really listening. For reasons I would never admit to anyone I had never found the courage to do this before – to pry into my father's administrative tomb. Perhaps it was because I'd always sensed the pain it would regenerate. Oh,

45

he was never close to me; he'd died when I was six years old and my only memories of him were of a dignified, soft-spoken man who occasionally disturbed the relationship between me and my mother, and who caused her a fleeting happiness when he came, spoilt by a much longer sadness after he had gone. But he was still my flesh and blood, my cause for being, and my mother's grief had amplified my own childish misery when we'd learned of his death. I'd always shied from the stark reality, I shrank from visualising the detail of his passing.

But suddenly there was a need to know. Everything. Because the fact of his sextant's resurrection had devalued what little knowledge I thought I had possessed of his death ... cast doubt, even, upon the true resting place of *Highlander* herself; and of all the men who'd sailed in her on that black day in 1941.

I opened the lid of the file, and found myself staring down at her.

It was a standard photograph, that monochrome print surmounting the neatly clipped and yellowing papers. A routine record taken for her builders during her acceptance trials. They'd taken place in the Clyde; I recognised the Tail O' The Bank in the background even before I turned the photograph over and read the neat legend inked on the reverse.

Motor Vessel *HIGHLANDER*: Yard No. 361.

September, 1938.

I flipped it back and gazed at it, the tightness in my throat mingling with professional appraisal. They'd built ships to look like ships in those far-off pre-war days – not shaped like floating blocks of flats, but with a grace and proportion which made them as one with the sea; a complement to their natural element instead of an alien presence on its surface. My father's *Highlander* had been the first of the Company's then-new class of motor ship; twin screw diesel-powered general cargo liners of ten thousand gross registered tons and a service speed of around fourteen knots.

The Chief Clerk coughed politely behind me and I came back to the present. 'If I might be of help, Captain? Possibly I am a wee bit more familiar with the contents of these boxes than you might be. Now, was there anything you wished to see in particular?'

I shook my head helplessly. How could I tell him when I didn't know myself. 'Just the circumstances of her loss, Arthur. Whatever we have on record – the exact time; weather conditions . . . what messages she transmitted before she went down. Anything pertinent.'

He was already leafing through the papers, eyebrows raised as if to levitate his spectacles clear of his nose. Already he was reliving the past; savouring the musty sweetness of history and tradition. 'I seem to remember . . . Yes I do remember now. She was outward bound for Iceland when it happened. Sailing north from the Clyde here.'

'Iceland?' I echoed in surprise. He dropped his head and peered at me; over his glasses this time.

'Oh, yes. We had a substantial British garrison in Iceland in those early days – before the Americans took over. Your father's ship was carrying military supplies, I would imagine.'

He stopped abruptly and leafed rapidly through the pile again. 'Oh dear! For some reason we do not appear to have a copy of the cargo manifest on the file . . . might it be important, Captain?'

I shrugged. 'I shouldn't think so. I suppose I could always get one from the Ministry of Defence records if it seems necessary.'

He smiled dryly. 'They were called the War Office in those days. And the Ministry of War Transport . . . We British didn't simply defend ourselves then; we went to war.'

Riffle, riffle . . . 'Ah! The weather at the time.'

I glanced at the scrawled note he tendered and then felt my own brow crease in shock. 'Force eleven! Nor' westerly wind force eleven, Arthur? That's practically a hurricane. Sixty knot winds coming straight down from the North Atlantic . . .'

I broke off abruptly. He could see what I was visualising, and the horror of it.

'Indeed,' he murmured gently. 'You can understand why there were no survivors from the *Highlander*. They were very brave men. Very brave.'

Brave? I couldn't help thinking of those resolute, eternally-fixed expressions of the bronze seamen silently surveying all from their marble memory upstairs. Could their flesh and blood models have been so calmly acquiescent? Had they really waited for death without whimper or fight, in the dignified attitudes presented by post-war sculptors?

Or might not more truth have been portrayed through staring, terrified eyes, and shattered limbs still dragging themselves towards the boats. By men bowed in prayer or contorted in panic; still fighting for survival even as their ships reared and began to fall over on top of them?

'Is there a transcript of her last message? There was one, wasn't there?' I asked, hating myself for equating their reactions to what I feared might be my own in such an event. My father must have been stronger than I; surely *he* would have borne his courage even into *Highlander*'s last moments as an anchor to those around him on that listing bridge? I had to believe that. Passionately.

Riffle, riffle, riff . . .

'One,' Davidson said, extracting yet another paper. 'Only the one, Captain. How did you know there was anything?'

'My mother was told. I remember her eyes . . . it confirmed there could be no room for doubt. Or for hope.'

And there it was in my hand. As uncompromising as the

eyes of some anonymous U-boat commander on that fearful night so many years ago.

SSSS . . . SSSS . . . *Highlander*'s shrieked submarine warning prefixing her war call sign and text . . . GBZQ . . . GBZQ . . . HIGHLANDER HIGHLANDER . . . TORPEDOED AND SINKING 22 MILES ENE BUTT OF LEWIS. ON FIRE WITH AFTER HOLDS FLOODING. AM ABANDONING NOW. GOD BE WITH U . . .

I found myself blinking. And then my eyes met the old man's beside me, and his spectacles too magnified moist and brimming lids.

He smiled. Only a little smile.

'I shed a tear every time I come down here, Captain,' the Chief Clerk said without a trace of shame. His hand encompassed the rows of silent, forgotten ships and men. 'Perhaps if more of us still cried for them the world would be a wiser, safer place.'

I focused on the copy signal form again. It had been forwarded to the Company for information from the Naval Officer In Charge, Loch Ewe. Its time of receipt was still legible: 131925Z JAN 41 – twenty-five minutes past seven on the evening of the 13th January, 1941.

It would have been dark then. Pitch dark and freezing in the banshee screech of a severe storm force eleven.

'So there was no doubt.' God, but she must have been sinking fast for them to have no option in that weather.

'And you also have her last known' position – twenty-two miles east nor' east of the Butt of Lewis . . .'

Davidson hesitated. Then he looked at me quizzically. 'I fear I am no navigator, Captain; but does that strike you as significant?'

I screwed my eyes up, trying to visualise the west coast of Scotland, and where Iceland lay in relation to it. 'Not as far offshore as one would imagine, d'you mean, Arthur?'

He shrugged. 'Not only that. But it may not be pertinent.'

I saw it then. 'That would put her *inside* the Hebrides. Just north of The Minches. Yet if she was bound for Iceland I would have expected her to pass west of Barra Head Light, heading up into the Atlantic with the Hebrides on her starboard hand.'

We weren't getting any further by speculation. Naval Control of merchant ships was very tight in those days; they might have routed her to avoid what they believed was a U-boat threat . . . or simply because they didn't always do the obvious, sensible thing. Submarine commanders could work out the obvious, sensible thing too, and lie in wait. It was a gigantic game of global poker, war at sea – and sometimes you were dealt a bad hand.

'Anything else, Arthur?' I asked, with the empty frustration growing within me. I'd got nowhere. Far from being pointed towards an understanding I was discovering additional problems at each step.

He had another riffle and pulled out a last offering. '*Highlander*'s crew list on her last voyage, Captain? Might it help?'

I took it from him with little interest. I'd already seen all those names before – up in the entrance hall. I'd never studied them; they wouldn't have meant anything, apart from one.

The rest were just names; not laughing, cursing, loving, real people with families and problems and joys.

. . . Jonathan Herschell; *Master*. William McLeod; *Chief Officer*. James Devlin; *Second Officer*. Jan van der Kroon; *Third Offic* . . .

'Van der Kroon?' I queried. 'On a British ship?'

Davidson held his glasses delicately and peered at the list. It took him a moment to nod, not without a touch of pride at his own retentive powers.

'I remember, Captain. I'd forgotten the young man's name, but I do remember him now. A free Dutchman. One of those who escaped the Nazi occupation and came over here to fight. Der Kroon. Yes, several of our allies helped to man the Company's ships in that period.'

Forty-three names in total. Forty-three mute participants in an ever growing enigma: a sudden death of witnesses!

I thanked old Davidson and left him to put *Highlander*'s file back in its final resting place while I wearily climbed from the cellars of the Scotia Steamship Company, as it once was. My mind was clouded with a vision of a stricken ship that lay further and further on her beam ends, with monstrous Atlantic seas, all white-streaked and roaring, breaking over her; and boats and spars and drowning men smashing together in a bloodied, raging foam.

I hadn't solved the riddle I had come to research; I'd found, instead, good cause to find it still more inexplicable. If *Highlander* had sunk in that particular place and on that awful night then there was no conceivable way by which any part of her or her crew could have reached the shore other than as fragmented and unrecognisable flotsam.

Yet at least one part of her had.

My father's sextant. Untouched by the ravages of the sea.

*

They were already waiting for me in Scuddie's when I arrived. It was packed with one-fur-the-roaders pouring out of the Queen Street offices and shops, and I had a job to find them for a few moments. Then I caught a glimpse of Charlie's height surfacing above the jostling, good-natured press of heads, and fought my way through.

Fran managed as ever to make one more aware of the form concealed beneath her black leather coat than most starlets are able to do while topless on a beach at the Cannes Film Festival. She was an enchantress in carefully composed camouflage; a winter-necessitated covering which still, miraculously, managed to emphasise her sensuality against the unisex sway of anoraks and jerseys and fur around her. When she kissed me I couldn't help wondering cynically if her

51

so casual allure had been designed to captivate me or Detective Sergeant McQueen. It didn't make me any better disposed towards him.

'I'll remember to call you "Captain",' he said, and to give him his due there was more attempt to be friendly than I'd seen on our previous meeting. I forced a smile back.

'John's easier.'

'He's a Donald; darling; Donnie to his friends,' Fran said, turning wide-eyed intimacy on to D.S. McQueen. 'It's a *super* name – Donald!'

'Ohhhh, come on!' Charlie jeered at her, but without raising the slightest flush of contrition in her high-boned cheeks. He pushed an amber glass across the crowded table towards me. 'I put one up ready for you. It's an Islay malt – they say it's not just whisky; it's pure dreams in palatable form.'

Of course he wouldn't have known from experience. I'd never seen Charlie drink anything stronger than grapefruit juice all the years I'd known him, yet there was no surprise at meeting him in a pub – pubs appeared to be the mandatory information-gathering environment for news reporters. And policemen.

'Did you get any further?' Fran asked anxiously. Apart from her inborn curiosity I could understand her concern; after last night's disappointment she must have been hoping to find me in a more settled frame of mind. I could only shrug, though.

'Negative. Just more confused than ever.'

I hesitated, glancing towards McQueen. I didn't know how much Charlie had told him, and whether or not he was taking it seriously even now. He'd obviously noted the way the sextant had shaken me yesterday, but a lot of odd people turn up at police stations; he was bound to develop a certain cynicism. Certainly he didn't do much to encourage me, whatever he thought.

'I've got the bones of it,' he acknowledged shortly, giving

nothing away. It may have been intended as an informal meeting but there was still an uneasy defensiveness between myself and McQueen. I got the feeling that he'd been railroaded into this confrontation; that if he'd known I would be there, he wouldn't have come.

I think Charlie could sense our mounting wariness.

'Tell us what you found out then, Johnny,' he encouraged quickly. It was obvious he wanted co-operation from McQueen and was nervous that I'd jeopardise the delicate relationship between press and police by getting uptight. Swallowing my reservations about D.S. McQueen, I related as much as I knew myself. Oh, I didn't dramatise it – there was no way any of them could have even began to visualize the scene, and the ultimate fear that must have been abroad on that screaming night of four decades before; only another seaman was competent to imagine the horror of a thing like that – but another seaman couldn't help me solve the riddle of its aftermath. I needed information now.

Of course I should have guessed that, like every other detail concerning the loss of my father's ship, it wasn't going to be straightforward.

'Presumably I have to tackle things backwards?' I hazarded tentatively. 'Start from the present – from where the sextant was actually stolen – and trace it back from there?'

Charlie and Fran nodded agreement, but McQueen looked strangely displeased again. It was that curious reaction which stirred my premonition of heavy weather ahead; that and the way he said flatly, 'Aye, well you realise I'm not bound to give you any background information regarding the recovery of your father's sextant? Especially as I now have reason to believe you may take it further.'

I frowned uncertainly; not sure whether he was being serious or not. Fran wriggled closer along the seat and laid her long fingers against his arm, shamelessly allowing them to trickle downwards to rest upon his hand.

'Oh , ou could tell John a little bit more, Donnie? And I'd love to find out, too. About where it was stolen from, and who actually stole it?'

He eyed her impassively; I noticed he didn't withdraw his hand though. 'No you wouldn't, Francine Templeton. For one thing Charlie wouldnae be buying me a drink if that's all you needed: and you're in the game too – you know fine you can get all that by looking through the records at the Sheriff Court.'

'I did,' Charlie interjected smoothly. 'This morning, first thing. So you're right, Donnie lad; that is why I'm buying you a drink – to find out the real truth.'

Truth? I stared at the three of them uncomprehendingly. Where did *truth* come into it? McQueen had already told me all I needed to know yesterday, hadn't he? I hadn't hoisted it in fully at the time, but he'd certainly mentioned a village . . . Laichy, that was it. And then it registered – the anomaly which had previously evaded me.

'That's a point. Why did you return the sextant to *me* when all you had to do was hand it back to the person it was taken from? Why did you go to all the trouble of tracing me when, for all you knew, I'd maybe sold or given it away years ago?'

'That's what I mean,' Charlie reinforced me. '*That's* why you're drinking on my tab, Detective Sergeant Donald McQueen. So Johnny here at least knows what he's up against when he starts to trace back.'

'When *we* start to trace back,' Fran said. Her hand went to my arm, and this time I knew she wasn't kidding. I also knew I was getting lost; lost and not a little irritated.

McQueen suddenly nodded. It was almost a kind of surrender; as if he realised he'd been cornered and accepted defeat. He wasn't too pleased, though.

'You're too bloody clever, Charlie,' he growled. 'What did you do – look up the list of productions?'

'Ve haf our vays . . .' Charlie smirked in a thick, mock-teutonic accent. He saw me staring and gave me a funny grin. 'Aye, you may well look, Johnny. But it never was produced as evidence in court at the trial: your dad's sextant – whatever Donnie here told you. But then at that time he never realised its recovery was more significant than the usual run-of-the-mill thefts he handles.'

He turned back to McQueen, who was sitting grimly silent. 'It's important we get the full facts, Donnie. This is one time the C.I.D. can't close a file wi'out tidying up the rough edges.'

I'd had enough! I felt Fran's fingers grip my arm warningly, but I couldn't stop myself. 'Wait a minute. Rough edges . . . Not produced as evidence in court? Maybe you should tell me what's going *on*, McQueen! Or do I need to come to the station tomorrow and formally demand a precise statement of how and why my father's property came to be in the hands of the bloody police . . .'

'Easy, Johnny,' Charlie urged anxiously. He knew McQueen, and exactly how far he could go with him, but I was different – I wasn't in the club. Maybe it wasn't politic to lean on any police officer but I could afford to offend McQueen's dignity where a newsman couldn't.

I shook my head doggedly. 'No, I want to know, Charlie – where it was stolen from. And I'm going to find out.'

McQueen said tightly, 'There was some doubt.'

I stared at him. 'Doubt? You send a man to prison for it . . . and now you say there's some doubt?'

People were looking at us now and looking quickly away again, embarrassed. McQueen was getting pretty uptight as well now. My inference had got him on the raw.

'You'd better believe me, Herschell; I don't give evidence before the Sheriff that puts men in Barlinnie without cause. Not even nasty wee villains like McGlashan.'

'McGlashan? Was he the man that stole it – who maybe was and maybe wasn't guilty?'

'Oh, he was guilty, Johnny,' Charlie assured me hurriedly.

'He pleaded guilty on all counts. Admitted to the theft of every item recovered from his address.'

'Including the sextant?'

'Aye,' McQueen snapped. 'Including the bloody sextant.'

'Then why the doubt? Why not produce it at his trial, McQueen, and why not tell me where it was stolen from?'

'Because the party McGlashan alleged he thieved it from denied point blank he'd ever seen it before, Herschell. And I've got a file of serious crime *that* thick waiting back in the office – I've no bloody time to nit-pick at an already proven case.'

I blinked at the angry detective sitting opposite. They were all watching us now, everybody in Scuddie's Bar, and suddenly I felt embarrassed. McQueen looked uncomfortable too, and I realised we weren't getting anywhere.

'I'm sorry,' I said tightly. 'But I still don't understand. This McGlashan – you mean he did admit that he'd stolen it. Presumably up in Laichy, somewhere?'

McQueen shrugged, his flash of temper dying too. 'Aye, he did. And exactly whereabouts he'd taken it from.'

'Yet they denied they'd ever possessed or even seen it?'

'Aye. Quite positively.'

Fran turned to him. 'I don't see the problem. Surely McGlashan must have been lying, Donnie. He's a self-confessed villain anyway from what you say.'

D.S. McQueen shook his head slowly, uncertainly. 'Not necessarily, Fran. Usually they're only too keen to tell all once we've pinned a few jobs on them; ask for everything to be taken into account. It doesnae add that much to the sentence they're going to get anyway – and their slate's clean when they come out; the wee bastards can start their thieving all over again from fresh. In fact McGlashan even admitted to having lifted other items from the same address, come to that, and the owner confirmed them as having been stolen.'

I picked his meaning up immediately. 'Then he had

56

nothing to lose by including the sextant? Therefore the suggestion is that the person he claimed to have stolen it *from* is lying instead.'

McQueen was shaking his head again.

'Only that's not likely either,' he said with certainty. 'He'd have even less reason to cover up having seen it than McGlashan.'

'You can't be sure, Donnie,' Fran put in. 'Maybe he shouldn't have had it either. Maybe *he'd* even stole it himself, originally?'

'According to the records there were six cases of forcible entry heard against McGlashan,' Charlie probed. 'Which one of those *was* the one he said he got the sextant from, Donnie?'

That was when McQueen started to smile, but it wasn't the smile of a contented man; just the rueful grimace of a policeman who'd spent his young life trying earnestly to understand people's motives, and only gradually accepted that he never, ever would.

'That, Charlie, is the nub o' the whole problem. And the reason why the police have grounds to believe that it *is* nothing more than a crooked wee opportunist's error; mistaken or not . . .'

He turned to me, and for the first time there was a trace of apology in his eyes. 'McGlashan swore blind he thieved your father's sextant from the *church* up in Laichy – yet the claim that he did is even more strenuously denied by a man we have every reason to believe.'

I didn't need to hear anymore. But I listened all the same.

'A man of the cloth, John,' Detective Sergeant Donald McQueen stated with an emphasis that left no further room for discussion. 'Laichy's very own Presbyterian minister!'

CHAPTER FOUR

—— *1941* ——

For a full minute after *Highlander* became a part ship there was a terrible silence. Even the North Atlantic itself seemed to hesitate in its fury; the shriek of the storm to diminish as if appalled by the awareness of some cataclysm within its domain, yet not of its own making. It was a shocked and dreadful perception.

During the millisecond flash of the torpedo's detonation a gash had been torn in her hull through which two double-decked buses could have been driven side by side. The expanding fireball had then raced onward, igniting the cargo stowed in her port 'tween decks and melting the steel bulkhead separating those upper spaces of five and six holds before finally erupting skywards, spewing hatch covers and a behemoth spray of steel higher than the truck of her fractured main mast. Even before she had fallen-off into the valleys which threatened to capsize her, *Highlander* was tumbling a vomit of glowing scrap from her wound. Over the void a tracked Bren-gun carrier, its white camouflage paint peeling in blazing strips, see-sawed with the fine-point balance of a ballerina, teetering on raddle-edged deck plates tortured in frozen form.

To her crew, realisation came as a slow dawning. To a great many of them there was no time for any understanding that they *had* been attacked; in some cases they didn't even *hear* the explosion which killed them. Blast created the initial horror – Second Cook Johnstone, who had been waiting at the head of the centrecastle ladder in company with Steward Sangster for a break in the incoming seas, was blown straight through the guardrails and out into the blackness as cleanly as if he'd never existed, yet such were the vagaries of high explosive that less than an arm's length from him, Archie Sangster was left with a cigarette dangling from his slack mouth and not even the woollen hat disturbed from the crown of his head.

Blast also caused the death of the youngest member of *Highlander*'s crew in that initial split-second. Fifteen-year-old Apprentice Jolly had been standing outside the half deck door on the after end of the boat deck when the torpedo hit. He'd been standing there with eyes full of youthful excitement; staring out at the North Atlantic seas as they careered almost to a level with his platform at one moment, then fell away with a giant sucking to be lost to sight in the next. He'd never seen waves anything like those, not ever in his whole short life; or maybe once when he'd been on holiday with his dad to Blackpool and they'd both raced the spray back to the shelter of the promenade stances as the breakers exploded with monstrous glee across the windswept beach. Then a proper explosion had come without any glee at all, whereupon the blast picked the boy Jolly up in its fiery clutch and forced him headfirst down a ventilator column only half the width of his shoulders.

The blast pounced upon another first trip victim, too – Standby-man Jimmie Beattie who at that moment was half way through being sick again in the lee of the poop housing. But in Jimmie's case it was a gentle caprice; a typically teutonic bit o' jiggery-pokery only tae be expected of they bluidy Germans that wis tryin' tae kill him. One second he was manfully giving his all on the main deck level, doing no harm to no man . . . an' then FLASH! An' he found hisself sittin' spook-eyed an' vague one whole deck higher – up on top of the housing itself with his brain rattling like castanets an' a bluidy great four-inch gun pointing out over his head at naething in particular, an' wi' no one there tae fire it even if there had been a target in sight.

Christ, but would *he* hae somethin' tae say tae his mum once he got back tae the Gorbals . . .

But blast without debris is like a tiger without teeth; it can overwhelm only by its weight. *Highlander*'s own massive protection from the storms she encountered provided the teeth and claws for the tiger – the hatch covers originally securing numbers five and six holds from the onslaught of the breaking sea.

Each gently round-backed steel H-beam weighed over a ton, yet the devil's luck of U-boat 236 had sent them spinning aloft on the puffball crest of that detonation like matchsticks flicked by a contemptuous finger. Having reached their zenith they glittered and cartwheeled, reflecting the holocaust below, and then returned seawards, spearing into the depths with only the slightest plumes of foam in an ocean of foam to mark their ingress. Or most of them did. Others never even soared particularly high, simply scattering across the after well deck in a scything flail to uproot winches, sever ventilators, carry away a large part of the rigging which secured the mortally stricken main mast. One even flew with comical accuracy to split *Highlander*'s tall funnel where it lodged, protruding from either side with the macabre aspect of Frankensteinian electrodes.

One solitary beam was expelled from its seating in number six hatch coaming and deflected aft towards the adjacent break of the poop. The foremost accommodation space at that point formed the greasers' mess aboard *Highlander*. Normally a favoured refuge immediately after the evening meal, that night had already seen the mess packed to capacity by the addition of those of the deck department who were seeking escape from the aroma of Bosun McColl's gastronomic self-indulgence.

The beam struck precisely at right angles on a level with the crowded settee, penetrating the half-inch plating with the ease of a javelin passing through cardboard. As it breached the bulkhead, so a vagrant comet tail of the torpedo's fireball followed; instantly expanding within the confining steel box in the micro-flash of its entry.

There were fourteen men in the greasers' mess when U-236 committed her somewhat optimistic act of war. None of them survived. Even for those not relaxing in the path of the imploding missile it was an instantaneous end. One sharp, incomprehending intake of breath in that superheated atmosphere was all the co-operation that death required.

In the awful quietude which followed there was only the muted scend of the sea outside, and the steady roar of the flames.

*

At seventeen minutes past seven the sudden jangle of the bridge telegraph electrified the ship; jolting even the most badly shocked into reaction.

Second Engineer McKechnie had been the first to respond to the emergency. As soon as his unthinking hands had cut the throttles down below he found himself pushing roughly past those gaping football *afficionados* Cullen and Eadie, and reaching with calm precision for the shiny brass handles of the engine room telegraph repeater above the control platform.

Numbly he swung them in parallel. BOTH ENGINES STOPPED! His training had informed the bridge of his action even before the echo of the detonation had faded, and while the strangled revolutions of the abruptly severed port shaft were still decreasing. Only then did fear strike Second Engineer McKechnie. He stood there in his white boiler suit and stared uneasily up through the spider's web maze of near-vertical ladders to where the only means of escape lay; and muttered, 'Christ!'

Greaser Eadie said shakily, 'Och, man, but we've copped an awfy packet down aft.'

Fireman Cullen simply started to run for the ladder until McKechnie's hand grabbed him, spun him round. They stared bleach-faced at each other across the platform as the ship fell off and began to roll alarmingly. Cullen was a big man; much bigger than the officer.

'Wait, Cullen!' the Second snarled, struggling against his own terror. 'You'll wait for bluidy orders fae the bridge the same as me.'

And so they waited. Already they could hear water rushing into the ship from somewhere close at hand.

*

Even the Captain had been stunned into momentary inaction when the event which he'd dreaded for the past eighteen months finally occurred. He felt *Highlander* lift bodily on the crescendo of the blast, then sensed the tremor of the turning screws suddenly cut and the deck heel as she slipped beam-on to the seas. He blinked as a crack zigzagged across his reflection in the mirror; dividing the shocked frown with sardonic mischief. 'Seven years bad luck,' he thought vaguely. 'Seven bloody years of bad luck to come . . . !'

Then the grey eyes staring blankly at him widened as his dazed brain slammed back into gear, and Jonathan Herschell was running for the door. Oddly, as is the case in times of stress, he suddenly realised he was still holding the shaving brush. Skidding to a halt he turned and carefully replaced it in the soap mug. Then began to run again. Still in his shirt sleeves.

The first thing he heard as he dived into the alleyway was a frantic banging at some nearby door . . . Third Officer van der Kroon's. Whirling for a second time he threw himself aft, smelling the reek of cordite hanging in the air even as he lunged for the handle. It was jammed fast by the force of the explosion. Herschell cursed, placed his back against the opposite bulkhead and kicked savagely. The door flew open with a rip of splitting wood and der Kroon stumbled out with a wide-eyed stare and a book in his hand.

'Use the hook next time,' the Captain roared, already moving again. 'That's why we keep the bloody doors hooked back, Mister. Just for times like this . . .'

'Oook?' van der Kroon muttered dazedly, beginning to leaf stupidly through the phrase book. 'What is der *'ook*, please?'

But Third Officer van der Kroon had gashed his head badly when the torpedo flung him bodily from his berth, and it would take him a few moments to think positively. Especially in English.

Just before John Herschell reached the door leading to the boatdeck and bridge ladders Chief Radio Operator Trent came rushing out of the Third Engineer's cabin in a black fury.

'They've upset my bloody draught board!' he raged. 'Three crowns I 'ad, Captain . . . an' them bastards scatter the bloody lot. It's bloody intolerable!'

'I'm sorry, Mister Trent,' *Highlander*'s master said as sympathetically as if they'd accidentally bumped each other during a heavy sea in peacetime. 'Terribly sorry about it all.'

'Bastards!' the Chief Sparks echoed again. Then he stared at the Captain, and the Captain stared back at him; and Trent squealed, 'Christ, we've been torpedoed . . .'

'Standby for a distress position!' Herschell's roar hung in the alleyway of the officers' accommodation. But the Captain himself had already gone.

*

After the torpedo had struck, and even while fourteen sailors were brewing-up directly below him in the greasers' mess-deck, Bosun McColl was still chewing on the most lethal onion there ever was. There had been a BOOOOOOOM, and a horrific flash and a sudden contraction of the air within the seamen's mess on the poop; whereupon Lamptrimmer Arnott was scrabbling on the compo deck with a mug of near-boiling tea thrown over him, cursing and squealing in fright all at the same time, and the whole bloody ship was rearing high in the sky before falling back with a thunderous crash of displacing water.

McColl bit into the onion again without being aware of what he was doing. There was a pain in his back which felt as if he'd been kicked by an Irish stallion, and a convex bulge had suddenly appeared in the centre of the deck while the atmosphere had gone all fuzzy, with a choking fog of smoke hanging motionless in layers resembling the fug of a Macao opium den. The other two men who'd braved the Bosun's company – Ship's Carpenter Livie and A.B. Gillan – sat frozen on the opposite settee, eyes blank with temporary incomprehension. Gillan only had three fingers on his right hand where, a moment before, there had been five. A rivet, driven upwards from the deck by the force of the explosion had taken off the other two as cleanly as if shot by a .303 bullet.

Then someone began screaming from below them, and all four men – Lamps still steaming gently in his marination of hot sweet tea and Gillan spraying flecks of blood with careless abandon – collided at the door. The force of the explosion had torn it from its dog; slammed it tight shut. To McColl, wrestling with the handle, it felt as if they were locked inside the Bank of England.

'Gerroff! Stan' back an' let me gettagoodkickatit!'

'Torpedo!' Chippie was yelling. 'We been fished . . .'

'Lifejackets. Whaur's ma bluidy lifejacket?'

A giant sea left the after end hanging in space as it sighed astern. Then *Highlander* fell into it, wallowing monstrously. The deck angled to port and seemed to take a very long time to recover. The screaming from without reached a new peak of intensity.

'She's *going* f'r Christ's sake . . .'

'Get yer ass outa the way, Arnott!'

McColl still managed to think straighter than his Captain when he finally got a clear run at the door. The kick-out panel at the bottom, especially weakened for just such an emergency, neatly fell out when his boot took it.

There was smoke blowing freely up the internal ladder from the black gang accommodation below theirs. The keening wail of someone's misery was coming from that direction too. Ahead of them they could see the red glare of fire on deck, flickering from the oblong hatch where once there had been a watertight steel door. It outlined their only route to survival should the ship be on the point of foundering immediately . . . none of them took it. Maybe each of those four shocked men realised that, if he did, then those squeals of supplication would stay with him for every waking moment of whatever life he had left. Bosun McColl reached the bottom of the ladder first . . .

The whole line of the internal bulkhead separating the greasers' mess compartment from its service alleyway had disappeared; its flimsy structure uprooted and carried bodily across the intervening corridor by the deadweight of the imploding hatch beam. There was no individual recreation space now; simply a charred open-plan shambles extending from the bottom of the ladder forward to the buckled plating still roughly forming what had been the break of the poop. They could recognise it as being the transverse skin of the ship facing on to the well deck because, through the ragged breach caused by some missile's entry, they could detect the flames jetting from the open mouths of five and six holds.

But they didn't spend a lot of time staring at *that*. Not when the other things before them demanded such immediate attention.

The below-deck crowd and their seamen guests still remained in the postures held at the moment of their passing;

a black and scorch-red tableau of jolly bonhomie. A space –
approximating to the width required to accommodate, say,
three closely-seated bodies – had been cleared in line with the
beam's superheated ingress; otherwise the blast had done
little to disturb those dead men from the pattern of their
comradely togetherness. One hairless, shiny-macabre
voyager still draped his arm around the shoulders of his
shrivelled friend; another held a sooted mug of tea to
carbonised lips, still clenched in daintily hooked claws. A
third had died in the process of yawning; teeth white as snow
against the gaping mouth with arms outstretched in
luxurious abandon never quite completed.

The only survivor of that cremated host, who had stayed
conscious and screaming for the eternity after the torpedo hit,
expired as the appalled watchers reached the scene; for even a
miracle cannot keep dehydrated lungs inflated for very long.
And as he sighed a grateful appreciation of his going, a whisp
of smoke escaped his tortured maw.

'Check the cabins on both levels; collect anyone still alive;
make sure you an' them 'ave got a lifejacket . . . then follow me
to the deck, lads,' the Bosun said with disciplined calm.

And then he vomited. For the first time in forty years at
sea.

*

Herschell took the starboard bridge ladder three rungs at a
time. Fourth Officer Findlay was already waiting for him at
the top. The glare from the fires aft illuminated the tightly-
controlled fear on the youngster's face, but at least it *was*
controlled. The Captain felt grateful for that; panic could be
a contagious weakness which would kill men just as surely as
any high explosive bomb. Even more surely, given the
weather they were currently experiencing.

'Where's Mister McLeod?' he shouted.

'Chart room, sir. Taking off our position.'

'Any word from the engine room?'

'No, sir. Apart from telegraphing both engines are stopped.'

'Get them on the phone. Anyone hurt up here?'

'No, sir.'

Herschell swung round briefly, looking astern for the first time. Everything was red, flickering red as if a piece of the setting sun was flaring on the after well deck. Except for the forward face of the poop housing; that was black; twisted black and shimmering through the heat haze rising from the holds. Everything between it and his eye was etched in stark silhouette; the mangled rails lining the after end of the boat deck, the main mast ominously tilted, the ready-swung out davits hooked vacantly over the empty space where number two starboard lifeboat should have hung.

He knew there would be casualties reported very soon. A lot of them.

It was light within the wheelhouse itself. The watchkeeping apprentice – Beedie wasn't it? – stood scrutinising him with huge round eyes and Herschell felt a pang of inadequacy as he realised the look on the child's face was one of implicit trust. As though the presence of the master meant that suddenly everything would be all right again.

'Why haven't you got your lifejacket on, son?' he asked kindly; hesitating despite his urgency.

'I'll put it on if you'd like me to, sir,' Beedie said helpfully; true grit showing clear through the apprehension.

'I'd like you to,' the Captain confirmed. 'It's a handy thing to have, even if you don't need it.'

Secretly he knew Beedie would, and before much more time had passed. His one brief glance astern, allied with his knowledge of the nature of their cargo, suggested that much. Whether the lifejacket would help Apprentice Beedie live for much longer than it would take a small boy to drown without one was pure speculation; sometimes a North Atlantic storm can fill a man's lungs with water even if he's lucky enough to be sitting erect in a lifeboat, such is the density of its spray. But it offered Beedie something a little more practical to pin his faith on than simply having his Captain on the bridge.

Quartermaster Hotchkiss was still struggling with the wheel. His yellow sou'wester had slipped sideways on his head giving him an unusually jaunty appearance. Festive. Like at a party.

'Wheel's jammed, Cap'n. Ah gied her twenty o' starboard helm while she fell off tae port, then the bluidy wheel jammed solid.'

'We've lost steerage way by now, anyroad,' the Captain growled philosophically. It was a curious feeling – this unexpected self-control; the way in which his mind was flashing through the options open to him at high speed. Yet his outward calm was easy to maintain. Herschell had always had one fear above everything else; that he wouldn't be able to cope when the unthinkable happened. But already he knew he could, and he felt tremendously grateful to . . . well, to God, he supposed; for allowing him the privilege of dignity.

Not that he believed implicitly in God. He'd never really thought about Him much before. But he was perfectly ready to accept assistance from any quarter, and already he'd received a demonstration that some forms of supernatural power did exist, hadn't he? For surely only the Devil Incarnate could have guided the hand which fired that bloody torpedo!

He met Mister McLeod face to grim face at the chartroom door. He noticed the Mate didn't bother hooking the blackout curtain back in place. It didn't seem to matter a great deal any longer.

'Twenty-two miles east nor' east the Butt of Lewis!' McLeod said flatly. 'It's a gey long swim.'

Herschell glanced out past the Mate, through the open wheelhouse door to where another giant sea, higher than the

68

angled bridge wing, reared curling and white as the skin of a dead man.

'If it comes to swimming, the distance is a wee bit academic.'

'I was aye one for the jokes,' McLeod grunted, but he didn't smile. Neither did the Captain.

Highlander toppled sluggishly sideways into the following trough and brought up with a jolt. The Fourth Mate, angled at fifty-five degrees and clinging to the engine room phone, muttered a startled 'Christ!' while only Hotchkiss's experienced hand prevented the young apprentice from galloping downhill and out over the exposed port wing. Even McLeod's expression betrayed an uncharacteristic unease. The motion also emphasised the urgency in getting a distress call under way; the ship was lying badly – any unnecessary delay and she was likely to make up his mind for him. Yet he still needed information; the Chief Engineer's assessment of the damage below was essential to any decision he took on whether to abandon.

He swung. 'Mister Findlay!'

'Sir.'

'I'm going aft with Mister McLeod but I won't be long. If the Bosun or Chippie find their way up here, send 'em down aft again.'

He didn't say, 'If they are still alive'. They all knew how close the detonation had been to the poop accommodation; the facts would make themselves known before long without underlining the horror of their situation to Findlay.

'. . . when Mister Devlin and the Third Mate arrive, hand over the bridge to Jolly and you go with van der Kroon; clear the covers from all boats and ease the gripes ready for immediate launching. Muster all hands you can find on the boat deck and break out the lifejacket lockers for anyone who's lost his own. Understand?'

'Aye, aye, sir.'

Then Findlay hesitated, looking worried. 'But what about Chief Graham when I contact him? What d'you want me to tell him, sir?'.

'Give him my compliments. Ask if he would kindly stand-by the phone until I get back. Two or three minutes only.'

The youngster frowned. 'Say he can't wait. Say the engine room's already flooding, sir . . . what'll I tell him to do then?'

This time Herschell did manage a smile. It was a dry one.

'In that case I don't imagine you'll have to tell him anything, Mister Findlay. I rather imagine it'll be the Chief telling *you* what to do.'

Second Officer Devlin and a bloody-faced van der Kroon tumbled anxiously through the starboard door as the Captain whirled to follow McLeod, already clattering urgently down the port bridge ladder towards the fire. He didn't wait; the time for formalities was past. As he slid down the ladder rails, arms braced to ease his weight, he nearly collided with the Mate. McLeod had stopped abruptly, eyes fixed towards the sky above. Herschell followed his stare in curiosity. With a sense of shock he recognised a steel hatch beam spitted clear through the funnel, spiralling wildly against the black scudding clouds.

'Me an' the lads were lucky,' McLeod grunted sombrely, 'a few feet lower and that would've carved straight through the bluidy wheelhouse.'

Herschell didn't answer. But then he wasn't entirely certain that McLeod's luck was all it appeared to be. Maybe, just maybe, under the present circumstances both he and his fellow watchkeepers on the bridge would decide it would have been easier if that beam *had* followed a slightly lower trajectory and killed them cleanly.

They began to run, stumbling and sliding over the debris strewn across the upper decks by the force of the blast. It was a nightmare passage under the flickering light of the flames, with armoured glass windows blown in as if made of sugar crystal and rails twisted into unbelievable contortions.

The Captain halted once more; only briefly, to stare upwards again but this time with stunned revulsion. There was a ventilator situated to port of the engine room skylight, high above the apprentices' half deck. It wasn't a very large ventilator as ventilators on big ships go, but nevertheless it appeared to have a pair of legs protruding stiffly from its bell mouth. Human legs. Like a metallic boa constrictor with a half-digested prize . . .

'Holy Mary, Mither o' God,' Chief Officer McLeod breathed, shocked to the core of his hardbitten soul.

The Captain grabbed his arm savagely; fighting to maintain his own equilibrium. 'Come on, Mister!' he snarled above the roar of the flames. His voice, for the first time, held a terrible anger.

But it was only when they reached the after end of the boat deck to hang, disbelieving, over the blackened, torn rails to gaze into the very heart of the torpedo wound below, that they confirmed how grievously stricken their ship was.

For Captain Herschell's ultimate fear had indeed come to pass. Irrespective of the great gash ripped in her port side, *Highlander*'s upper holds were already blazing with an intensity which dried the sea-sweat from their faces and caused them to flinch at the searing heat. Instantly they became aware that a third element now had to be set against their prospects of survival; even more critical than any factors affecting general storm-worthiness and the likelihood of restoring engine and steering power.

Yet they also realised that neither ship's officers nor engineers were any more qualified to speculate about the hazard they faced than a daredevil small child who buries a firecracker in the base of a bonfire, and then lights the top and hovers, wondering how long it will take for the heat to expand downwards and explode the cracker – a sort of time, temperature and ultimate detonation experiment, for which the necessary ingredients were already available. And the process triggered.

They undoubtedly had the heat source at the top of the bonfire – in this case situated in the upper tween decks of *Highlander*'s after hatches.

They also had a firm time base from which to begin their count-down. It was now seven twenty p.m., only four minutes after the torpedo had struck the hull.

They even had the firecracker; conveniently buried at the core of their experimental oven. It was a very large firecracker, and would leave no doubt at all when the moment of revelation came. It had been placed precisely, almost as if in anticipation of the great pyrotechnic gamble; distributed evenly throughout the lower holds of numbers five and six before they sailed from Gourock.

Six hundred and fifty tons of ammunition. Various calibres.

CHAPTER FIVE

'Shugie McGlashan committed six thefts to subsidise his June tour of the west coast resorts,' Charlie said musingly. 'Three up in Ullapool; one from an Oban hotel room; one from an old biddie's croft out by Lochinver, the conscienceless wee bastard, and . . .'

He passed the notes he'd taken from the Sheriff Court records earlier, summarising a petty Glasgow crook's holiday with pay, '. . . and the one that seems to be favourite for the moment, according to the word of McQueen the Polis!'

'Laichy Church?' I muttered, taking the pad and glowering at it as though trying to terrify it into revealing all.

'Where is Laichy anyway?' Fran asked from the doorway. I turned and eyed her across the big Victorian living room of the flat. She'd obviously decided that tonight, mystery or no mystery, my concentration on matters concerning the sextant were to be channelled into a direction not unconnected with its first three letters. Charlie hardly bothered to glance at her – four-inch satin mules, a purple silk emphasis of curves and a sweet sophistication of shining, high-coiled hair could have been superseded by seaboots, boiler suit and a fisherman's sou'wester for all the attention he paid.

She'd still have looked just as desirable to me, though. If it hadn't been for a cretin called McGlashan.

'Yeah, where is it exactly?' I put in gloomily.

'Laichy? I spent the *Citizen*'s time looking that up too,' Charlie said, all pleased with himself. He slipped into a sonorous monotone. 'Beneath the breaking of anger, my children; above the finger of Stoer . . .'

'Don't be bloody childish, Charlie,' Fran snapped. Childishly. But I had to agree with her – it was one of Charlie Sullivan's more irritating habits; answering questions with riddles. And we had enough riddles already.

'She's right. Don't mess about,' I echoed with feeling. 'Where *is* this Laichy place. And how big is it when you've found it?'

'The breaking of anger . . .' Charlie explained with laborious insistence on playing the game to the bitter end. 'Cape Wrath, see? The waves breaking on . . .'

'Oh, very droll. And finger?' I surrendered wearily. But when you had Charlie for a friend you had to tolerate a lot of odd facets to his character. Well, he had to find *something* to utilise those dormant brain cells which would have been fully occupied in the case of most blokes living with an Aphrodisian beauty like Fran.

'Finger . . . point? Point of *Stoer*, Johnny lad. Which lies south of Eddrachillis Bay. Laichy is a wee crofter community right up north between Eddrachillis and Cape Wrath.'

'How wee?'

'Two hundred-plus Heilandmen. And maybe a dog or three.'

Fran came over and sat beside us, studiously covering her legs while staring pointedly at me. The withdrawal of privilege didn't concern me too much, though; the straining robe fell away again as fast as silk would slide over skin.

'That's *really* way up north,' she commented, yielding to the inevitable.

'About as far as you can get without a boat,' Charlie confirmed. 'According to the gazetteer there isn't even a proper road to the loch; there are still places up on that north-west coast that are practically as isolated now as they were when Prince Charlie met Flora MacDonald.'

'You said "loch",' I queried. 'Is Laichy far inland, then?'

'Sea loch, I should've said; Loch Fhadaig, Johnny.

Smaller than the others in that area – Laxford, Inchard an' those – but still a big, deep, wild hole in the coast. According to the map Laichy's at the head of it . . .'

'Not quite my idea of a swinging town,' I reflected vaguely.

'Oh, I dunno,' Charlie said. 'There's good climbing there. Ben Stack; Foinaven; Quinag – most of the Sutherland peaks are within staggering distance.'

'That's hardly what I meant,' I retorted. As a fairly lethargic seaman I found that other facet of Charlie Sullivan the most baffling of all – the way that, when he wasn't battering himself to a pulp on a rugby pitch, he was heading north, with a coil of rope and spiked boots and a Tyrolean hat in the car, just so's he could spend his free weekends pretending to be a bloody mountain goat.

I was glad I didn't live with him permanently; I'd never have managed to keep up – apart from in the field of feminine conquest, that is. Maybe I'd been wrong all the time; maybe I knew now why Charlie Sullivan could ignore even Fran's most unsubtle invitations to cavort, and had been capable of refusing all those other female advances over the years.

He wasn't odd at all, Charlie wasn't: he was just too bloody tired!

'Give us the list again,' he said, reaching over. I handed it to him and he frowned down the neatly spaced column of addresses.

'One thing for certain,' Fran remarked. 'The sextant must have come from *one* of those places. McGlashan may have got mixed up about which one, but as Donnie said – he'd have made very sure he admitted to all the jobs he'd done so's the police couldn't come back at him again later.'

'So where do we start?' I appealed. 'You're the fact-finders; what would you do?'

Charlie chewed his lip pensively, then shrugged. 'Still with the obvious. In Laichy.'

'Obvious? Like McQueen said, Charlie, it was the minister

himself up there who denied having seen it before. *He* wouldn't lie.'

'Anyone lies,' Charlie retorted cynically, 'if their motive's strong enough. And remember McQueen told you the local police had received the same denials from everyone else on this list. They're maybe no' all ministers of the Church of Scotland but, until we can prove different, they've no more reason to cover up than the holy man o' Laichy. So it's back to the gospel of McGlashan. At least he's *specific*, and it's the only specific thing we've got in the whole of this Chinese bloody puzzle.'

'So what next? Go and see McGlashan?' Fran hazarded.

'Do you know him, this McGlashan? Isn't he supposed to be in prison?'

Charlie shrugged a Glasgow-weary dismissal. 'I know a thousand Shugie McGlashans in this city, Johnny, and they're all the same . . . but there's no point; not yet. McQueen's got as much out of him as anyone would. He's probably back in his wee bog of iniquity by now anyway, with Barlinnie a fond memory. He went down a fair time ago, mind; while you were away.'

'Then what?'

Charlie looked at the two of us, then his eyes fell to the elegantly uninhibited cross of Fran's long legs and followed them up; expressionlessly taking in the taut silken curves and the swell of her breathing. Finally his eyes met hers and something passed between them; something understanding; a wistfulness for what ought to have been.

'You two need a holiday,' Charlie prescribed with avuncular gravity. 'A short time to retreat; a period of reflection, for the consolation of both the spirit and the flesh . . .'

He saw me opening my mouth to protest – I couldn't leave this now; not even for Fran – but he held up his hand commandingly. Then he grinned.

'The less refined among us might call it a dirty weekend,

my children. Or sin by the sea loch. Like in a wee Highland village, maybe? Not all that far from the finger o' Stoer?'

*

We left early the next morning; Fran's MGB wolfing the rain-swept miles up through the Trossachs, Crianlarich, Fort William . . . It was mild weather for a Scottish November; certainly there was snow blanketing the Grampians and huge sparkling drifts still piled high by the roadside, slabbed and scattered by the snow ploughs which had battled with some more seasonal blizzard of a few days before, but it was melting steadily now under the thawing caress of a sou' westerly wind. Even the rain gave way eventually to a bleary sun struggling to maintain altitude over the great shoulder of Nevis. We stopped and let the hood down like kids on a careless adventure, and snuggled together for warmth while we ate rolls and butter and yellow cobs of Orkney cheese, and washed it down with plastic cups filled from the bottle of *Niersteiner Gutes Domtal* Charlie had presented to us before we departed.

It was our happy time.

We even had a bed to go to. Despite Charlie's conviction that it would still be a community sheltered from progress, we'd discovered that not only did Laichy boast a four-bedroomed hostelry but that it also had at least one telephone; the voice which had answered my call had been soft and feminine and quietly Highland.

It was odd, though – the way I'd hesitated when she'd asked what name I was booking under. I don't know why I did what I did; what possible connotation could the mention of Herschell – Captain John Herschell – have held for a distant voice in a Sutherland village I'd never even heard of before yesterday. But I did hesitate for a brief moment; and then I'd answered, 'Templeton. Mr and Mrs John Templeton!'

I couldn't help thinking back to Charlie's earlier cynicism after I'd hung up. What was it he'd said about truth, and a man of God? Anyone will lie if they feel their motives are strong enough . . . Yet I had no apparent motive. Unless . . .

. . . Unless some sixth sense within me already DID suspect that Laichy held the key to the riddle I had embarked upon. And that, in itself, presupposed that a churchman HAD lied deliberately. Yet *that* suggested that the Church itself might be involved in obscuring the truth about *Highlander*'s manner of dying . . .

*

It was dark by the time we turned off the Durness road; dark, but with the unpolluted clarity of a northern Scottish night. High ghostly hedges of glinting snow drifts reared familiarly in the glare of the headlights; the MGB's tyres crackled a growling swathe through the crisp ice-diamond lane leading towards the head of Loch Fhadaig. And the remote secrecy of Laichy, the village.

It was well below freezing now, but it wouldn't snow again; not for a few days with any luck. If it did, we'd be marooned as surely as castaways on a deserted island, but I had three weeks' leave and I had to take that chance – I had to locate a starting point for my journey into the past.

Or had I already entered upon that strange undertaking? From the moment we left the metalled ribbon of the A838?

As we grumbled down that winding mountain, skidding over what was little more than a hard-core snake of wheel tracks descending towards the black edge of north west Sutherland, I began to realise that Charlie hadn't been so far out in his initial assessment. This really was a land fashioned by the original hand of God; an ageless, savage grandeur where change demanded the passing of centuries, and history was a whisper from behind every ridge and every boulder. To my left I could still envisage the silent ghosts of a thousand clansmen filing bravely on their sad road to the battlefield of Flodden; from my right came the skirl of the pipes across the darkness, a joyous passing from glen to glen of the rising of the

Jacobites; ahead and from astern still echoed the cocky militarism of Wade's fife and English drums.

'There's a light,' Fran remarked suddenly. 'And some more . . .'

'Stop the car,' I said, regaining the twentieth century, yet with an odd reluctance. Maybe I had been unconsciously waiting for the more recently dead to follow that spectral procession: the proud kilted Argylls en route for the corpse-strewn nightmares of Flanders and the Somme; the khaki-clad Jocks leaving the wee crofts and the hamlets yet again to fight, and die, at Dunkirk and on Crete, and in the burning sands of El Alamein; the young Highland boys who had scarcely seen a motor car by 1939, yet who would fly Spitfires and crew Lancasters and fall out of the shrieking sky on to cities they'd never imagined the likes of in life. And the Scottish fishermen from their crabbers and cobles and tiny inshore drifters, who volunteered only to perish in the turrets of the *Hood* or the riddled engine spaces of *Jervis Bay* and *Kelly* and an armada of other gallant Royal Navy ships, because it was a tradition up here – up in this wild and ancient place – that, when war came, the young men went with a fierce pride. And fought like their fathers had before them. And *their* fathers before them.

Aye, and they went to the Merchant Navy too. Under the snap of the defenceless Red Ensign. *And* they suffered and died as well; in ships called *San Demetrio* or *Ohio*. And *Highlander* . . .

'Laichy,' Fran's voice spoke again from a great distance. I stirred. She was already out and standing before the car with the wind tugging her hair into a whirling, dimly-seen black cloud against the faintly purple sky.

Clambering out stiffly I walked round beside her, looking down.

With the MGB's engine stilled, it was the silence which made the loudest sound. Because the whisper of the sea and the moan of the wind through the mountains which enclosed us from three sides weren't separate entities in that mystical place – they *were* that place. They themselves created its silence. It was an exquisite loneliness; a disembodiment; a beautiful apprehension.

Fran must have felt it too. Her hand stole into mine and gripped it tightly. 'It's . . . frightening,' she said in a tiny wonderment. 'It's welcoming, yet so eerie. Frightening in an inexplicable way.'

I strained to make out detail. I had a seaman's eyes, accustomed to the dark, but even so I could only trace the faint curve of high cliffs stretching on either side of us, with the lighter falling-away of the track leading down to our left and towards the cluster of lights themselves – into Laichy. There was little snow here, right on the coast where the salt Atlantic air hung heavy with its familiar tang. Only the frost survived its salinity, a sparkling dust like the aftermath of a fairy's wedding, with a crisp fragility that made even the blades of grass crack like snapping twigs as I moved my foot.

I could discern the roofs of the houses clearly because of it; white rectangles from our elevated vantage point with the occasional yellow glow of an uncurtained skylight like some unblinking eye staring back at me. A flashing light apparently suspended above the village at first caused me to frown, disoriented, until I realised I was gazing down the length of Loch Fhadaig, and that the white flashing light – three every twelve seconds – was the beacon of Sròine Riabach – Bridled Point – at the seaward entrance nearly a mile away.

It was a big loch, just like Charlie had said. A big, deep, wild loch when the wind howled from the west and the great Atlantic rollers came roaring and exploding a hundred feet high as they battled in majestic fury for the right of entry. I could make out the dim line of the tiny harbour breakwater on the far side of the houses – they'd need it in a winter gale, I reflected grimly; by God but they'd need protection, for even seas fragmented by the entrance to Fhadaig would race the length of the loch like express trains, and every bit as high, before they finally burst on the foreshore of Laichy.

I shivered suddenly. I don't know why; I was well wrapped up and still relatively warm from the car, but I shivered.

'Come on,' I muttered. 'Let's see if we can get something to eat.'

It was only after I'd spoken that I realised I was whispering. As though all those phantoms of the mountain had been warily listening.

*

There were no curtains drawn in Laichy as we drove slowly through the single street. The privacy was the privacy of communal respect which, remarkably, survived despite occasional abuse from alien intruders. I knew it wouldn't last forever though - McGlashan the thief had already been there, while the fact that Laichy supported even a small hotel like the *Sutherland Arms* made it a certainty that other predators would follow. Among every annual influx of decent holidaymakers seeking only to commune with the sea and the sky and the mountains there would always be an animal like Shugie McGlashan.

But for now there was only the silence of winter. Even the occasional mutter of voices escaping from the public bar entrance to the hotel seemed muted; absorbed by the freshening wind and the acoustics of stark granite walls.

As we entered through the studded main door we took another step back through time. The sweet earthiness of peat smoke hung tantalisingly between low blackened rafters which had already contained it for a century of welcome to the weary traveller. There was a remarkable space to the hall which belied the *Sutherland Arms'* seemingly narrow frontage to the street; and it presented a quietude of traditional Scotland by its very simplicity of decor. Only the glint of mounted claymores and swords and the dark drape of plaid, broke a rough casting of plaster on walls as thick as the length of a clansman's arm.

There was a small dining room opening to the right with the suggestion of bright tablecloths and silver and faded prints. To the left the connecting door stood wide from the public bar, and the sounds of conversation and laughter were louder. It was already half past ten – but Laichy seemingly stayed awake a while yet.

A movement from the back of the hall caught my attention and I turned. A girl stood smiling at us. 'Mr and Mrs Templeton?' she asked. I nodded, uneasy already through the knowledge of my lie – and then I simply looked at her.

She was lovely; a Celtic vision which only the pen of Burns the Master could have hoped to translate into adequate description. There was no similarity between them – between Fran standing beside me and this unexpected Caledonian paragon – for where Fran bore her sophistication blatantly the girl radiated a subtle grace; with Fran the impact of her presence was that of the statuesque, magnificent in its rounded fullness; in the girl it captivated by her sonsy elegance, her unblemished symmetry prevailing even over the reticent deception of chunky Shetland wool and thick-pleated kilt, and the heavy walking brogues with the shine of fondness. With Fran the sexuality was open, in the girl it was as if deliberately restrained, yet equally disturbing by that very confirmation of her own self-awareness.

'My name is Fiona,' she greeted us, and her voice – the voice which had answered my telephone call – had indeed the soft lilt of the Western Highlands. 'May I welcome you both to Laichy.'

I felt Fran's sardonic gaze on me and I knew what she was thinking. And she was right.

'What time do you serve breakfast?' I asked, after we had signed the registration book.

The girl looked at me with brown eyes which seemed as if they could convey everything, yet admit to nothing. What *was* there about this innocence that appeared so open and yet so brittle? Or was I already subconsciously pre-conditioned to a suspicion of Laichy? Had my ghosts become too real, and the sextant mystery too obsessive?

'Whenever the guests rise from their beds, Mister Templeton,' she said disconcertingly. I blinked, a little lost.

'Oh! But what time will that be, Fiona?'

She smiled a fractional smile. 'What time will yourself and Mrs Templeton be getting up? There are no other guests tonight. Laichy is an out-of-the-way place for most in the winter.'

'Say we get up about eight-o-clock, then?' I suggested. Before adding idiotically, 'In the morning!'

It was clear as a mountain lochan what Fiona was thinking while she looked first at me, then appraisingly at Fran, then back to me again . . . that I hadn't been over-doing it when I specified a.m. rather than p.m.

It also indicated that I'd been right about the brittle innocence of this Bonnie Lass o' Laichy – there *was* a worldly sophistication – whether deliberately or unwittingly in-hibited I didn't know, but certainly at odds with her outward naïveté.

Fran didn't seem to sense it. She gestured towards the sounds of conviviality from the adjacent pub. 'And what time does the bar close, Fiona?'

Fiona smiled softly. There it was again – that damnable, wide-eyed ingenuousness. 'What time would . . .'

'Let me guess,' Fran enthused. 'What time would we *like* it to close?'

'Och, well, there are no policemen in Laichy either,' Fiona added mischievously.

I couldn't resist it. 'Then does that mean there's never any crime. Not even the odd theft?'

Fran nudged me warningly but Fiona had already turned away as if she hadn't heard. Or had she?

'I will go and see what my mother can offer you for a meal. You must both be very hungry.'

'Your mother?'

She looked back. 'She and my father own the hotel, Mister Templeton. It has been in our family for many years.'

'And yourself?' I probed, determined to discover why she was so self-possessed; a Highland lass who'd very likely never been outwith the borders of Sutherland, yet who managed to make me, master mariner and international man, feel so ill at ease.

'I . . . have another job. This is my holiday. I enjoy spending it at home.'

I must admit I showed surprise. Even a so-obviously provincial girl must surely have felt the desire to get away from the place of her birth sometimes? I tried not to appear condescending.

'But surely you try to get out of Laichy occasionally, Fiona? Inverness; even down to the shops in Glasgow or somewhere?'

I think it was the expression of resignation on Fran's face combined with the twinkle of merriment in my country bumpkin's lovely eyes that caused the first flush of crimson to appear above my collar. There was a gentle kindness there too, though – the sort professional people-handlers showed when they were dealing with the old or the inane.

'Occasionally,' she smiled. 'You see I'm an air hostess, Mister Templeton . . . a senior stewardess on the international routes. With British Airways.'

*

Our happy time was to continue, despite my idiocy.

In a way it made that first evening in Laichy supremely enjoyable. I had learned one lesson already – that because my father's sextant *had* grown to haunt me, then so had every factor associated with my quest. Because of what could well have been the confusion of a small-time thief under police questioning, I had been directed to this unlikely starting point and I had gradually allowed the village itself to assume a sinister aspect out of all proportion to the little we knew of it. But not anymore. After my ludicrous conjecture about Fiona's background, I resolved there and then to turn my back on *Highlander*'s ghosts and to close my ears to their clamouring suspicion.

Laichy would remain a place of innocence until I had some other reason to believe in its guilt. Yet why did that reflection in itself raise such a strange unease within me? Why did I invariably insist on thinking about guilt in collective terms? Why consider my mission as an investigation of Laichy the *place*; and not of any individual who might reside within it?

I mean, a *village* couldn't possibly have guilt to hide; not a whole community!

Could it . . . ?

CHAPTER SIX

—— *1941* ——

Gazing aft, even from the height of the boat deck, the heat radiating from *Highlander*'s ruptured holds was intense enough to cause them to shield faces behind upflung arms. Whorls of glowing fire-flecks gusted and soared continuously; twinkling red comets rioting against a rushing Cimmerian sky.

Herschell was remotely conscious of the moisture evaporating from his Chief Officer's oilskins in a fine haze immediately snatched by the gale. His own thin shirt clung chilled and wet to his back, yet the front was already bone dry.

'The ammo . . .' he shouted, bawling above the clamour of the sea and the wind, and the thunder of the fire and his own accelerated heart beats. 'How long would you reckon we've got?'

There were shouts from the boats behind them now, and the glimmer of a shaded torch as figures moved around the davits. They ignored them.

'Twenty minutes,' McLeod hazarded. He didn't take his eyes from the white-water hole that had so violently appeared in *Highlander*'s port side aft. 'Or then again . . . maybe twenty hours.'

'Or maybe twenty seconds, eh?' The Captain shook his head savagely. 'It was a daft question, Mister.'

The Mate glanced sideways at him then, bushy brows creased in rueful ferocity. Herschell was grateful for his sardonic grin, even if it did hold more the look of a sickness.

'Five minutes ago I'd have said the whole bluidy situation was daft and couldnae happen. Now ah've given up on the guessing games.'

The ship took another gigantic roll and they could hear heavy things tumbling below decks. More water thundered into the gash, generating a mini-explosion in itself; blowing crates, dunnage, drums, clouds of hissing, black-sooted steam into the sea. A run-away Bren-gun carrier screeched into view and projected from number five upper tween deck, tracks snarled by the upward blasted plates ringing the cavity. Herschell had seen bombed tenements down by Clydebank looking just like that – as if a huge fist had smashed vertically through the structures leaving each floor exposed with furniture hanging pathetically in space for everyone to ogle at in wonder . . . but Glasgow tenements weren't built of steel. And they didn't swing through sick-crazy arcs all at the same time.

The ship felt sluggish, too. You'd expect that; she was taking a lot of water and had to be slightly down by the stern, but she shouldn't sink. Not unless her engine room had been opened as well, and the Chief would soon enough let them know about that . . . Then the Captain momentarily forgot about the longer term threats from water and fire as he noticed a movement in the port mast shrouds. They had gone slack, curving high above them; seemingly red-hot themselves as they reflected the fire.

Highlander fought shudderingly upright and began to fall the other way, sighing to starboard. McLeod followed the master's eyes to the base of the massive steel mainmast as the shrouds snapped taut and began to thrum . . . it was actually moving; pivoting fractionally while sparks were tumbling and bouncing into the grue covering the deck. It was beginning to buckle!

They both took an involuntary step back from the rail as tons of fabricated metal teetered above their heads, but it wasn't fear which caused them to stare so grimly, it was a desperate understanding. They both realised the need for decisive action had slammed from urgent to immediately vital – when that mainmast collapsed, then so did *Highlander*'s triatic stay and H.T. wireless aerials. Their only link with the shore was about to be severed; from that moment on they would be screaming for aid in a vacuum.

Men began to scramble from the poop accommodation; hunched figures shimmering behind the flames, bending low and shying from the heat; some supporting others as they struggled forward, running the starboard deckway gauntlet between the seas creaming outboard and the holocaust roaring inboard of them. Yet there was *still* someone up on the gun platform; a lonely shambling silhouette wandering vaguely in circles. And someone else climbing the vertical ladder towards him. The gun platform? What the *hell* was anyone doing on the bloody gun platform in a force eleven with a U-boat they couldn't even see?

Only now there wasn't time for speculation; not even to wait for the Chief Engineer's report. Herschell found himself faced with the demand not only for an impossible, but an instantaneous choice. *Highlander* would detonate beyond any doubt – his own eyes told him that; the only indeterminate factor was precisely *when* the inevitable explosion would occur. It was a grim certainty that when it did happen, every last man aboard would die in that violent tick of the clock; there could be no eleventh hour opportunity to save themselves at that stage.

Yet the alternative offered an equally bleak prospect – to take to the boats while they still had the maximum possible time to prepare. For they were all big ship men aboard *Highlander*; indeed there were few professional boatmen in the whole of the deep sea merchant fleet. Owners of peace-time shipping companies weren't prepared to subsidise training for the unlikely event of their crews abandoning; there was no profit in encouraging the abandonment of a ship, and safety came expensive when it involved stopping in mid-voyage to exercise boatwork. So the average steamer-hand, officer or rating, was permitted merely the Board of Trade statutory minimum when he gathered, usually complaining bitterly anyway, for his once-weekly boat deck station call or his even more occasional in-harbour routine of lowering a boat all the way to a flat-calm waterline and hoisting it back aboard again.

But once clear of the ship they at least had a chance – those who made it. A lifeboat, even in a force eleven, is still a miraculously buoyant sliver of hope able to look after its occupants long after they've given up caring for themselves. And running before the wind the Scottish coast was little more than fifty miles away . . .

Herschell racked his already-overstressed brain in search of any factors which he'd overlooked, and which might tip the finely-balanced scales of probability. Oddly it was an almost casual remark from McLeod which forced him to a decision.

'One more torpedo,' the Mate growled, eyes peering distantly outboard to where the U-boat might still be prowling in the darkness, 'and we'll no' have any problems left.'

The Captain swung round. The prospect tipped the scales in favour of the devil they at least knew – the sea itself. One more strike by their human enemy would consume them quicker than the fires already burning. Neither he nor Chief Officer McLeod could have guessed that U-236 was already heading away from them, returning to base with empty weapon racks.

'Then we'll abandon . . . but softly, softly, Bill,' he temporised. 'One boat only at first with the best crew we can provide; not more than the minimum to handle her, and all volunteers.'

McLeod looked at him steadily. 'You mean, "see if it's possible", eh? To launch a wee boat in yon mish-mash?'

'Do *you* know if it is?'

The Mate shrugged expressionlessly. 'I told you earlier – ah've given up on the guessing games. It depends on your first boat. If she does get away safe, then lying down wind at least the others hae a slim chance of being hauled out if theirs don't make it.'

'Then we signal we're abandoning, and try with the one boat, like I've said . . .' The Captain hesitated; the next part came harder than any other. 'Will you take it away yourself, Bill?'

McLeod showed his teeth in a sardonic travesty of a grin. 'Ah thought you said "volunteers", man.'

'Will you?'

Chief Officer McLeod turned slightly, to stare out at the monstrous creaming seas which he knew would probably kill him in the next few minutes. Then he swung back to face *Highlander*'s master.

'You'll be well advised to put on a warm coat, Johnny,' he said quietly. 'It'll be gey cold out there. When it comes tae your turn.'

*

When Bosun McColl – for he was one of the remaining afterguard observed by the Captain from the boat deck – reached the topmost rung of the access ladder to the gun platform, he stuck his head cautiously above the edge. And gaped.

Jimmie Beattie, very ordinary seaman just joined, was wandering around the exposed deck like he was a first class passenger taking the sea air on the promenade deck of the *Queen Mary* or somethin'. And singing!

'Ah belong tae Glasgae . . .' Jimmie crooned in a cracked and tremulous voice. 'Dear auld Glasgae toon . . .' But the outlandish unconcern didn't tally with the lonely stroller's eyes. For Jimmie Beattie was crying.

'Beattie!' the Bosun bellowed, still sick at the thought of

those incinerated men lolling in ghastly array below him in the greasers' messdeck.

'There's naething the matter wi' Glasgae 'cept it's . . .'

'Beattie! Get off've that fucking deck!'

'. . . goin' roond an' roooooond.'

'I'll kill 'im,' the Bosun promised in a moment of near-hysterical wistfulness. 'Oh, I'll bloody *kill* that bloody Beattie even if the bloody Jerries don't . . .'

But he still scrabbled and hauled himself erect on the gun deck and fought his way through the scattered wreckage towards the last shell-shocked survivor, because deep down Bosun McColl recognised when fear had driven a man dangerously close to the outer limits of sanity; and he also realised that something unbearable must have happened to lift Beattie up on top here, and that the idiot-smiling creature would never find his way to the boat deck alone. In fact, from what he already knew of the most recent addition to *Highlander*'s complement, Beattie wouldn't have been able to find his way to the boat deck anyway, not even on a guided tour of the bloody ship.

There must've been fourteen, fifteen of 'em in the black gang mess when that torpedo hit. Fourteen shipmates . . . Christ!

Beattie draped his arm over the barrel of the gun and beamed hollowly at McColl as he approached. It was funny, the way he was scared gutless inside, yet on the surface he sensed he was acting like he'd been on the booze all night. Of course he didn't know what had happened to the ship; he just prayed it wasn't like this every day with the fires and the shouting, and the general disconcertion.

'Ye ken ah wis goin' tae be a fighter pilot, don't ye?' he said conversationally as McColl gently led him aft to the ladder, steadying him with enormous control against the violent movement of the ship.

'Easy, lad,' the Bosun encouraged, taking Beattie's pitifully trembling hand and placing it on the ladder handrail. 'One step down at a time, son . . .'

Six minutes had now passed since the initial explosion. And Beattie was the sixth man McColl had led towards the comparative safety of the centrecastle.

Yet all he'd really wanted to do since he'd gazed upon those pork-crisp men was to curl up somewhere alone. And pretend the nightmare wasn't happening.

*

It was easy to see how scared Second Engineer McKechnie was. His hand shook uncontrollably as he replaced the bridge telephone receiver just as Chief Graham slid down the ladder to the control platform with an urgency which belied his sixty-eight years.

'Fourth Mate, sir,' the Second shouted nervously. 'Says the Old Man's gone aft. Asks if you'll hang on here a few minutes.'

Graham ignored him. Typically. 'Why did you stop engines, Mister? I didnae give you permission to stop bugger all; and I know fine it wasnae an order fae the bridge.'

McKechnie stared at his senior. It had been a long and terrifying six minutes since the torpedo, and the frantic squealing of the run-away port shaft; a sweating long six minutes as he'd used up all his courage – and Cullen's and Eadie's – to keep them standing-by down there with the knowledge that, at any moment, the ship might not recover from her next roll, and they would drown as a thousand tons of Atlantic cataracted into their funeral cathedral. And now Graham . . . misery-faced sarcastic old Chief Engineer bloody Graham wanted to know why he hadn't waited for orders!

'Why?' he bawled carelessly, ignoring the fact that two ratings were drinking in every word he said. 'Why? Because I got three rings on mah bloody arm, Chief. An' three rings in *my* book says I c'n do whatever I think bloody fit while I'm in charge of a watch, see? So when I knows the bloody ship's goin' round in bloody circles under one engine, wi' her steering crook an' a bloody torpedo up her backside, then I stoppem! Bloody dead!'

'Oh aye? Well thank you, Mister McKechnie,' Chief Engineer Graham said calmly. Then his lined face wrinkled into the first smile the Second had seen in two years aboard *Highlander*. 'So now we'll all go doon tae the bedplates and see if we can find where yon water's coming from; and mebbe even fix the engines, eh?'

It was only when the older man had already gone, heading for the bottom of the ship with that gleam of unaccustomed happiness in his eye, that Second Engineer McKechnie realised that the Chief was actually enjoying himself.

He suddenly became aware of something else, too. That he wasn't frightened anymore.

Just bloody angry.

Which only went to prove that not only was Chief Engineer Graham a perceptive, but also a very cunning old man . . .

*

The fact that van der Kroon's English was inadequate didn't prevent him from taking charge of the starboard side boats – or boat, as number three aft had already been blown clean from its davits by the same radiating blast as had killed Apprentice Jolly so cruelly, and flung Second Cook Johnstone outboard, never to be seen again.

Certainly there was no question of deliberate mis-understanding when the shaken survivors from the after end arrived to prepare for what they already considered would be the order to abandon ship. Under war conditions all boats remained permanently swung-out and readied for immediate launching anyway; it took moments only to strip away the covers and spreaders and insert the plug. The ready-rolled boat ladder was kicked over the side to plummet vertically, hitting the water with a splash lost against the vortex. Van der Kroon himself knocked off the gripes which steadied the

93

heavy open boat, and gestured urgently to the two seamen manning the falls to lower away to deck level – and that was when the communication void first became evident. The bow of number one starboard dropped jerkily, its rope fall eased hurriedly through the bollard . . . the stern stayed precisely where it was. Jammed solid.

'Sod it.' Third Officer van der Kroon roared in nervous frustration. But the best school in the world in which to learn how to swear in perfect English is found aboard a British merchant ship. The technical phraseology takes a little longer.

Struggling to ease the after end, Lamptrimmer Arnott offered his own technical explanation for the delay.

'Bluidy radial davits . . .' he bellowed back. 'Mickey Moose Land; thon's whaur they come fae. Mickey bluidy Moose Land!'

Which, even to an officer born and bred south of the Scottish Border, would have presented a certain difficulty in translation. Van der Kroon was totally lost.

'Mickey Moose?' he said dumbly. 'Vas is the Mickey Moose, man?'

'Disney!' Arnott screamed in ever-mounting fury as he kicked at the turns snarled around the bollard. The ship rolled heavily again and the top of a wave swamped high above the boat, blinking whitely at him. 'Disney, that's whit we're up against, laddie! *This* disnae work . . . that disnae bluidy work . . .'

'Disney . . . ?' van der Kroon muttered to himself over and over again, long after the jam was cleared and the boat finally ready for launching. 'Vat kind of part voor der reddingsboot is a Disney?'

His phrase book wouldn't have helped him, even if he'd remembered to carry it with him. Phrase books simply weren't written to cope with Lamptrimmer Arnott.

*

Highlander's radio room was situated on the after end of the boat deck, just to starboard of where the Captain and Mate had taken their critical decision. When they parted, McLeod hurried across to authorise their distress transmission before preparing himself to take the first boat away.

He had no illusions. It would only require one false move – one error on the part of those charged with the synchronised disengagement of the falls – and the crest of the sea would drop away to leave the boat itself hanging vertically above a fifty foot abyss, while every last man in her tipped down to the sucking grave below.

Curiously there was little fear of the death to come in Chief Officer McLeod's mind at that moment – just a dour cynicism; and it was all to do with the unlikely subject of money. The rate for the job. Oh, maybe it was just a mental defence against fear, to occupy oneself with resentment about something so apparently irrelevant as wages . . . but there *was* good cause for ironic reflection, all the same. Because apart from a few of her officers contracted permanently to Scotia Steamships, from the moment that *Highlander*'s crew took their places in the lifeboats and formally abandoned her, their pay from the Company ceased. Even as they choked their lives away under the suspended hulk of their flotsam lifeboat they would already be unemployed, their articles of service terminated. Paid off and entitled only to the statutory war survivors' compensation should they ever reach the shore . . .

. . . He didn't think there would be a very large claim for survivors' gratuity from the sailors about to abandon the Motor Vessel *Highlander*. Still, it did keep your brain busy; getting bloody mad just thinking about iniquities like that.

The wireless room door was already open and firmly hooked back. Even as McLeod stumbled across the coaming there was another rumbling explosion from aft as the ship wallowed to port and ice water flooded red hot steel. Both radiomen whirled round at his entry. Trent had taken over the operator's chair, Second Sparks Stronach was standing white-faced beside him. Both officers wore their bulky kapok lifejackets.

Bill McLeod didn't think he would bother to wear one when he got into that bloody boat. It hardly seemed worthwhile.

'We're abandoning, lads,' he snapped. 'Get the signal off.'

'Jesus!' the Second Operator muttered. Neither of his companions could have guessed at the real reason for the fear which curdled in his belly. Stronach still couldn't rid himself of the memory of those putrefied voyagers he'd once looked upon ... for someone must have said precisely the same words to them, once – we're abandoning! Maybe they'd even smiled a little in relief, at the promise that order had offered?

Trent's hand was already on the key. 'Torpedo?' he asked, though it was hardly necessary. But he had to be sure. He had to warn of the U-boat's presence in the area for other ships which might pass in that hellish night.

The Mate nodded. 'Aye. But dinnae waste time with fancy messages, Davie. The mainmast's ready to go over the side ...'

'Jesus!' Stronach blurted again.

'... Twenty-two miles east nor' east Butt of Lewis. On fire an' sinking ...'

The Chief Operator's fingers keyed even before McLeod had finished. The splurge of static from the speaker over the desk dissolved in a twitter of Morse unintelligible to the layman; even to McLeod.

SSSS ... *Submarine attack; submarine attack* ... SSSS ... SSSS from GBZQ HIGHLANDER.

'Answer,' Stronach muttered tightly. 'C'mon you cloth-eared bastards ... *answer!*'

The aerial output needle flickered on its meter. The Chief Sparks looked at his junior grimly. Something up top was already giving way. He keyed again with icy calm precision.

'The Old Man said as soon as you get an acknowledgement get the hell out o' it . . .' McLeod hesitated. He wasn't a dramatic man by nature and the words came hard. 'If I dinnae see you for a while . . . Guid luck tae ye both.'

When they turned, Chief Officer McLeod was gone. Only the glare of the fires reflected through the open door of the radio room. 'Damn!' Operator Stronach said as the magnitude of the disaster finally hit him. 'I've left my bloody draughts board down in the Third Engineer's cabin.'

He didn't stop transmitting though. Not even when there was a crack and the chilling screech of rending steel from outside, while the needle of the meter deflected crazily across its dial.

. . . GBZQ HIGHLANDER HIGHLANDER . . . TORPEDOED AND SINKING 22 MILES EAST NORTH EAST BUTT OF LEWIS. ON FIRE WITH AFTER HOLDS FLOODING . . .

*

Captain Herschell burst into his cabin and crouched before the safe under the tiny desk in his day room. Opening it, he reached in and removed the confidential war books issued before they'd sailed from Gourock. There were a large number of them manuals of codes; convoy procedures; alternative routing plans; zigzag patterns; operation of the DEMS 4.6-in gun sitting so uselessly on the ravaged poop deck. There was a neatly-folded canvas bag in there, too. When he lifted it out it felt heavy; there were lead weights sewn into the bottom of it. One of his final responsibilities as master of the Motor Vessel *Highlander* would be to ensure that those secret documents were ditched over the side to prevent any possible recovery by the enemy. Quickly he bundled the books together and inserted them, snapping shut the D-ring through the neck.

Impassively he surveyed the cabin. His uniform jacket still lay across the bunk where he'd placed it prior to the explosion, the shaving brush glistened wetly in the mug before the cracked mirror. Almost absently his hand found its way to his chin, fingering the stubble. He wouldn't be shaving tonight . . .

Stirring, he opened the door to the wardrobe. The four gold stripes on each epaulette of the heavy bridge coat caught the light as he slid it from its hanger – they made him think of little Johnny again, and of how delighted he would have been to see those emblems of command on his own boy's shoulders.

He didn't think he would live to see that day, though. Not anymore. Not when he thought about the fire above *Highlander*'s ammunition cargo; and the giant seas outboard.

Moving fast again he slipped into his uniform jacket and shrugged the thick blue coat about his back. His cap, with the braid edging its peak and the Merchant Navy badge at its centre dull green from the salt spray of many seas, sat squarely across his brow as he reached for the picture of his wife and son still lying on the berth. Quickly he removed the back of the frame and withdrew the photograph. For the first time, he found himself hesitating as he stared down at it. Rothesay had been the place where it was taken; in the last year before the war had come, when he'd treated Mary and the boy to what the Glasgow folk called 'a trip doon the watter' – all the way down the Clyde to the Island of Bute by paddle steamer. Even then Johnny had gazed with a fascination far beyond his years at the tumbling wake astern, and at the wheeling seabirds cartwheeling above the taffrail, and at the bearded, majestic officer who gravely paced the postage stamp bridge; and Captain Herschell had smiled to himself, and nodded his satisfaction.

Carefully folding the photograph he placed it firmly in his pocket. He was almost ready for the trial to come.

Almost.

The last thing Captain Herschell did before he continued

to the bridge was to reach into the bottom of the wardrobe and remove the wooden box carefully placed there against the motion of the ship. It was a rosewood case, polished with age and affection. He squandered one precious moment more in gazing down at it; feeling the same thrill of ownership, never lessened, that he'd originally sensed when he bought it as an apprentice so many years before. The brass plate inset into its lid gleamed as warmly as his master's rings, and just as proudly:

JONATHAN HERSCHELL
Scotia Steamship Company
Glasgow

Tucking the box firmly under one arm he lifted the bag of confidential books. That weighted bag would go out over the bridge wing, ditched as soon as he had made sure he was the last living soul aboard. The rosewood case would go with him in his lifeboat.

For his navigator's sextant was in that lovingly tended case, you see. And his sextant symbolised the life he had chosen, and which had been so good to him; his life as a seaman. So if it should come to pass that Captain Jonathan Herschell ended that life at the bottom of the North Atlantic on a winter's night of war, then it was only right that his precious sextant should be with him when he died.

He blinked, and for a brief moment there was an unfamiliar moisture in the corner of his eye. Oh, there was grief there for the ship; an even greater sadness for those of her crew already gone and for those about to perish; but it was also a time of personal sorrow for *Highlander*'s master, triggered by the satin feel of that closely-guarded box. For of all the aspirations Jonathan Herschell had cherished, perhaps the most dear was that of handing over his sextant to his son on the day that Johnny, too, became a sailorman.

The Captain knew, already, that it was a day which could never come.

He swung abruptly, and left the master's cabin without a backward glance.

CHAPTER SEVEN

On that first blissful night in Laichy we dined on grilled brown trout, so fresh that the glazed shock of their catching could only just have come over their eyes. Her father had caught them, Fiona said, as she piled the table with oatcakes and scones and crisp rolls still warm from the oven; earlier that same evening, up in the lochan on Dubhail Leirge. Because he had captured them himself, and because they were winter fish and should never have been caught at all, there would be no extra charge on our bill.

We sat there for a long time after, Fran and I, holding hands and talking in low voices before the glow of the great peat fire, with only the occasional gust of laughter coming through the open door across the hall and the distant sigh of the seas breaking strongly at the head of Loch Fhadaig to orchestrate our musings.

For a time I forgot all about the sextant. For that very happy time.

Eventually there was the sound of an outer door slamming, and the clatter of receding steps from the street. The late men of Laichy were finally away to their beds. I stirred and glanced at my watch; it was one o'clock in the morning and it didn't matter at all in that peaceful, remote place that the licensing laws of Scotland had been broken with such blatant cheer.

Then the door swung wide and a giant of a man came smiling into the room, and we saw that he was wearing the kilt and that he was as handsome at maybe sixty years of age as any strapping Highland boy. And that he only had one arm.

'I am Fiona's father,' he said. 'My name is Donald MacFaid.'

'You must be the fisherman?' Fran smiled back. MacFaid grinned; a grin that set his whole face alight with mischief.

'In and out of season, that I am. Ye'll not tell the policeman in Glasgow, Mrs Templeton?'

'We could hardly do that, Mister MacFaid,' I countered. 'Now that you have made us accessories after the event. They were delicious.'

'Och, you were just lucky that the pool was not already covered with the ice,' he said. Then he pushed his shoulder forward, with its empty, pinned-up shirt sleeve, and grinned again. 'And that a single-winged man like myself also happens to cast the most sneaky dry fly in the whole of the county of Sutherland.'

We laughed, and he looked at Fran with the same glint of devilment; a little boy being cheeky. 'Are you desperately anxious to get to your bed, Mrs Templeton? Maybe even to sleep eventually?'

She grinned straight back. 'Eventually. But every nice prospect is the better for a bit of waiting. Tell us what you have in mind, Mister MacFaid?'

He slapped his bare knee with a gusto that no man of sixty should show at one in the morning. 'A nightcap, then. To welcome you both to the Sutherland Arms, and to introduce you to the bonniest flower ever to be found in the Highlands of Scotland.'

'We've already met Fiona,' I responded thoughtlessly. He eyed me with forbearance.

'Fiona? Och, man but she's nothing but a skinny, unformed lass. I am talking of Margaret, my wife.'

He strode across to the door and called loudly while we exchanged surreptitious grins across the fire. MacFaid of Laichy was more than a hotelier; he was a towering infection of humour and hospitality. I wondered how he had lost his arm; and why a thing like that should happen to one such as he.

He turned, holding the door. 'There's one wee condition attached to your dram, mind.'

'Oh?'

'That you call me Donald,' he boomed. 'For whisky and formality make poor companions.'

'Then it's John and Fran in return,' Fran countered. 'For Mr and Mrs Templeton are very stiff people indeed.'

It was then that our hostess entered the room while I, for the second time that evening, could only stand and stare.

Fiona's mother carried her years with all the elegance of a white swan. But where her daughter's attraction had been that of supreme and fresh-faced comeliness, Margaret MacFaid presented a delicacy of inner beauty. Yet there seemed a fragility about her that was disquieting; a fragility as compelling to the eye as the brittle stem of some exquisite wine glass. Even more alarming than that – there was a translucence to her skin as clear and as striking as in the purest of all lead crystal. And as ominous as the calm which forewarns the approach of a killer typhoon.

When I saw the look in Fran's eyes as she gazed on the woman of Donald MacFaid, I noticed a shocked sadness which mirrored my own. And a depth of compassion.

For Margaret MacFaid was dying. Already she bore the mark of that ultimate knowledge. We could see that it would only be a very short time before Donald MacFaid of Laichy would have lost not only his arm, but the companionship of his obviously beloved wife.

But she would be leaving him with dignity. And with an unquenchable spirit. We could see that, too, in her erect tranquillity.

'My Maggie!' MacFaid announced with an enormous pride and as if nothing were amiss. And that, in itself, told more than a volume of words about the courage of that irresistible Highland man.

Yet, do you know, we recovered our composure and the four of us began to talk, and within a few minutes even Fran and I had almost forgotten that death was but a mountain slope away. Margaret, mother of Fiona, was as stimulating by her serenity as was MacFaid, the unrepentant fisherman, with his massive zest.

'And now you must tell me what brings you to Laichy?' he beamed, before he lifted his dram in traditional Gaelic salute. '*Slàinte-mhath!* To yourself, John, and to your beautiful lady.'

'*Slainte*, Donald,' I echoed, while Fran smiled a flushed little thank-you. I moved uncertainly in my seat, praying he wouldn't notice my awkwardness. While I had already prepared the deception in my mind, I felt the meanness of my falsehood even as I uttered it.

'Partly chance, Donald. A sort of working holiday. I'm . . . ah . . . an engineer with oil-related business in Durness. And I . . . I . . .'

'He's here to appease *me*, Margaret,' Fran broke in; shamelessly supporting my inept floundering. 'He works far too hard and I insisted on his taking a few days off. Laichy is perfect for him to get away from it all . . . and anyway; he happens to be indulging me at the same time. I'm searching for a flower, you see. Not terribly exciting, I know . . . just hunting for a flower.'

'A flower, Francine?' Margaret queried. 'Is it a naturalist that you are, then?'

The wicked challenge Fran implied in her sideways glance towards me was inexcusable. 'I *love* natural things, Maggie – don't I, darling?'

'In an amateur sort of way, yes,' I hissed back warningly. 'It's only a sideline for you, isn't it, darling?'

'What kind of flower would you be looking for, lass?'

Donald asked blankly, and I could tell from his polite confusion that fate had saved us from a confrontation with a horticultural expert. My sigh of relief must have been almost audible – Fran might have been a mine of irrelevant information, but reporting on the exhibits at the Drumchapel flower show hardly equipped her for esoteric discussion on the flora of Scotland.

I'd underestimated her, though. I should have known that whatever Fran entered into, she did so fully prepared and with a devastating enthusiasm.

'*Primula scotica*, Donald,' she thrilled. 'It's only found in parts of Sutherland and Caithness; invariably up on the north coast. That's why I wanted to come somewhere as unspoilt as Laichy, here in the west. It would be *marvellous* to be the first person to discover it here, wouldn't it? Don't you think it would, Margaret?'

'Indeed Laichy would be a famous place at last,' that Highland lady smiled gently. MacFaid just shook his craggy head and sniffed.

'Aye. Och well, I have to admit to a preference for the fishing, myself. But I wish you luck, lassie . . .'

And that was how we at least came to establish our interest in Laichy; and incidentally prepare the ground for wandering freely round the area with my 'wife's' hobby as excuse and no doubt a humorous talking point within the local community.

It was an efficient deception. Even though it did cause me shame through all the hours we spent in that friendly village at the head of Loch Fhadaig.

*

An inner warmth cheered us during the whole of the following morning as we explored the immediate environs of Laichy. Initially it had been the after-glow of a true Highland breakfast, when we sat and finished our coffee and gazed at each other wordlessly; remembering the way in which Fran's earlier anticipations of the previous evening had proved well-founded. But it was maintained when we ventured into the crisp, cold air by the nods and the shy smiles of the few people who passed us by as we walked together hand in hand. It was the euphoric culmination of our happy time.

We stopped to look at the church first; the cause of our visit. It wasn't a particularly attractive example of ecclesiastical architecture; just a weathered granite building fronted by a neatly severe graveyard, with a small annex to one side which we presumed to be the community centre, and the manse on the other in a state of dignified dilapidation. There were a thousand churches like it in a thousand Scottish villages, and no apparent sign that this held any greater significance. Certainly McGlashan *had* been here, there was no dispute about that, but according to the word of its present incumbent – one listed as the *Reverend Hamish Watt Stewart M.A.* in fresh gilt letters on the notice board at the gate – Shugie McGlashan's little desecration had amounted only to the theft of two silver candlesticks, a brass collection plate, two pounds sixteen pence in cash from the Congregational Treasurer's tin box and the Reverend Stewart's own ornithological 12 × 50 binoculars taken from a cupboard in the vestry.

No sextant. Merely the unequivocal denial of that bird-watching man of God that there ever could have been. Not stolen from St Andrew's Parish Church of Laichy.

We didn't enter the church; it didn't seem necessary. Instead we strolled briskly on the long exposed path towards the sea and the entrance to Loch Fhadaig a mile away. The awful beauty of that desolate place was even more evident as we finally scaled the point of Sròine Riabach and stood staring out into the grey Atlantic ocean, and watched the swell breaking in thunderous tumult on the rocks below; terrifying even on this calm and frosty day. Then we turned and faced back up the loch to stare at Laichy itself, and saw only a distant, innocuous hamlet of tiny houses dwarfed by the overhang of cliffs, and rising behind them a vast mountain bulk of brown and purple with the dazzle-white blanket of snow crowning every ancient top.

I tried to marshal my thoughts as I gazed entranced. There *was* some secret about in the real circumstances surrounding the loss of the Motor Vessel *Highlander* so many years ago – I sensed that now as surely as I felt my ever-increasing love for the woman beside me. But how could such an evil have any link with a community so open and so welcoming?

Then the winter sun was shadowed by a cloud, and I shivered suddenly; as I had done when I first set eyes on Laichy. But it could only have been because the temperature dropped an abrupt five degrees, and because the point of Sròine Riabach would have been an uneasy, lonely place even in the heat of summer.

Or had I suffered the first chill of premonition? Had I foreseen, somehow, that our happy time was already nearing its end?

The telephone message was waiting for me when we returned to the *Sutherland Arms* for lunch, leg-weary and flushed after the bracing snap of our sharp walk back from Riabach.

Curiously I had never regained my earlier sense of well-being. As we strode down the path into the lower end of Laichy, skirting the quiet harbour with its few unattended fishing boats and its battered granite breakwater, Fran had suddenly cried, 'Oh, look, John.' We halted before the slender white column of the most beautifully kept village war memorial I had ever seen.

It was then, as I allowed my eyes to travel downwards from the bronze soldier-statue bowed eternally over his inverted rifle which surmounted the marble plinth – a lonely, kilted sentinel in high-buttoned jacket and the puttee'd hose of the

First Great War – and down past what struck me even then as a disproportionately long list of names of the dead, especially for a village as small as Laichy; and finally blinking for a long time at the wreath of oh, so fresh poppies which had been placed at the stepped piers of the memorial's base. It was then that I thought again about my father's own death in the service of his country. And wondered why it, and the quiet marble plaque in the hall of Scotia Container Lines, and now this immaculately maintained tribute to a Scottish village's past grief; why they all seemed inextricably linked.

Lest we forget . . .

But I'd discovered already that I couldn't, no matter how hard I tried. And that was why I was strangely sobered when I returned Charlie Sullivan's telephone call from Glasgow.

'We have to leave this afternoon,' I told Fran bitterly a few minutes later. 'Scotia have been trying to get me. Bill Parton, master of *Lowlander*, has got himself clobbered by a Mercedes taxi over in Hamburg and they've asked me to take her up to Rotterdam to complete loading for the Far East. Oh, they'll get someone else to sail her outward, but it'll take about ten days. I'm sorry.'

Her face reflected her disappointment; maybe she sensed too that the happy time was about to end.

'But what about the sextant, John? Do you still think it has anything to do with Laichy? With the people here?'

I looked at her. 'Do you?'

She frowned and shook her head. 'No!'

Then she looked defiant, screwing her lovely eyes into fierce aggression. 'And I don't want to either. It's too nice a place; *they're* too nice – Donald MacFaid; Fiona; poor Maggie . . .'

'We'll come back. One day soon, darling,' I promised. 'McGlashan gave five more addresses – I've got to weed them out first and try to solve the riddle; then we'll both come back to Laichy. And the next time there'll be no suspicion to spoil it.'

*

It was late that night before we arrived back at the flat in Alexandra Parade. It hadn't changed; it still matched our mood. Wetly depressive.

The shame I'd felt when I made our excuses to our late host and hostess of the *Sutherland Arms* still rankled – my vague apologies for change of plans; business arrangements; must come back again some day . . . And the look of what I really believed was sincere disappointment on their faces, and their guileless encouragement to us to return.

'I shall be looking for your flower, Francine Templeton,' Margaret had said. 'So you come back now; just as soon as you are able.'

But we knew as we waved goodbye that the frail wife of MacFaid had little time left to look for anything at all. Death was indeed present in Laichy but there was no mystery to it; no long-concealed history. Just the open mark of cancer that shrieked of tragedy to come.

Charlie was waiting with the sizzle of grilling steaks in the air and a curiosity shamelessly ill-concealed. Yet even after we'd related the tale of our inconclusive visit to Laichy, and the lessening of our suspicions – Fran with certainty; myself with a little less conviction – he didn't seem at all crestfallen. But Charlie Sullivan loved an enigma. I think he'd have been bitterly disappointed if we *had* solved the riddle of the sextant without his help.

'What time d'you need to fly to Hamburg, Johnny?'

'Early afternoon tomorrow would do, probably. I'll check with the office first thing . . . Why?'

Charlie rose from the table and began to gather the plates with casual domesticity. 'Because in the morning we're going on a McGlashan hunt, that's how. I talked McQueen into giving me his hiding places while you were away.'

Fran picked up an apron and tossed me the dishtowel. 'Where?'

'Not far. He lives just off the Gallowgate, between Camlachie and Bridgeton. When it isn't care of Her Majesty's penal establishment, Barlinnie.'

Fran pulled a face. 'Hold John's hand when you cross the frontier. The only quiet part down there is the Eastern Necropolis – or Parkhead when Celtic have an away match. Otherwise it makes the no-go areas of the Shankhill Road look like a tourists' paradise when the pubs empty out.'

'Maybe I should catch the earlier plane,' I muttered uneasily.

'We're only going to have a chat wi' the wee bastard,' Charlie growled reassuringly. Then he gazed reflectively at his fist. Even to my eyes it looked like something blasted from the base of a granite quarry.

Gently he slipped the knot of Fran's apron and took the dishtowel from me. 'It's your last night here for a while,' he said, looking pointedly towards the door. 'You might even get a wink of sleep, if you get to bed now.'

*

It was after eleven by the time I'd finished my briefing and collected my travel documents from Scotia Containers. Then Charlie drove me back along Argyle Street and through the Trongate. When we got to Glasgow Cross he took the right fork down London Road. I frowned in surprise.

'I thought you said McGlashan lived off the Gallowgate?'

'The pubs are open now,' he explained condescendingly. 'And Shugie McGlashan was due to come into money at nine-thirty this morning. Until they pour him back into the gutter at closing time there's no way we'll find him in the cess pit he calls home.'

'Money?'

'It's his booking-in time for the social security. An' the unemployment. An' the supplementary benefit . . . It's enough to cover his alcoholic overheads in between looking for old biddies' windows left off the snib.'

'You seem to know him.'

'Like I said – I know a thousand Shugie McGlashans. I don't like any of 'em.'

I stared uncomfortably out at the uncompromising, crumbling tenements; acres of depression and neglect and social deprivation. Here and there bright curtains stood as a symbol that there still remained people with pride and fight left in them, but it was mostly black-corroded grey. And hopeless. A group of youths hung around on one corner, anything from twelve to eighteen years old; their heads were shaved, except for a couple who seemed to fancy bright green with a middle track of yellow-spiked hair. Their tattered jeans were an ankle length too short with great big boots at the base of each spindle leg. Most wore bomber jackets or scuffed jerkins with more zip fasteners than leather; half of them had crude swastikas painted across them. One kid had laboriously scripted *Belsen was a gas* across his back. It wasn't even an obscene joke; just sad.

'That one I do know,' Charlie said. 'They found his wee brother on a pile of trash in the backlands a couple of weeks ago. He'd been glue-sniffing. A Safeways plastic bag over his head an' the empty tube still in his hand. He'd been dead for three days before his mother bothered to report him missing.'

It was the first time I'd felt like a stranger in my own city. The world was changing too much, or maybe I'd been away too long. Charlie saw my expression as we began to slow down. 'Don't get too depressed. There's still plenty of nice people live around here – the ones the post-war planners didn't manage to lock up in multi-storey concentration camps or overspill schemes that'd be closer to Sauchiehall Street if they were on the bloody moon.'

I looked at the pub across the road from where we'd stopped. It seemed to be the only occupied cave in the block;

the rest of the property glowered back through empty eyes of broken windows and graffiti-sprayed boarding. The faded, peeling sign proclaimed we were about to enter *The Braw Covenanter*.

'It's a while since they actually had one as a customer,' Charlie said enigmatically. 'He must've had guts, the lad that called it that originally. There's more Catholics round here than in the Vatican; only time you'll see a Protestant now is when Celtic are playing Rangers at home. An' then they need a special dispensation from the Pope and a lot of courage.'

'Let's get it over with,' I muttered, masking my nervousness with irritation.

'Just don't turn your glass upside down by mistake,' Charlie cautioned, getting out of the car. 'It's like inviting the start of World War Three to a Glasgae hard man – Scotia Container Lines would need to post you to Hamburg wrapped up in grease-proof parcels. Quite a few of them.'

Even when he grinned I wasn't sure whether he was kidding or simply enjoying my discomfiture. I never was, with Charlie. Not even after all the years we'd known each other.

The only difference between the interior and the exterior of *The Braw Covenanter* was that it wasn't raining inside; or only in a couple of places where the ceiling had sagged. Otherwise the degree of mouldering obsolescence was broadly the same. Once upon a flourishing time the wallpaper had been scarlet-flocked and rich; now it was nicotine brown, continuing a decade-long struggle to part company with the bulging plaster and strategically reinforced by blistered Sellotape where the plaster had attained brief superiority. The knots in the creaking, uncovered floor boards protruded like ringbolts from a ship's deck to trip the unwary; eroded into bas-relief by generations of steel-capped working boots diverted on their way home from work. Or the Brew. The chairs and tables had been broken in so many brawls they were just repairs with a touch of the originals; the long bar-counter a relic of early cocktail plastic, the laminates long separated around the edges and faded by a distillery of articulated elbows.

'They'll be demolishing it soon anyway,' Charlie said philosophically.

'It looks like they've already tried,' I growled. Quietly.

There was an old man sitting in rheumy contemplation of an empty half-pint glass, over in the corner between the *Ladies'* and *Gents'* toilet doors. His eyes briefly surveyed us in watery optimism before flickering back to the glass, presumably classifying us as nae guid f'r a soft touch. Two equally ancient contemporaries never even afforded us a moment of recognition; motionless as graven images they bent over a part-completed game of dominoes with the intensity of concentration usually only seen in a world chess tournament. But it was the group on the other side of the room, staring at us with open insolence, which gave me the greatest cause for apprehension -- conditioned as I already was by Charlie's black humour.

There were five of them; four more or less clones of the youths we'd passed earlier with the mandatory leather and denim rig of the well-dressed yobbo-about-town, and each slouched in a semi-horizontal tilt across the scuffed seating with hands stuffed deep into side slit pockets and cracked boots resting on worn steel heel pieces. And Number Five. Only he was different. He was smooth and clean as a well-fed reptile, and he wore a yellow shirt and a black tie and a light grey suit and the cold arrogance of a tiger shark. Even I knew that Number Five was the pseudo-sophisticated face of Glasgow violence; a sordid little Pretender holding petty court in his anti-social realm, who needed the fealty of his moronic courtiers to bolster his ego as much as they needed to feed from his carefully calculated air of contempt. And according to the gospel of Charlie, the East End Kings like Number Five would cut you for no reason other than as a public relations exercise if you so much as gave them a sideways glance of challenge.

I tried not to look at Number Five. The deck of a ship was my world, and I'd dealt with plenty of hard case sailors in my time, but an alien code of conduct governed the Glasgow backlands where authority provided the red rag to a bull, and even policemen like Donnie McQueen walked in the middle of the street after dark. I could still feel his eyes on us, though; and sensed he was wondering why we were there.

The barman didn't hurry. When he was ready he came over and leaned on the counter with a shoulder-spread as wide as Charlie's. I didn't imagine there were many little publicans left who ran hostelries like *The Braw Covenanter*. He didn't exactly smile in welcome either.

'What're you fur?'

'Pint of Tartan and a Coke,' Charlie said cheerfully. The barman gave him a funny look to make sure he wasn't having him on, then turned away to search for the Coke. It wasn't a drink he sold every year. When the beer came it slopped over the edge of the glass and the barman wiped it away with heavy irony. It seemed he was wondering why two foreigners like us were there as well.

He didn't have very long to wait. 'I'm looking for a lad, McGlashan,' Charlie announced without a lot of originality. The barman stopped wiping.

'You the Polis?'

Charlie placed a pound note on top of the bar. 'If ah was, ah wouldnae be offering to pay mah hand, would ah?'

I noticed how his accent had broadened; adopted the Glasgow sing-song chant. The barman took it and slid the change back across on a bow wave of beer.

'The Sheriff Officer, then? The tally man . . . ane o' the hire-purchase collection lads?'

'No,' Charlie denied virtuously. 'Ah'm a human being. Looking for Shugie McGlashan.'

'Then ye'd be better off lookin' someplace else,' the barman advised in a whisper. 'The furniture in here doesnae break itsel' – it collides wi' strange faces. Askin' questions.'

I began to drink my beer. Quickly. It seemed like a good idea. Charlie didn't hurry, though. This time he raised his voice so everybody would hear.

'They tell me Shugie McGlashan drinks here. Ah want to see him.'

The clattering of the domino needle match stopped dead. Out of the corner of my eye I could see the old man with the empty glass watching us again. Now his watery stare had a gleam of animation; an animal cunning. But the response came from the other side of the room.

'You the Polis?'

We turned, slowly. I felt a ridiculous urge to giggle. It was like being a film extra in a scene from *High Noon*. Then I saw the cold challenge on the face of Number Five, and the sniggering anticipation of the zip-fastened clones flanking him; and lost my sense of humour again.

'We've been through that already,' Charlie sighed. 'No, ah'm not.'

'Ah think he's a poof,' one of the clones said and looked slyly round for approbation. Charlie frowned in mystification.

'Did you pull the strings then,' he asked Number Five, 'or can the dummy work its mouth a' by itsel'?'

The youth began to get up, crimson and uncertain. Charlie smiled intimately at Number Five, who hadn't stirred, and remarked, 'If he does make it to his feet, it'll no' be for long. You'll be able to take him tae the Royal Infirmary inna bucket.'

The man in the grey suit eyed Charlie's bulk expressionlessly, but now there was curiosity there, and a grudging respect. Meanwhile the leather clone froze even more doubtfully, then flopped back in his seat when no moral or physical support appeared imminent.

'You lookin' f'r aggravation, pal?' Number Five queried calmly but, again, the malice was muted. It was simply a desire for a mutual understanding. I realised then that Charlie had skilfully stuck to protocol; acknowledged Number Five's leadership and neutralised the juvenile opposition all in one go.

'No,' Charlie shrugged while managing to give the impression that he wasn't too fussy either way. 'Ah'm just lookin' for Shugie McGlashan, like ah said.'

'What fur?'

'It's personal.'

'Face-stitch personal or a'-pals-thegether personal?'

'Ah just want to see him. Friendly.'

Number Five considered a moment. I got the impression there was something else on his mind; something which mildly amused him; but I kept quiet and let Charlie do the running.

'It's worth a few quid,' Charlie prompted cautiously. 'Just to save my time an' petrol, o' course. Not that a smart lad like yoursel' would need charity.'

'Twenty quid?' Number Five hazarded. Charlie looked sour.

'A tenner! Ah'm no' wantin' his body for science.'

One of the clones began to snigger again and Number Five gave him a look bleak enough to wither a pine forest. The sniggering stopped as if it had been guillotined. Or severed by an open razor. I noticed Charlie frown but he was committed now; it was too late to backtrack.

'Ten notes, right?'

'Right!'

'Just tae see Shugie McGlashan?'

'That's all ah want,' Charlie verified.

'Nae guarantee he'll agree tae speak to youse?'

Charlie shrugged confidently. It was a routine obstacle in the life of a newspaperman, and apart from the fact that Charlie could charm the worms out from under a stone, he had big fists. It was always open season on the Shugie McGlashans. He reached for his wallet and Number Five waved a lofty hand.

'Just look on me as the local Oxfam do-gooder. Gie a couple o' quid tae Jeemie there for takin' ye, and the rest tae Shugie's wife afore she lets youse see him. Ah'm trustin' ye, pal.'

Jeemie came shuffling over at a greedy trot as soon as Number Five called. He was the old man with the empty glass. His rheumy glance devoured the money in Charlie's hand.

'Tell Shugie's old lady ah said they wis tae see him,' Number Five commanded. 'And, Jeemie?'

'Aye?'

'You try on fiddling ony o' thon eight quid off've the woman f'r your boozin', an ah'll cut ye intae jelly. Right?'

The old man smiled, and there was an evil in it that chilled me more than any look on the faces of the young yobbos. 'Ah mind when ah wis King, McQuade. You wouldnae hae been man enough tae lick the soles of mah boots.'

But Number Five just stared at him until his drink-wet eyes dropped. And I'd learned a little bit more about the social structure of the Glasgow gutters. Then we left without another word; while something in me screamed a warning.

That when we'd found him, Shugie McGlashan would find a way of covering for the riddle of my father's sextant. A way that would defeat even the wiles of Charlie Sullivan.

*

The close off the Gallowgate offered the gloom of the crypt.

The acrid stench of urine hung thick to muffle our footsteps on the stone-flagged stairs while spider-webs of filth reached down to clutch at us as we strode grimly by.

McGlashan's lair was the third landing right. Most of the other doors had long been stripped from their hinges as firewood by the remaining tenants; only the no-hopers and the never-hads still existed in that catacomb obscenity long overdue for the demolisher's hammer and giant grab. Even Charlie was uncharacteristically quiet as we followed the shambling footsteps of a toppled king of violence.

The door opened a crack; no more. The one eye peered out bright with suspicion, yet strangely dulled with the apathy of constant fear.

Jeemie smiled his toothless, wicked smile.

'They've come tae see Shugie, Jesse. McQuade sent them.'

The voice from the darkness was tremulous. 'Is it the Polis, Jeemie?'

'Och, it's no' the Polis, woman! McQuade sent them, ah telt ye.'

'Then whit dae they want wi' Shugie?'

'I just want to see him, Mrs McGlashan,' Charlie called gently. His accent had gone; now there was just a kindly note as if understanding the woman's terror. 'Just to ask him one question.'

There was a long silence. 'They're gaun tae gie you money, Jesse,' the old man wheedled. 'Eight pound. Just tae see Shugie, f'r a wee minute.'

The anonymous woman began to cry and I gripped Charlie's arm fiercely. 'Forget it,' I snarled. 'There's something bloody odd, Charlie. Just forget McGlashan . . .'

I could sense Charlie's uncertainty too, now. Things had gone wrong ever since McGlashan the Thief had been missing from where Charlie had been certain he would find him – in his daily drinking den. And then the curiously obliging attitude of the sophisticated cretin, McQuade; and his secret humour; and the suddenly-muffled sniggers of his idiot courtiers. And now this. A sobbing, besieged woman in a slum plagued by an ancient villain, all for the price of a few more drinks.

The door opened slowly, creakily. A short hall ran away from us and at the end was another empty door frame. A child squatted within the rectangle; perched on a cracked, brown-stained toilet with grubby trousers around spindle-shank ankles and a thin grey face gazing blankly and without embarrassment. In the gap separating us the ceiling had given way in a tumble of sodden plaster; the mildewed laths hanging like the black bones of a gutted fish.

The woman was grey, too. And crumbling. The dark rings around her eyes shadowed the essence of misery.

'Eight pound?' she whispered. 'Just tae see mah Shugie?'

'Just for a minute,' Charlie muttered. 'I won't hurt him.'

'Gie her the money first,' the old man cackled. And then began to laugh; scuttling sideways through the door and down the cracked stone stairs like a hideous giant crab.

Charlie entered what had, long ago, been a bedroom once. Before the animals and the insects had taken over.

'Ohhhh, *shit*!' I heard him say. But it was with such sadness; such a terrible sadness for the woman clutching the money.

Shugie McGlashan looked so small and so inoffensive, lying in the matchwood coffin. I didn't think he'd been a particularly striking man even when he was alive – not many people who prey on old ladies and rob churches for a career do – but I'd never wanted to see him like that.

'A bus,' the woman said pathetically. 'Ootside of the pub twa days syne. And they all knew. They a' knew afore they sent ye doon here . . .'

But we could hardly blame the patrons of *The Braw Covenanter*.

McQuade with the grey suit and the black morality never

had guaranteed that Shugie McGlashan would actually speak to us, had he?

*

Charlie had more or less regained his usual equanimity by the time we got back to the flat; but I could see he was still ruffled by the macabre blind alley his over-enthusiasm had led us into. And the dent his pride had taken from the sick humour of hard man McQuade.

He still tried to cheer us up, though, while I packed my bags before leaving for the airport.

'Look, children,' he persisted with lofty reassurance. 'I've got a week's holiday long overdue, and as a newsman and fact-finder I can honestly claim to have no peer in this land of our fathers . . .'

'Excluding certain pubs off the Gallowgate,' Fran jeered, professionally waspish. But not unkindly, mind.

'So once again I shall confront the challenge of your mystery object, Johnny lad. I and my trusty Tyrolean hat, armed with the address list of McQueen the Polis, shall sally north while you're playing with boats, and unravel all.'

'What he really means,' Fran translated with caustic humour, 'is that the *Citizen* needs a rest from him and, because he's just as determined as you now and twice as pushy, he's hoping that if he makes a damned nuisance of himself with the rest of the people McGlashan robbed, one of them might admit to having owned the sextant just to get rid of him.'

'My quest shall begin 'neath the Folly of MacCaig,' Charlie intoned, very much back to his old form. 'And proceed to the shadow of sugar loaf . . .'

'Charlie,' I murmured ominously. I needed him to help with my riddles, not to bloody aggravate them; and so far he hadn't exactly proved infallible.

'The Folly of *MacCaig*,' Charlie explained laboriously as if to a child. 'That unfinished edifice which stands above Oban, Johnny. God, you are ignorant, even for a sailor – and Oban was where the late unlamented McGlashan pulled his first job. Right? Then I'll go see the old biddie he robbed up in Lochinver. Sugar loaf, pal? The shape of Suilven mountain that overlooks Lochinv . . .'

I reached for Fran before picking up my bag. 'Cheerio, Charlie,' I said pointedly. But he knew I was only disguising my gratitude: if anyone could uncover a link between the sextant and *Highlander*'s loss it was still Charlie Sullivan.

Two hours later I was aboard a Lufthansa flight into Fuhlsbüttel, Hamburg.

And the happy time was ended.

CHAPTER EIGHT

1941

The engine room telephone was ringing as the Captain returned to the bridge; struggling to climb the reeling ladder while still clutching his sextant box and the weighted confidential bag. Behind him on the boat deck the activity had reached a peak of stunned confusion, lifejacketed figures moving uncertainly around the three remaining boats; some men simply slumped and staring silently outboard as if trying to come to terms with the nightmare which had hit them, others fumbling with unfamiliar gear under the anxious commands of Fourth Officer Findlay and the clipped alien direction of the Dutchman, van der Kroon. A third uniformed shape now fussed among the crowd – Chief Steward Paton, trying desperately to supervise the loading of additional emergency stores, tally the names of those still alive, and advise an already-disenchanted Lamptrimmer Arnott on how to dress the gaps in Able Seaman Gillan's mutilated hand. But Wullie Paton never *had* learned how to delegate . . .

Hotchkiss came hurrying from the wheelhouse, still tying the straps of his lifejacket. The apprentice followed obediently behind the bigger seaman, already wearing his. Beedie looked like a fat baby penguin with eyes wide at the excitement and the fright of everything; arms sticking awkwardly outwards and the peak of the first-trip flat cap giving the small white face a strangely bird-like quality.

'Now you stay wi' me, young sir,' Hotchkiss was saying,

'and ah'll see ye right. No' that there's naething tae be feared of anyroad; not wi' just the wan wee torpedo in us.'

The Captain dumped the confidential books against the corner of the bridge wing and stepped quickly into the chart room, placing the sextant securely within the fiddles of the book rack above the table. His eyes fell to the ship's Deck Log lying open before him. McLeod's scratchy writing had made the last entries so far, under the heading 13 JAN 1941:

1916 GMT. *Torpedoed port quarter. Both engines stopped.*

1917 GMT. *On fire 5/6 holds. Steering reported inoperative. Master to bridge.*

Herschell automatically glanced up at the brass clock over the chart table. It was now seven-twenty-five . . . only nine minutes had actually passed since the explosion. It seemed more like nine bloody years.

Second Mate Devlin was holding the telephone receiver anxiously towards him when he hastened back into the wheelhouse. As he snatched it he felt the younger officer's eyes boring into his, desperately trying to read his intentions. He didn't have the right to keep them in suspense any longer. Covering the mouthpiece he said as gently as he could, 'We're abandoning, Mister Devlin. Or at least sending one boat away; to test the temperature of the water, so to speak.'

Captain Herschell couldn't really understand the look of relief in his Second Officer's expression. Surely the decision didn't offer as attractive an alternative to staying as *that*? But Herschell didn't know that, just as Radioman Stronach had his personal nightmare, so did 2/o Devlin – though the fears of both men derived from different ends of the spectrum of terror. Second Sparks's horror was based on being forced to leave the ship: the Second Mate's was at the prospect of remaining on board. To await the sort of holocaust he had witnessed once before, when that Norwegian tanker had detonated.

The Chief Engineer's dry voice greeted the Captain at the

other end of the phone. Even as his opposite number shouted up from the bottom of the ship Herschell could detect the background clamour of the slowly idling main engines, and marvelled at the courage of those men down below who still stayed at their posts until he gave the word to leave.

'Ye've been a bluidy long time in condescending tae speak to me,' the Chief roared, with total disregard for the majesty of command. But John Herschell was used to that, and tolerated it out of respect for his Chief Engineer's age and temperament. Which was bloody dour, to say the least.

'Sorry,' he said foolishly, and then immediately got angry at himself. Why was it that an oil-stained old man in a baggy white boiler suit always made him feel guilty? Like a kid in front of his teacher.

'Aye.' Graham's tone was only slightly mollified. 'Well maybe you'll be kind enough to listen tae what's goin' or doon here now, Captain. Your port engine's buggered. Snafu! Shaft's been sheared like it wis a slate pencil. We're making a wee bit water through the glands but there's naething the pumps cannae cope with at the moment . . .'

'I'm abandoning,' Herschell interposed determinedly. 'Get your lads up out of there, Chief. Right away.'

'. . . but ah can gie you slow speed on the starboard screw. Nae mair than a handful o' revolutions, mind. There's a gey chancy bend on . . . WHAT did you say, Mister?'

The Captain took a deep breath.

'I'm ordering "Abandon Ship" Mister Graham. We have a fire over explosive cargo aft, which could go up at any time. McLeod's taking the first boat away in a matter of minutes; if he makes it safely, then I want everyone else on the boat deck and ready to follow immediately. Get them up now, Alec.'

There was a long silence, apart from the whine of the wind storming through the open wheelhouse, and the shouts from the boat deck.

Then Graham's voice came back grimly.

'And what if they don't make it, Captain? You'll not get many offers tae try a second time; orders or not.'

Herschell squeezed the receiver tightly. It was the nearest he could get to a prayer. 'I'll not force a choice in that event, but by God I'll not deny any man that wishes a further opportunity to leave. We're going to blow up, Mister Graham. *Explode*, man! And there's no way I can steam her back to the coast even with slow speed on the one engine – our rudder's locked, too, Chief. We'll just sail round in bloody circles.'

'I'll away to the tiller flat an' hae a look.'

'Get up here, Mister Graham! That's an *order*, do you hear? I want every last man up from that engine room now; and ready to abandon when his time comes.'

'You'll have my lads. Ah'll pass the order now . . .' The Chief's tone hardened and Herschell knew he was wasting his time. And there wasn't any time left to waste. 'But I'm still going to take a look at the steering engine, Johnny. On fire, stopped, and a sitting target you're right tae try the one boat – may the Guid Lord be at the tiller and ye get them all away and safe. But happen you lose your first crowd, then you'll want the alternative of trying for home . . . ah'll see if ah can gie it to ye.'

The Captain stared sightlessly at his reflection in the wheelhouse windows. Graham had never used his first name before; not in all the time they'd sailed together; and abruptly he found it very hard to speak.

'You're refusing to obey an order, Alec? Is that it?'

Chief Engineer Graham chuckled at the other end. The ship lying over with each gigantic roll promising to be her last; ahead of him only the self-inflicted prospect of struggling alone in oil and slowly rising water until the virtually inevitable blast ripped monstrously through her double bottoms and compartments – and the most humourless man aboard *Highlander* was actually amused.

But then again, Herschell could never have been expected to understand how Alexander Graham's fear of retirement had, for a long time, been much greater than any fear he'd ever held of death.

'Apart frae this misbegotten crew of ours, Johnny, ah've nae family. And ah'm sixty-eight years old, man. Ah've lost all the taste I ever had for the wee boats.'

'Hang on f'r God's sake!'

Herschell heard Second Officer Devlin's choked warning even as he caught a glimpse of the rushing mountain of water bearing down on them. Slowly, shudderingly, *Highlander* began to crab beam-on up the side of the roaring white slope as her port side dipped crazily into a valley already lost in the blackness. Her bows reached the crest and she faltered, hanging with fifty feet of her forepart suspended in space, and then she swooped; fo'c'sle dropping sheer with the stern of her suddenly pointing to the sky and the flames jetting out horizontally as the savagery of the storm screamed across her open decks.

There was a singing noise, and a crack from high above.

The Captain was already whirling round; dropping the telephone and shying involuntarily away from an only half-sensed danger when the port window blew back in a razor-edged shatter of fragmenting glass. At the same instant what appeared as a writhing black snake sliced the far corner of the wheelhouse; ripped the port door clean from its mountings; caused Herschell to drop flat in shock even as he heard the first shouts and running footsteps from the deck.

And then, from astern, came a reverberating rumble accompanied by the screech of tortured steel. *Highlander* seemed to wince as the energy died from Herschell's snake and he recognised the slowly writhing coil for what it was – a fray-ended wire, still with a white porcelain insulator spliced into its length. Struggling to his feet he hurled himself through the starboard door, already searching aft with cold certainty at what he would see.

The mainmast had finally succumbed to that last violent plunge of the ship. But while the radio aerials had parted instantly to lash across the wheelhouse, the triatic stay had held; and as the massive column had teetered, sheared, begun to fall, then the weight of wire between both masts had taken charge, directing its collapse precisely along the fore and aft line of the stricken vessel.

The mast now lay amid a monstrous web of tangled rigging, embedded in the after end of the boat deck housing. Urgently men were gathering, running across the angled deck, picking through lethal snarls of wire and shattered planking to reach the point of first impact.

It would take time; time which they didn't have, and cutting equipment stowed far below in the engine room to release anyone still alive within that imploded compartment.

John Herschell prayed that Chief Officer McLeod had already left the radio room before the mast carved through it like a crowbar through a cardboard box. But he didn't think Trent could have made it clear, nor Second Operator Stronach. In fact he might never be certain now that their only distress call had even been completed.

*

SSSS . . . GBZQ . . . GBZQ . . . HIGHLANDER HIGHLANDER . . . TORPEDOED AND SINKING 22 MILES ENE BUTT OF LEWIS. ON FIRE WITH AFTER HOLDS FLOODING. AM ABANDONING NOW . . .

Chief Operator Trent had hesitated only one second longer after the sharp acknowledgement came; a crisply professional key from an unknown shore station. Then his fingers had rattled again. An afterthought of unfamiliar prayer from the recesses of child memory.

GOD BE WITH U . . .

He never even heard the topmast explode through the deckhead immediately above his operator's post; the headphones clamped firmly over both ears rendered Chief

Operator Trent deaf to any sound generated less than a wireless frequency away. His supple fingers were still keying that last desperate entreaty when a behemoth fist smashed him, his chair, his Morse key and most of his Marconi equipment, down through the radio room deck, the passenger verandah immediately beneath, and onwards into the engineer officers' lavatory situated at centrecastle island level.

And there the scarred masthead of the Motor Vessel *Highlander* finally came to rest amid an obscene porridge of valve parts, coloured wires, gaping dials and the smeared debris of what had been, less than a blink of an eye before, a draughts player of high repute. The pulsing sprays from fractured sanitary plumbing quickly cleansed the more ghastly features of that violent impact . . . it was a hygienic passing; a total surprise of a death, and one with very little discomfort for Radio Officer Trent.

But Second Operator Stronach? Well, he'd been standing slightly to one side as Damocles fumbled his sword. The plummeting mast folded the deckhead inwards; flailed him stare-eyed into a corner; continued on through the radio compartment, collecting his Chief on the way; and left him shocked but relatively unmarked, yet unable to move more than a finger as it imprisoned his legs and the lower part of his torso within a cocoon of buckled steel and snarled wire rigging.

When the first ashen faces peered tentatively through the metallic maze which now substituted for *Highlander*'s radio room, every jaw dropped in disbelief at how lucky, and yet how unfortunate a man could be after a dreadful accident like that. Imagine surviving the fate of a bug under a hammer in one second, only to discover in the next that you have a ten-thousand-ton millstone gripping you; and one which might well founder before a helping hand could penetrate the mess which imprisoned you?

If any helping hands stayed long enough to try.

But at least Second Operator Stronach did have one faint consolation – he wouldn't turn to jelly slowly, as his nightmare had suggested. Whatever happened to him now would happen very quickly indeed.

*

While Captain Herschell's prayer was answered in part – in that Chief Officer McLeod had indeed left the radio room before the ultimate collapse of *Highlander*'s mainmast – the event still had an ironic aftermath. For the whip of the carried-away aerial, which had so nearly decapitated the master himself, also caused one further casualty as it lashed the length of the boat deck – and that casualty was none other than . . . Chief Officer McLeod.

Mind you, he wasn't mortally stricken. You wouldn't have needed to be a qualified medical man to diagnose that fact – the language which met horrified rescuers converging on the seeming corpse of First Mate McLeod after the tumbling wire had slammed him to the deck was, to say the least, selected by a brain in no way dulled by the anaesthesia of approaching death. In fact even Bosun McColl, bearing a still dazed Jimmie Beattie in resentful tow, stopped abruptly and listened as the Mate sat up and roared vitriolic confirmation of the life spark still within him. Whereupon the Bosun smiled a beatific smile of approbation; even in the midst of the holocaust, sweet learning still there was.

But McLeod had been injured all the same. His right arm and side were savagely bruised and cut where the aerial had struck him a glancing blow as he hurried unwarily, intent on preparing his boat for that first critical escape. As soon as Herschell raced aft, pushing through the stunned groups of men at the boarding stations, he knew Mister McLeod could no longer be responsible for the safety of any lifeboat on such a desperate mission. Apart from the blood and the torn oilskins, the Chief Officer couldn't conceal his pain at the slightest movement.

Then Herschell's original decision was frustrated even further as he ran on to gaze with tight-lipped sympathy at the agonised radio officer trapped within the wreckage. Despite the hands which plucked at the razor-edges of Stronach's cocoon it was barely possible to make out the boy's face deep amid the tangled web, and that only by the light of the fires raging from the afterdeck. Immediately the Captain realised that only a volunteer with a cutting torch and time and luck and a lot of courage, could hope to extend the life of Radio Operator Stronach.

He accepted without question that he would have to be that man; and for as long as the ship gave him time. Because the mast which imprisoned the young officer had just as surely captured Jonathan Herschell; those four gold rings of command upon his arm demanded more from him than any other man aboard could be expected to give.

'Mister Devlin,' he called urgently, rising to his feet.

The Second Mate eased his way through the press of ineffectual helpers.

'Sir?'

'Mister McLeod isn't able, now. Will you take the first boat away?'

There was relief evident in the Second Officer's answering nod; almost gratitude. 'It's funny,' Herschell reflected vaguely, 'how we're all scared; yet we're all scared of different things.' It struck him then that maybe courage didn't really exist in the minds of men under threat – only fear dictated their actions; a fear which drove them to attempt desperate things in order to avoid their even greater terror at doing nothing at all. 'Concentrate,' he thought savagely, 'philosophy is for quiet nights alone on the bridge, when the moon is bright and the path ahead clear; not for now, when men are dying and the end of our world is but a white-hot flash away.'

But it would still be his own personal fear which would force him to stay aboard with the trapped Operator

Stronach, not his bravery. Because Captain John Herschell's private nightmare was that of being seen to fail in his responsibility to those under his command. The prospect of being drowned or blown to bloodied lumps was secondary to a terrible wound like that.

Highlander rolled crazily again and sea met fire with rumbling malice. Clouds of smoke-steam and whirling embers played among the anxious group and Stronach shrieked aloud from his lobster pot of iron.

'You'll not be left, son,' the Captain called with a steady voice. 'I promise you'll not be left alone.'

Then he swung round. 'Ten volunteers at the oars, Mister. Two more of the most reliable manning the falls. Get them aboard and ready to lower. I'll be along in a minute.'

'That leaves you with two boats, sir,' the Second Mate said, and Herschell could see that he was already excited, the adrenalin colouring his pinched face at the promise of getting away. 'Will you be taking one of them?'

The Captain shook his head. 'Mister van der Kroon will be in charge of number two; the Fourth Officer in number three . . .' He hesitated; he was about to say *if*, but then he changed it. 'When the three of you are launched you'll do your best to stand-off a safe distance. The Chief's already decided to stay aboard, and there will be myself and the Radio Officer when I get him free. I'll flash instructions from the bridge about picking us up one way or another.'

There was a stir from the back of the group. The Mate shoved his way through, careless of his injured arm. 'You're holding back the truth an' ye know it, Captain. There's no way a boat's crew can hold their position in this; they'll be blown away down-wind soon as they hit the water.'

'That's enough, Mister McLeod,' Herschell snapped.

Another figure stepped forward – Second Engineer McKechnie, fresh on deck from his earlier place in the now abandoned engine room.

'There'll be four o' us staying, anyroad. I'll away and get the cutting gear now, wi' your permission, sir.'

'Permission refused,' the Captain growled, startled. 'Get it up here by all means. Mister – I'll be glad of that much help – but then you leave in van der Kroon's boat, McKechnie. Along with the rest.'

'With respect, Captain, ah couldnae trust a master with a delicate tool like an acetylene torch for ony reason.' The Second Engineer grinned – weakly, yes – but nevertheless he grinned. 'You're liable to blow the ship up, sir; using a dangerous thing like yon . . . apart fae which the Chief'll need a hand wi' the steering engine, and Christ knows he's in a bad enough temper a'ready.'

'And I'm no' going,' McLeod said with dour petulance. 'I've gone off the yachting. And beside,' he leaned over, wincing as his shoulder caught a vagrant spear of wreckage, and peered fiercely into the mess wherein Stronach lay, 'ye'll need a man wi' a sense o' humour, eh, son? To make ye laugh.'

'You, Mister McLeod,' the Captain snapped, ignoring the next roll and the way all eyes flickered outboard to expose their fear, 'are aiding and abetting a mutiny, and should know better.'

But he didn't mean it. Only the choking sensation at the back of his throat wouldn't let him put his real feelings into words.

'Aye, sir,' his Chief Officer nodded complacently. 'So if ye'll guarantee to put me safely back ashore, ah'll be only too happy to hang for it.'

Bosun McColl was the next to step forward. 'You'll need a strong man to 'elp the Second pull the stuff apart, sir. And engineers – beggin' your pardon, Mister McKechnie, sir – shouldn't oughter be left wi'out a proper seaman's eye on 'em. I'm stayin' as well, if it's all right by you.'

'Well, it isn't, McColl,' Herschell roared. 'None of it is!'

'Ah,' the Bosun frowned, and looked sad. 'Then it's me for the 'anging too; alongside the Mate. Sir!'

'Here,' a voice exclaimed in outraged suspicion. 'Ah'm no' goin' in one of they wee matchstick boats an' that's a fact.' Whereupon everybody turned and glared at very ordinary seaman Jimmie Beattie; almost-fighter-pilot and the primary target of every German in Hitler's *Kriegsmarine*. But Jimmie was getting over having been blown-up for the first time and his natural Gorbals wariness of the motives of other men was rising to the fore – if a' they *officers* wis wanting tae stay aboard the bluidy ship, then there wis bound tae be some subtle, selfish reasoning behind it.

'Ah'm no' going, ah tell ye,' Jimmie reaffirmed, quailing only slightly under the disapproval of his superiors. 'Ah signed on tae sail inna big ship. If ah'd wanted tae float aboot onna wee bit wood I'd've been a bluidy lumberjack, so ah would.'

'That makes six of us staying,' the Mate said emphatically; ignoring blatant rebellion by a seaman for the first time in his life. Then he went down on one knee and bellowed into the hole. 'Sparks! Are you stayin'?'

The voice was thin with horror, but the trapped boy tried very hard.

'For a while, sir. If it's a party . . .', but then he started sobbing with the fear of it. Mister McLeod snapped severely, 'Stop that now, laddie, or ye'll spoil everybody's day!' before shrugging.

'Seven of us, Captain,' he announced inflexibly. 'Plus any others that change their minds once they've watched the Second Mate play roller-coaster.'

'You're a bloody disgrace,' the Captain muttered with an alien glint in his eye. 'All of you – a bloody disgrace.'

'Yessir,' they agreed. Except for Second Operator Stronach, who was still crying his relief at not being left alone, and hadn't really been included anyway; and Jimmie Beattie, who didn't care *what* the Old Man thought of him just as long as he didnae have tae face goin' in one of yon wee coble things.

The Captain turned to stare down into the crackling breath of numbers five and six. Even as he did so the ship lurched heavily yet again with the white water frothing and rumbling over the lee bulwarks of the well deck, and cascading explosively into the gaping rift. For a brief moment the fires shrank back, retreated as if in hiding from an enemy even more voracious than they; but the ship was an island over which the fire still owned control, and Herschell suspected that the only way in which the sea could regain sovereignty was by overwhelming the ship itself. Then the flames blazed in glaring counter-attack, and the Captain knew the fire would take *Highlander* long before its competitor, the sea.

It was now seven-forty in the evening, and there were still twenty-five men left alive aboard the ship – twenty-five and a half, counting Stronach. That was when Fourth Officer Findlay came running down the port side boat deck and blurted, 'Mister Devlin's ready to abandon, sir!'

Captain Herschell forced his gaze from the fire.

'Thank you,' he said quietly.

It was difficult to determine in which direction his thanks were really aimed. For his grey eyes were firmly fixed on the blackened, bloody-minded ring of mutineers which surrounded him.

Grimly he followed Findlay's trail to where the lifeboat hung with its tense and strangely silent cargo; oars already up-ended and clutched in bone-white fists.

He hoped they would get away. Oh, he prayed so desperately that at least *they* would get away. And be safe.

CHAPTER NINE

There was no one in the Glasgow flat, half dressed or otherwise, when I returned from Rotterdam nine days later. But it was only three in the afternoon which meant that Fran – unless she was on nightcall for the paper – wasn't due home for another couple of hours at the earliest. I hoped she *wasn't* working nights; I hadn't forgotten my sombre mood of the previous time, and the way the sextant's traumatic appearance had spoiled our first reunion.

Charlie wasn't due back from his great northern sleuthing tour until the weekend, which gave us two whole days alone together; but love in the still of the night holds an intimacy never matched during the waking hours of the city. I toyed with the idea of phoning the *Northern Citizen* reporters' room and checking where she was, then decided to wait. Maybe I remembered Fran's impish retort to MacFaid of Laichy – every nice prospect is the better for a bit of waiting. I put the kettle on instead and wandered aimlessly through the empty flat.

The sextant was still as I'd left it, sitting innocuously on the sideboard in the living room; an enigma boxed in ageing rosewood and a reminder of questions unanswered. I'd come to terms with the fact of its continuing survival now, while I'd spent nine days in a separate world, shielded from idle speculation by the pressures of commanding an unfamiliar ship – and that had its curative effect, too. No longer was I so obsessed with the mystery that existed regarding the sinking of the M.V. *Highlander*; instead I had developed a grim resolve to unearth the real truth . . . but not at the expense of loving Fran. That was for today, and for the future. She was my life, I knew that now. Never again must I allow the still-spreading ripples of a forty-year-old torpedo explosion to take precedence over something as coveted as that.

Anyway, Charlie wouldn't be back until Saturday so there was no point in tilting at phantoms. If there was any connection between those remaining five addresses and my father's sextant, then he'd have traced it. And that would be the time for us to decide what to do next. My eyes fell on the postcard propped beside the rosewood box and I lifted it idly. It was a stereotyped view of mournful Highland cattle lounging on an unidentifiable hillside, staring blankly into the camera lens with bovine disinterest – and of course, it was from Charlie.

Typical, original, laugh-a-minute Charlie.

I turned it over and glowered resignedly at the scrawled, practically unreadable cryptogram on the back. The kettle began to whistle readiness from the kitchen and I replaced the postcard, grinning fondly. Wandering through, I turned the gas off and then caught sight of the old man and the fat black and white dog down on the Parade. They were the same pair I'd watched previously, only this time I could afford to smile at the tongue-lolling exuberance of that canine tow; on the last occasion I'd still been numbed by the implications raised by the act of one Shugie McGlashan.

But even that had had its consolation – at least we'd found Laichy because of it. Thinking of Laichy made me ponder on Charlie's postcard again. Fran would be able to read it; Fran knew Charlie's appalling reporter's hand . . . but it wouldn't help much; it'd be so obscure that we'd still have to wait for the sleuth's return to understand the bloody thing.

Laichy. Maybe *we* could go back there, though? Just for a few days. Just to enjoy its friendly beauty, and each other. I was still dreaming of our last happy time when I heard the door open behind me. I turned, waiting pleasantly for her shriek of delight, only it never came.

Fran was standing there, just standing, and staring at me; and there was a terrible pain in her face, and the black-mascara tears had washed unheeded rivulets of sadness all the way down her cheeks. I think I anticipated what she was going to say before she actually spoke.

'It's Charlie, John The police phoned me at the office. Don McQueen. He wanted to tell me himself.'

She began to cry but I couldn't go over to her. I couldn't do anything.

I said tightly, unnecessarily, 'He's dead. Isn't he?'

She bowed her head and the black shining hair fell unheeded across her lovely face. I wanted so much to go across then, to hold her, but her shoulders began to shake and I was too much of a coward. I knew her soft helplessness would only trigger my own grief and I had to find something out first. Something which I was already terrified I might hear.

'How? How did he die?'

'They say it was an accident. There were witnesses . . .'

I turned away from her, feeling the pain of my nails biting into the palms of clenched hands. The old man and the fat black and white dog were blurred now as they'd been when I first saw them. Only it wasn't the rain on the window that was causing it. Not this time.

'Where, Fran? Where did it happen?'

There was no answer; only the lonely sounds of her misery. I swung round, impatient for the bad news I felt was coming.

'Where was Charlie killed, dammit?'

Her eyes burned into me, wide in their accusation. Yet when she spoke it wasn't only Fran's voice I heard – it was the spectral clamour from the throats of a whole crew of long dead sailormen. My ghosts of the Motor Vessel *Highlander*.

'Laichy! Charlie must have gone there because of your sextant, and now he's dead. In *Laichy*!'

*

'Obviously it was an accident. There were no suspicious circumstances,' D.S. McQueen said uncomfortably, floundering under our uncompromising stares. Fran and I both sat silently, almost detachedly, while he read through the report relating, in impersonal officialese, the manner of death of another Highland climber who had made one fatal mistake.

'Mister Sullivan's body was recovered from the base of Creag Fuar cliffs, some half mile south of Laichy village. Preliminary Police Surgeon's examination indicates death caused by impact, injuries compatible with a fall from some thirty metres; this would confirm observations made at the scene by attending officers.'

'. . . Climbing equipment noted (Itemised Annexe A) as being neatly placed in the boot of the deceased person's vehicle, and later found parked in Laichy itself. No roping or other preventive equipment was attached to the body of the deceased.'

McQueen allowed his voice to trail off, then recovered. 'I'm sorry! There's little else at this stage. It didn't even happen in Strathclyde Police area – the Highland Region Force conducted the enquiries; copy report to us because Charlie lives . . . lived in Glasgow here. But it was an accident. The Highland bobbies have no conceivable reason . . .'

Fran stirred, forcing herself out of her slump of misery. 'You used that expression once before, Donnie. When you said a minister of the Church would have no conceivable reason to lie about the stolen sextant. But neither did McGlashan, remember? Yet one of them *must* have done.'

'Or McGlashan did make a genuine error, Fran.' He shrugged cautiously. 'But this is different – this time there are three people to give firm statements. Three witnesses to the accident, all of whom state that they actually saw Charlie fall while climbing that cliff alone.'

'Who were they?' I muttered. 'Those unimpeachable witnesses?'

I could see him eyeing me in a funny way – he'd obviously read my emphasis on the word 'unimpeachable' – but he didn't query it right then; just leafed through the file on his desk and shrugged again.

'All local people. Alisdair McLeod, fisherman; David Scott-Watson, retired naval officer; and a Miss Fiona MacFaid, air stewardess.'

'. . . and daughter of the *Sutherland Arms* hotel,' I completed grimly. I caught the look of shocked disbelief in Fran's red-rimmed eyes, still glistening with her grief for Charlie, but I didn't care. I was convinced now of Laichy's involvement. Charlie's death had proved one thing already in my mind – that the true manner of *Highlander*'s disappearance was being concealed somewhere up there on that bleak Sutherland coast. And somewhere not too far from the head of the sea loch of Fhadaig.

And also that a certain Reverend Hamish Watt Stewart, M.A., Minister of the Presbyterian Church of St Andrew's in Laichy . . . *that* particular man of God had been lying in his teeth as well.

But why? Why should such people lie; now perhaps have gone even further? To conceal an event which must have happened forty years ago? Before Fiona MacFaid, at least, had even been born?

'Do you want to read the witnesses' statements, Johnny?' McQueen said, holding Highland Constabulary Report Annexe B towards me. I ignored it bleakly.

'I never read fiction,' I muttered with contempt.

'You are implying that a very grave charge should be considered against those three witnesses, John.'

I gazed at him steadily, 'More than that – I am *saying* serious charges should be brought, Sergeant, and that your buddies in the Highland Constabulary should get off their asses an' do their bloody job!'

He slammed the file on the desk. 'Look. Three witnesses.

Three totally unconnected and disinterested witnesses to an accident . . .'

'Not unconnected!' I snapped back. 'Not disinterested, McQueen. Hell, man, but can't you see it *yet*? That they, and their bloody man of God; they do have one common factor . . . they all live in Laichy.'

This time Detective Sergeant McQueen stared at me for a long time. When he did finally speak he chose his words with enormous care.

'You are claiming that all this goes back to the time of the war, aren't you? And that the sextant stolen by McGlashan, and the loss of your father's ship and now the death of Charlie Sullivan . . . they are all somehow connected. Not only that, but that the population of Laichy – virtually all of them, one way or another – are somehow connected with this too.'

Knowing how she felt about Laichy I glanced towards Fran and met her eyes pleadingly. They blinked back, pained beyond ordinary grief. But then she nodded imperceptibly, and I loved her for her support.

'Secrets can't be kept forever in an inbred place like that,' I persisted woodenly. 'So most of them must know of it – yes. Whatever *it* is.'

'Whatever it is?' McQueen echoed disbelievingly. 'Whatever it is : . .'

His chair cannoned against the wall as he jerked upright, slamming his fist on the desk in frustration.

'Christ, both of you, but how am I to go to my senior officers . . . to the bloody Procurator Fiscal, dammit! and . . . an' say to them I want a warrant for the arrest of . . . of a whole village that's not even in Strathclyde Region? And all based on some . . . some crazy sailor's conviction that a sextant which most certainly does exist isn't supposed to. Because it ought to be lying in some sunken wreck God knows how far off the coast instead. And on those flimsy grounds, a minister of the Church is alleged to have committed perjury; an entire community has been accused of withholding evidence; witnesses are automatically presumed to be lying . . .'

I rose from my seat and held the door open for Fran. 'Goodbye, Detective Sergeant,' I said stiffly. 'Thank you for your help.'

I knew he wanted to, but couldn't. The hurt and the frustration in his gaze as he watched us leave were more than enough to show that.

I never even bothered to mention the postcard from Charlie.

McQueen wouldn't have taken that seriously either. Not unless it had borne Charlie's blood as proof that something appalling really *had* occurred in Laichy.

*

Of course there wasn't any blood, I mean. On Charlie's postcard. But there was the splash of a tear after Fran had finished translating the enigmatic scribble backing those blank-eyed Highland beasts.

It was three o'clock in the morning and we'd hardly said a word; just sat in the silence of that strangely empty flat, and became ever more conscious of an estrangement between us that even our temporary alliance in the face of McQueen's scepticism had done nothing to overcome. Ever since Fran's shock had exploded into unintentional accusation the rift had been widening and, to my everlasting shame, I had never tried to rectify it.

I'd simply left the thing I loved more than anything else in the world, to stare hollow-eyed and miserable, and slipped back into my obsessive gloom; going over and over and over the words which blurred before me. Over what had originally been intended as Charlie's joke, but which was now Charlie's legacy.

To exercise your minds when you're not exercising each other, my children –

An excess from Flanders; a well in the loch;
The field of St George, yet served by pibroch;
The dating inscribed of their gallantry.
But the peaks of the bens – why washed by the sea?

See you Saturday. Love, Charlie.

Postmarked Tuesday. From Laichy, in Sutherland.

I read it again, and then again. It had to be all there . . . the solution; the true fate of a ship, a crew, a forty-year-old horror. Everything.

Turning the postcard over I blinked at the bovine vacuity which had obviously tickled Charlie so much. And I remembered the way he used to grin at me, and the way we'd been so close. So bloody close.

Ever so gradually my shoulders began to shake. And the merciful safety valve of grief finally lifted.

*

We left on the road to Loch Fhadaig early on the morning after Charlie's funeral: a journey without laughter or light. Even the grey skies were weeping, as if matching our reawakened sorrow for Charlie. We didn't stop to eat this time; neither Fran nor myself had any appetite, and despite our dual resolve to discover the secret that had already cost us so dear we were still a couple far apart.

Steadily I had become more aware of the gulf between us, and of the irony that the object which had first focused our love – the sextant – was now the only tangible thing to bond us together. But it couldn't be allowed to last; not that strained and sad seclusion.

It was only when it finally became night again, and the mountains' gloom drew a welcome blanket over the now crumpled drifts of dirty snow lining our path, that her hand stole tentatively – almost fearfully into mine. I stopped the car instantly, contempt for my own stupid pride overwhelmed by the gratitude I felt and my need for her. And I put my arms around her, there and then in the middle of that Highland road, and she gave a little strangled sob before we kissed. Afterwards I held her tight and savoured her perfumed warmth. And thanked God for a love I didn't deserve to regain.

It didn't bring the happy time back; there never could be another happy time for us, not in Laichy. But at least it gave us the resolution to conceal our outward mourning, and to act as though we really were the same unsuspecting couple who had left the *Sutherland Arms* a fortnight before; even to smile and to joke with those very people who were – beyond any reasonable doubt in our minds – practising a deception infinitely more sinister than any subterfuge of ours.

Yet being affable wasn't as difficult as we'd anticipated. Within minutes of our second arrival – and our reception from MacFaid and Fiona and poor smiling Maggie, who greeted us with all the warmth of hosts genuinely delighted – we really *were* talking and laughing as though we'd never left at all.

Only we had left, you see; and I couldn't free my mind of the thought that maybe Charlie Sullivan was dead simply because we had done so. And that in turn created a second, even more disturbing apprehension which I never once mentioned to Fran – and that was regarding what might have happened had I not been called to sail *Lowlander* to Rotterdam, while Charlie had probed for the truth in my place.

Could it have meant that Fran and I would have been lying cold in our graves by now, instead? With the only link between the sextant and an otherwise forgotten incident of war surviving, once again, as a barely perceptible gleam in the eyes of certain inhabitants of Laichy. Like one-armed MacFaid, for instance? Or even sweet, condemned Maggie, who would surely be taking her awful knowledge into her own sepulchral kist before many weeks had passed? Or, in the dark and innocent gaze of the lovely Fiona, who couldn't even have been born while the men of *Highlander* were dying?

Undoubtedly there was one person who *must* be lying – only in his case behind the mask of a holy smile. Because it had been through his denial, and therefore his certain involvement, that this whole awful quest had been initiated.

It meant we at least had a starting point.

Tomorrow Fran and I intended to go to church.

*

It was Donald MacFaid himself who gave us the perfect reason to call upon the Reverend Hamish Watt Stewart without giving rise to any suspicion. 'I have been thinking of your flower, Francine,' MacFaid had said after breakfast the next morning. 'The flower that you are here to look for? Yon *Primula Scottish*, was it?'

'*Scotica*, Donald,' she replied quickly. I glanced at her anxiously; was our host of the *Sutherland Arms* sincere – or probing? But he'd just nodded sagely and continued.

'Perhaps you would be well-guided to ask the advice of our friend, the minister . . . He is a great man for the bird life, is Hamish Stewart. It could well be that he may know of places nearby where a plant of that sort might be found.'

Half an hour later we were approaching the manse beside the parish church of Laichy. I was already conscious of a dull excitement rising within me – somewhere in that quiet precinct lay the key to *Highlander*'s secret; I was as certain of that as I was of my hostility, already acutely anticipated, towards its incumbent. Many a time I had tried to picture the Reverend Stewart, and failed. For how could I? What man of religion *could* be visualised who was associated with such evil? I could only imagine him as being old; even very old. Forty years had passed since the unimaginable had occurred; by now, he must be well into his seventies.

A figure was moving under the trees backing the manse

garden; a young chap belatedly gathering the last of the autumn leaves, now stiff with frost. A bonfire smouldered sullenly nearby and I watched the grey smoke curling and dissipating as it rose, whipped by the rising westerly breeze. We stopped at the gate beside the church notice board.

'We'd better ask for the Reverend Stewart,' Fran said, already seductively pink from the fresh cold air.

I called, 'Excuse me . . .' and the young gardener came over, wiping his hands on his jeans. The square chin lifting enquiringly was bedded in a polo-necked Fairisle jersey with holes in the elbows, and a long yellow and blue university scarf made several turns on a neck which would have been well employed in the front row of any rugger scrum. I couldn't help noticing that most of his curiosity was directed towards Fran, and not myself.

'Hallo,' he said as he came up to us. 'Can I be of help?'

I don't know why, but I hesitated. Something told me this was no Laichy-based handyman. I hazarded an educated guess. 'I think we must be looking for your father. Is he in?'

The young man looked blank.

'The Reverend Stewart,' I amplified. 'Is he available, please?'

His expression cleared and he grinned. 'Oh, sorry – yes.'

I waited. We all waited. Finally I said uncertainly, 'The Reverend Hamish Watt *Stewart*. We would very much like to meet him. Please.'

He stuck his hand out. 'That's right. How d'you do?'

I felt my lower jaw sag as I gazed at the smoke-grimed, slightly battered face watching my discomfiture with such cheery tolerance. Dazedly I found myself shaking hands with the sinister keeper of *Highlander*'s secret. Yet he couldn't have been a day over thirty years old.

'I'm Hamish Stewart,' he laughed. 'Unless you really do want my dad; but then you'll have to go south to Edinburgh. He's an executive with the Clydesdale Bank.'

As ever I was rescued by Fran's cool equanimity.

'No, I think we should stay with you,' she rejoined with cheeky composure. 'For it's a flower we are after . . . not an overdraft.'

*

An hour later and I still hadn't come to terms with my shock.

It was warm in the manse, and untidy with the homeliness of family. Odd socks, children's toys, magazines, even a half-eaten jam sandwich lay spread through the living room in a confusion of embarrassment for the young woman fussing before us round the blazing fire.

'Will you take another cup of tea, Mister Templeton?' asked Joan, the wife of the minister of Laichy. Then she looked round and said for the fifth time, 'Och but you must be thinking we live here like pigs, both of you. In such a mess as this.'

'It's a lovely manse,' Fran smiled. 'If the children were tidy they wouldn't be proper children, Joan. Tea, darling?' She nudged me out of my daze. 'Joan's asking if you want more tea?'

'Er . . . no. No, thank you,' I answered hastily. If Joan Stewart had been caught unawares by our unexpected arrival, *I* had been totally shattered. All my preconceived illusions about Laichy's man of God had disintegrated; in fact everything concerning the sextant's existence was proving crazier and crazier. Hamish Watt Stewart *had* to be the keeper of its secret, yet this craggy, pleasant young cleric – like Fiona MacFaid before him – couldn't even have been born when it first survived what should have been its end.

So why?

I had to probe further.

'Do you have a . . . well, a family connection with Laichy?' I asked diffidently. He swallowed a mouthful of cake and shook his head cheerfully.

'No. Nor the Church, John, for that matter. I'm the first of our line to enter the Ministry. Rest of them are bankers apart from my eldest brother – he's a solicitor in Inverness.'

'Have you been here long, then?'

He frowned, looking queryingly at Joan. 'Just over six years,' she said helpfully. He shrugged. 'Six years. And two bonnie kids.'

'Sometimes I think they must have wee horns,' Joan added feelingly, gazing round at the mess. Fran could see what I was driving at though.

'Does Laichy keep its ministers long, Hamish? Have there been many since . . . say . . . the last war?'

I held my breath; she was pushing it. Then I remembered Charlie and didn't care too much. Stewart didn't seem to notice anything amiss.

'I came to replace the Reverend McKail; he was a very sick man even though he wasn't old. I think he'd been minister of St Andrew's here since about nineteen fifty-eight or 'fifty-nine. It had been a Reverend Crombie before then. Since about the late twenties, I think. So to answer your question, Francine – not really. We small parish men tend to hang on as long as we can. We get close to our people, you see. And the West Coast Highlander really has to be the most perfect of all God's children.'

'Crombie?' I had to ask. 'Did you ever meet him. Talk to him?'

This time he did look at me with a trace of query. 'The Reverend Crombie? No, I never talked to him, but I still see him often enough. His grave is out there in the churchyard . . . he never gets lonely, you know.'

It was our turn to frown. 'Lonely?' Fran echoed.

'He was a dearly loved man. There's plenty still remember him, and bide a while with him after worship. Things have changed a lot in these wee coastal hamlets since the thirties and forties, mind. In those days communities like Laichy were virtually isolated; introspective; very dependent on their so-called educated residents like the doctor – and the minister.' He smiled, and there was a trace of ruefulness. 'There's times when I don't think they've changed all that much even now.'

Joan Stewart nudged him fondly. 'Och, that's just the remains of your Edinburgh upbringing struggling to get out, Hamish.'

I picked him up immediately. 'Then the minister – you – still do retain a pretty strong influence over your members?'

'Not only us Presbyterians. There's still a strong Catholic following in the Western Highlands, you know. And the Free Church became rooted up here after the Disruption. The "Wee Free's" as the irreverent would have them.'

'The Disruption?'

'Och, it's history, but important. Five years after the seventeen hundred and seven Union of the Crowns an act passed by the then English-controlled Parliament denied Presbyterian congregations the right to choose their own ministers – they were appointed by a system of lay patronage; by the local landowners instead, which many claimed struck at the fundamental democracy of the Church. Because of that, and over a century later, four hundred and fifty ministers finally walked out of the Scottish Assembly and formed the Free Church as a protest. Oh, the two Churches amalgamated again in nineteen twenty-nine after the official Presbyterian Kirk abandoned the system, but there's always been a strong resentment felt against outside interference since. Even now there still is.'

'Nineteen twenty-nine? Then the Reverend Crombie must have been the incumbent here at that time; and a pretty powerful force within the community? Therefore by definition as a clergyman, with a great responsibility towards it?'

The young Reverend Stewart definitely hesitated this time. It may have been my imagination but I thought I detected a note of caution. Or suspicion.

'I would hope that as his, and Jamie McKail's successor, I could also claim to honour my responsibilities towards my congregation in Laichy, John. Even in this age of transistorised comfort the Church still has a duty to guard the spiritual well-being of the people.'

'Guard?' I said, far too quickly. 'You mean protect, Hamish? In a still remote parish like Laichy, don't you have to protect more than just their spiritual well-being . . . ?'

For an uneasy moment he stared thoughtfully, almost appraisingly at me; but there was still a refreshing openness in the features of that most unlikely custodian of sinister intelligence. Then Hamish Stewart smiled apologetically and turned to Fran.

'I'm boring you with my talk of ecumenical history, Francine. You say Donald MacFaid thought I might be able to help you discover your flower; your *Primula scotica*?'

I chewed my lip in frustration, but didn't dare return to the subject I was most concerned with – the Reverend Crombie; who had been the minister of this remote Presbyterian Parish during the Second World War. During the critical time in which any link with *Highlander* must have been forged.

Fran nodded. 'Donald tells us you are an amateur naturalist yourself, Hamish.'

'Mostly birds. Though the Lord is a pretty resourceful architect; he gives us a world of beautiful things to gaze on.'

Joan dug him in the ribs caustically, but with love. 'He means Fiona MacFaid, don't you, Hamish?'

The minister of Laichy grinned unashamedly; it was an explosion of open boyishness. 'Only if I were in the Catholic priesthood would I have to deny an accusation like that. I can afford a momentary lapse in Fiona's case – all said and done I married the most beautiful thing of all.'

Joan Stewart blushed and gathered the plates hurriedly. 'Aye,' her husband kidded her, 'you go and perform your wifely duties, my darling. Remember it's not so many years ago that the women of hamlets like this used to carry their men on their backs out to the fishing boats, to save their feet from getting wet.'

Fran laughed. 'So chauvinism does still live in Laichy, Hamish? Even in the manse.'

Joan smiled at her from behind her husband. It was an intimate, female understanding. 'He likes to think so. But he'll still do the washing-up after you've gone.'

I found myself grinning in concert; it wasn't possible to remain hostile to those warm and surely sincere people. I still steered the conversation back to our rather less honest subterfuge for being there, though. Because I hadn't forgotten Charlie.

'Fran's flower, Hamish – can you help? I can't even pretend to be a chauvinist, you see; she'll make my life a misery if I take her home in frustration.'

'How would I recognise your elusive bloom if I saw it?' he was asking Fran. As ever she was well prepared.

'You probably won't; not in winter. But you may have noticed them earlier on in the year . . . it has a tight rosette of leaves on a short stalk, and a bluish-purple umbel of flowers; a sort of cluster with the youngest flowers in the centre. Look.'

She hauled a picture out of her bag and I wondered cynically if the *Northern Citizen* knew she'd borrowed it. Hamish Stewart eyed it doubtfully.

'I don't think so. Maybe I could have, up on the tops.'

I pretended to remember. 'Someone mentioned to us that they might have seen it in the . . . what area was it, Fran?'

She lied as straight-faced as I had, and with even more conviction. 'Creag Fuar, wasn't it? Is there a place called Creag Fuar here, Hamish?'

It was Joan Stewart who undermined our strategy. We were both watching closely for a reaction from the Reverend when she gave a sudden cry instead; distracting us.

'*Creag Fuar*? Oh, you mustn't allow Fran to go there at this time of the year, Mister Templeton. Only last week some poor man was killed on the same mountain.'

I fought to control my disappointment; by then Stewart was nodding sagely and I'd missed any involuntary response to our somewhat clumsy trap. He certainly didn't over-react, though, as he might have been expected to do if he was covering anything sinister.

'Aye . . . a climber from Glasgow, I believe. The police couldn't really understand why he was up there, and alone, but people do silly things out here in the wilds; silly, dangerous things. Even some of the most experienced who should know better. But I can't see your Primula being out by Fuar, Francine; more like the gentler slopes. Up on Dubhail Leirge, maybe, where the ground is flat. Or somewhere out by Sròine Riabach if it has a preference for the sea air.'

And that was . . . well . . . that. Nothing! In fact we seemed to have slipped even further back in our attempt to secure a starting point. Despite all my preconceived notions about the Reverend Hamish Watt Stewart of Laichy, I was beginning to have doubts. Maybe I had been wrong about the sextant, and Stewart's denial of any knowledge; maybe Detective Sergeant McQueen *had* been right all along, and the truth was locked away for ever in the dead mind of McGlashan the thief.

One thing I was certain of as we said goodbye to that warm young couple; the present incumbent of the manse at Laichy, the enthusiastic Hamish, really was a genuine man of God.

We waved again as they closed the door, and we breathed the good fresh air of Scotland while we hesitated at the church gate, uncertain where to look next.

Until Fran snapped, 'John,' and I blinked at her, surprised by the urgency of her voice.

'Look,' she added grimly. 'Look at the board.'

I frowned, turning uncertainly to face the church notice board. It was faded by the elements but the gilt lettering still showed plainly.

Church of Scotland

ST ANDREW'S PARISH CHURCH

Minister: Rev. H. W. Stewart, M.A.
Session Clerk: Alisdair McLeod Esq.
Church Officer: Cdr D. Scott-Watson, R.N. (Retd)

'McLeod . . .' I echoed, dredging fairly recent memory. And then it hit me. 'Alisdair McLeod and Scott-*Watson*, by God.'

It was Fran who confirmed I was right; and coincidentally destroyed any lingering doubt I may have had regarding Laichy's involvement with the sextant.

'The other two witnesses, John,' she muttered. 'The other two witnesses who swore they'd actually seen Charlie fall to his death. From Creag Fuar!'

CHAPTER TEN

— *1941* —

Second Officer Devlin could afford little room for fear in that time of the desperate escape. His dread of remaining aboard the volatile *Highlander* had already neutralised his apprehension of the dangers inherent in the act of abandoning her; all that existed now was a tight-coiled spring of concentration as he assessed the dimly-seen wave formations sweeping down past the parent vessel. The oil already seeping from *Highlander*'s ruptured double-bottoms had flattened the crests of the seas fractionally; there was little foam or spindrift to leeward as the tops succumbed to the viscous black film. But the mountains themselves still remained, the valleys between still yawned with bottomless malice. Devlin knew he had to slip the twin cords holding them to their dying mother precisely on the peak of one of those lumpish pyramids, or all the nightmares there ever had been in a sailorman's mind would explode in screaming reality . . .

'Are you ready, Mister Devlin?' the Captain called across the gap between. His voice was measured; deliberately calm.

'Aye, aye, sir.' Devlin's eyes were black-narrowed in a white strained face, but there was a cold certainty there.

'Then ease the falls together,' Herschell ordered, and lifted his hand in solemn salute. 'Get well away once you're slipped, Mister . . . and good luck to you.'

Slowly the boat began to drop below the level of the deck, and even then they tried; some of the hardier spirits.

'Ah'll see you lads in Scuddie's Bar,' the Chippie cracked

from the stroke oar's seat. 'Last wan in pays the round!'

'Then I'll pass ye on the row ashore,' Hotchkiss jeered down from his task at the forward falls. 'There's no' a man in this bluidy ship's ever been stood a drink fae the Carpenter.'

The ship came up from her last roll and hung, trembling. It was nearly time. The block on the after davit began to squeal as the rope slid steadily through. It was like a lament from the pipes, honing an edge to the cry of the wind.

'Remember the barley sugar's still to go in number two,' the Chief Steward roared up, faithful to the last in his inability to leave anything to anybody else. 'An' the extra case of condensed milk!'

And so they left *Highlander*, with terrible fright hidden under stiff-jawed humour; descending closer and ever closer to the maelstrom surface of the sea. The ship was still upright, balancing the range of wave crests. Captain Herschell's face gazed down at them from the receding height of the boat deck, a white expressionless orb now, already separated and observing from another world for their future lay in Devlin's hand, and his commands were the only authority to be recognised.

Lower the lifeboat squealed, and lower. The promenade deck passed, the centrecastle deck level with its chipped rails and the rust-bearded freeing ports. The gap between them and the ship's side began to close suddenly; the freighter was leaning to starboard again, sliding down the far slope of the mountain; faster and faster.

'Fend off . . . Fend off!' the Second Mate roared, half-standing in the sternsheets with the tiller vice-gripped in anticipation. The Lamptrimmer's boathook screeled for purchase on the rusted grey plates, levered the bow off, there was a crash as the stern swung in and someone yelped in muffled fear; then the Chief Steward aft got control as well; she steadied, slid ten feet more . . . and stopped abruptly. It was Herschell's final offering; he had controlled their lowering to the precise point where he assessed the next sweeping wave top would rise as *Highlander* struggled from the trough.

They were in the cradle of the valley now, with the towering cliff of the mother vessel rearing vertically above them and every man's eyes staring hypnotically outboard to where the great slope of the receding sea hissed away into the blackness. It seemed eerily quiet down there in the abyss; no wind, no rattle and clatter of halyards and unsecured debris as there had been on the upper decks; it was a period of anticipation, a detached limbo of apprehension as they waited for the inevitable.

And then it came. The separation between boat and ship yawned wider as *Highlander* collapsed towards them, her superstructure arc-ing to port. Abruptly she was staggering sideways up the face of the succeeding wave, lifting with ten thousand tons of inertia casually picked and flung sky-wards . . .

'We're *awaaaaaaay* . . .' a tremulous voice screamed. Devlin braced himself, hauled the tiller towards the ship's rusted grey side, readied for the supreme moment of truth.

'Stand-by the falls . . . OUT OARS!'

The clatter as the oars slammed into the crutches was a trigger to the drill already rehearsed over and over again in the minds of those committed to the attempt. Before Second Officer Devlin had time to bellow his next command the Lamptrimmer and Chief Steward Paton flung their boat-hooks down, clambered frantically over the thwarts tight with grim-set figures, lunged for the heavy blocks still suspending the boats.

'Watch yer hands, Chiefy. Watch yer bluidy hands!'

The peak of the sea detonated from below *Highlander*, creaming and rearing towards them. Suddenly there was wind again; screeching and howling, blasting with devil-breath to snap oilskins, flail bone-white faces with the skin taut and parted lips already rasping an anticipation of stress. A great bank of smoke and steam whirled crazily from astern, enveloping and stifling them even as the plates of the ship screeched in the agony of her once-again vomiting wound. Embers of red hot cinder settled sizzling on Devlin's exposed knuckles gripping the tiller, he never even felt the pain as his wide-eyed gaze searched frantically over the gunwhale, striving to estimate the ever-narrowing clearance between keel and soaring, humping water.

Twenty feet . . . fifteen . . . ten . . . FIVE . . .

'SLIP!' he screamed. 'SLIP THE FALLS!'

The hump exploded under the boat, throwing the stern violently upwards, a swelling black blister suddenly bursting into frothing tumescence. Only it kept on rising, monstrously out of control: throwing them with it. Someone was cursing in panic; someone else – the Third Engineer – fending off with the tip of his oar. 'Let her ride,' Devlin was shouting. 'Let her ride, man!'

Spray, now! Spray and steel plating zipping in a vertical blur, and the roaring of the still-climbing peak which lifted them. The aftermost rope falls suddenly relieved of the deadweight of the boat, tumbling and coiling on top of themselves, snarling around arms involuntarily raised for protection. Chief Steward Paton, purple-faced with strain, struggling with the after block; unhooking it; flinging it bodily outboard before tumbling backwards across a thwart. The Lamptrimmer fighting to do the same forr'ad; steel-bar tension still there in the purchase though . . . Get on, man, get on with it!

There was a chilling cry of panic – the Third Engineer, oar blade abruptly jammed in the gap between freeing port and steel plate along the deck line. Devlin sensed the sea leaving them too soon, a diminishing roar as if left in a station after a locomotive thunders through. He saw heads swivel compulsively; saw the butt end of the trapped oar spearing inboard as

the boat itself yawed madly towards the ship's side . . .
'Watch it,' he bawled, feeling the renewed slam of fear in that
hopeless moment. 'Watch it f'r God's saaaake!'

Lamps half-turned in shock, saw the butt of the oar coming
straight for him, opened his mouth far too late even to scream.
The oar took him cleanly like some diabolic spit; driving in
under his rib cage, whipping him clear out of the still-
penduluming boat and holding him, momentarily suspended
in black-gaping space, before snapping violently at the
fulcrum of the starboard crutch. And then there *was* no
Lamptrimmer; no time. No hope . . .

'Grab the falls. She's goin' . . .'

'Save yersel's, lads!'

The Second Mate's voice; already corpse-dull. 'Chippie!
Try f'r the *block*, man!'

The stern was plummetting, all support gone. There
wasn't any sea left under the after end of number one lifeboat
even before the old carpenter flung his own oar down and
recklessly scrambled, lunging for the remaining hook which
was killing them all. She was angled at forty-five degrees by
the stern with men falling and rolling downhill in a confusion
of shrieks before he actually did manage to grasp the falls;
fighting to bring his other arm upward.

'*Slip*, ye bastard . . .' he swore with his eyes staring and his
face a maniac terror. 'SLIP OOT YE BASTAAAARD!'

Devlin had his eyes closed now, clinging frozen to the tiller.
A body shot past him and jetted into space on a disappearing
curve of horror. Chief Steward Paton gave one strangled
croak as the slack lines coiled sinuously around his neck . . .
then exploded upwards, yanked out of the tumbling lifeboat
on the end of a monstrous noose. 'I'm sorry . . .' the Third
Engineer was crying hysterically as he, too, passed Devlin on
his way out. 'I'm sorryyy*yyyy* . . .'

A last excited flip of wavetop caught the bows as it
subsided, throwing them fractionally, opening a gap between

block and lifting ring. Chippie's clawing arm drove clear into the tantalising space as he scrabbled for grip . . . and then the wave withdrew in malicious mischief while the full weight of the now unsupported craft again came full on the forward falls, and the little gap snapped guillotine-shut with a chunk just above Chippie's wrist . . .

He passed Second Officer Devlin too, just as the forward falls finally parted and the whole bloody boat tipped backwards and over, and down on top of them.

There isn't any difference, no matter which way you die, Devlin thought just as he and all the other men who had abandoned *Highlander* to escape an explosion were pulped instead under their already-disintegrating behemoth.

. . . 'cause you're JUST as bloody frightened whatev . . . !

CHAPTER ELEVEN

An excess from Flanders; a well in the loch;
The field of St George, yet served by pibroch;
The dating inscribed of their gallantry.
But the peaks of the bens – why washed by the sea?

'Charlie,' Fran said tearfully. 'Oh Charlie!'

I put my arms around her and helped her to cry. It was cold down there on the path to Sròine Riabach, but it wasn't the snapping tingle of true winter now, just the grey bleakness of the North Atlantic being carried by the wind as warning of a coming gale. Even for the contented it was a day to blight the spirit; miserable as we now were after our visit to Laichy manse, it was the last stroke to underline our helplessness.

After a few minutes her tremors subsided and she sniffed woefully; just like a little girl. I kissed her with a reassurance I didn't feel, and ordered, 'No more tears. Not for Charlie. Promise?'

Gently I took her handkerchief and stuck my finger in it, holding it towards her. She licked it and carefully I wiped the smudges of mascara from her high cheekbones. She sniffed again, then forced a brave smile.

'He'd be upset if he thought I was still making a fool of myself.'

'He'd be bloody furious,' I grinned back weakly. 'And I don't want you to give Charlie an excuse to be annoyed, wherever he is now – 'cause I'm hopping mad with him.'

'Because of the postcard?'

'Because of the postcard!'

She took it from me as we huddled close together in the lee of a big rock. I felt a twinge of shame when I held her again. I'd been selfishly glad of her tears then; somehow they'd made me feel strong and protective for a change, and that in turn had helped to soften my own frustration.

'*The field of St George*,' she murmured vaguely. 'The *field* . . . but what kind of field — a battlefield?'

I shrugged. '*Served by pibroch*; by the pipes of the Scots? No way; not if he meant a real battlefield under the cross of St George . . . an English battlefield. Any true-blooded Scot would have been running that flag through with the point of his claymore, not playing it a tune.'

'What about more recent history? Particularly the Second World War, which *is* why we're here. Charlie must have been referring to that.'

I frowned. It didn't make sense as it stood; not in that context. 'Who fought under the *English* Flag, as opposed to the Union Flag though? And remember — Charlie was a Scot; thin-skinned as most of us are about the random use of the term "English" when people really mean "British". No, Charlie was being quite specific. He *meant* the cross of St George.'

'Maybe there is some old battlefield near here. Maybe that's what he was hinting at?'

'Maybe . . .'

We were silent for a while, Fran staring hard at the postcard while I gazed bleakly down the length of Loch Fhadaig, watching the steadily increasing sea already breaking white within the entrance, with fingers of spray reaching up towards the top of Sròine Riabach, and the swell bustling and pushing greedily to fight through the heads and into the loch itself where it spread in white-capped waves maybe six feet high and scurried down to meet us on the beach below where we sat. There was a hell of a storm brewing, my seaman's sense told me that — a westerly storm that was already screaming towards Laichy from the distant Atlantic.

It had been a storm like that on the night when *Highlander* took her torpedo. Poor bastards!

'*A well in the loch*, Charlie said. Do you think he meant this one, John? Fhadaig?'

I shrugged my ignorance. 'It's crazy anyway. How can you have a well *in* a loch? The only thing I can imagine is some fresh water spring opening into it. Being of a different density it might be possible to detect it on a flat calm day but . . .'

She saw the way I gestured and nodded. 'All right. Then what about the peaks of the bens – the mountain tops? How *can* they be washed by the sea?'

'Bloody Charlie!' I growled. And for the first time it didn't hurt. Not too much.

'Obviously he can't have meant the actual peaks themselves,' Fran persisted. 'So what else might he have had in mind? Charlie always was a little ambiguous, remember . . .'

'*A little?*' I jeered.

'So what else could be identified with the peak of a Scottish mountain, darling? What else might you expect to find up there?'

'Deer? Cloud? Mountaineers . . . ?'

'How about a cairn? A lot of the tops have stones piled on them; a kind of monument to mark success, I think. Sort of an "I have been there!" gesture.'

I was going to say something irrelevant, like not having the strength to build any pile of rocks after I'd been climbing something like Ben Nevis; but I didn't. There was a determined glint in her eye which made me hesitate; when Francine Templeton was on to something it was time for mere men to stand back.

'What d'you want to do then?' I asked tentatively.

'Say it is a cairn. That means that if it's also *washed by the sea*, then it has to be down here somewhere. On the beaches; maybe hidden at first sight.'

I stood up stiffly. 'Let's explore. It's better than freezing to death, and we've nothing else to do until we've cracked Charlie's code.'

'Which way first?'

I intoned, 'Eeny, meeny, miny, MO . . .' and was heartened to see her smile. 'Out to Riabach again. The hard way – along the tideline.'

'On one condition,' she stipulated.

'What's that?'

She came very close to me and I felt her arms encircle my neck while her perfumed form radiated all the heat I could ever need. And all the love.

'You kiss me first,' she commanded softly.

*

It took us nearly an hour of slipping and sliding, and sometimes even splashing into freezing puddles of sea water trapped from the receding tide. And we found nothing.

By the time I collapsed exhausted we were so close to the base of Riabach that we could actually feel the sting of the salt spray carried by the wind, and had to raise our voices above the roar of the breaking sea. Fran stood erect, her black hair streaming and whipping with a life of its own and the flush of excitement turning her face to the wind. I could only watch her and marvel at my fortune. God but she was beautiful. She stood there in the flail of that Atlantic breath for a long, long time before she finally looked down at me. I could see the almost aphrodisiac quality of that wild place reflected in her eyes.

'Do you feel it?' she shouted. 'Doesn't it turn you on, darling?'

'I'm a deep sea man,' I glowered back. 'Being within ten miles of a wave breaking on rocks scares the hell out of me.'

'Let's make love,' she said. 'Here. Now.'

I rolled over. There was sand in my shoes, clinging damply to my clothes, gritty even in my mouth. 'Now I know you're crazy,' I bawled. 'Save it till later.'

She was standing over me, hands on hips with even the padded thickness of her bright blue anorak moulding the thrust of her breasts under the pressure of the wind.

'It won't be the same, later,' she pouted.

'I know. It'll be warmer for a start.' I held my hand up to her. 'Give me a pull up. Take pity on an old man.'

After I'd struggled to the vertical I dusted myself down and kissed her. She tasted salty. The way she was moving against me it took an effort of will to ease her firmly to arm's length.

'What now?' she asked, only slightly mollified. I looked over her shoulder, across the turbulent entrance to Fhadaig towards the opposite point. Already it was getting dark enough for the loom of Sròine Riabach light above us to show as an intermittent reflection from the wet, distant face.

'Back to Laichy,' I said. 'There's one more beach on this shore to look at – the one near the harbour breakwater that we passed earlier, before we walked the tideline.'

I glanced down at the scuffed and salt-white shoes. 'And this time we go back along the path, Superwoman. The easy way!'

*

By the time we returned to that last beach on the Riabach side of Fhadaig there were lights winking on in Laichy itself. It was a pleasant walk; hand in hand with the wind now behind us and the detail of the village coming ever closer as we neared. Even the great bulk of the mountain, rising as a back-drop more awesome than any man-made amphitheatre, seemed to hold less menace than before as we revelled in our new-found enchantment with each other.

But that should have been a warning in itself. Because the mountain's name was Creag Fuar, and Charlie's ghost must now be wandering that remote, unsettling scene in company with all those other spectres from its past. And Charlie could never rest peacefully; not until we had finally resolved what surely must be Charlie's secret too.

There was a path leading down to what was more of a rocky cove than a proper beach. We half-slid, half-ran down it in temporary, giggling euphoria with the heather snatching at our ankles and the tiny avalanches of displaced scree tumbling and bouncing behind us. The waves building momentum down the length of the loch were already breaking white as we stood there panting, and I guessed that in a full westerly gale that isolated cleft would be a nightmare swirl of creaming water. Even in the part-darkness I could see, as I turned to look behind, that the almost sheer face of the landward wall bore a seamark far higher than the highest tide. I don't know why I did what I did, but abruptly I let go of Fran's hand and walked over to the base of the looming cliff, eyes straining to pierce the gloom.

There was nothing to see; only the dank wet stone and the green slime of sea moss; but suddenly I shivered. There was no reason for it – even the cut of the wind was muted compared to the air down at Riabach   but I still shivered. Uncontrollably.

Fran's voice was puzzled. 'What's wrong, darling?'

I didn't answer right away. I turned; walked as far back to the water's edge as I could, then swivelled again, neck angled to gaze up at the height of the cliff. There was a slight stepping to it when viewed from a distance; a few ledges where seabirds had left their white guano stark against the black rock, but nothing else to note until the precipitousness eased away into the scattering of heather edging the more gentle slope where we'd descended.

'I dunno . . . just a feeling,' I said eventually. 'It's nothing.'

I saw her trembling too, but it was only the cold finally getting to her. 'Come on,' I muttered, taking her hand again and leading for the upward track. 'Let's see what MacFaid the Fisherman can produce for dinner tonight.'

Her hands felt like ice and, as we slithered awkwardly across the slimy boulders at the base of the cliff, she missed her footing in the gloom. Her grip slackened as she flailed for balance while her open shoulder bag tumbled and bounced across the rocks.

It must have taken a good ten minutes for us to collect the typically female assortment of trivia scattered from it; feeling with numbed fingers in weed-strewn crevasses for lipstick; compact; a bar of chocolate; a pen; a bunch of keys. 'One thing,' I growled, emptying my latest finds back into the bag, 'you'll never need to worry about being burgled back at the flat. You've brought every bloody thing with you.'

Nonchalantly she dumped her own retrievals into the apparently elastic carry-all. Then still on her knees, she kissed my bad humour away.

'That's what I love most of all about you, darling,' Fran giggled. 'You say the most romantic things when we're alone.'

*

It was only after we'd returned to the *Sutherland Arms* and shrugged thankfully out of our bulky winter anoraks that she noticed the marks on our bedroom carpet. I was just about to collapse on the bed while she prepared to careen herself in the delightfully antiquated bathroom along the board-creaking hall, when she said sharply, 'Don't, John. You'll make the bedspread filthy.'

I looked guilty – normally it wouldn't have occurred to me to slump fully-dressed on any bed but I was a sailor, and sailors aren't designed to walk half way across bloody Scotland before dinner. Not my kind of sailor, anyway.

'It's your shoes,' she elaborated tartly. 'You've got oil or something on them.'

I began to grin and she faltered. 'Now what?'

'Your knees!' I retorted superiorly. 'You've got whatever it is on *them*, Miss Prissy.'

Straight-legged, she bent forward lithely from the hips and her hair tumbled down to touch the floor. When she straightened up she was frowning. She was a bit red in the face too, and panting with exertion.

'It *is* oil. All over my jeans. Damn! We must have picked it up from the beach; probably out on Riabach.'

I stopped grinning and screwed myself round, trying to see the seat of my pants. I'd been lying down on that particular occasion, which meant I must be covered with the stuff . . . but when I looked I found I wasn't, yet I *had* been in it as well; my shoes were proof of that. I began to mutter dark invective about irresponsible tanker masters who cleaned their tanks illegally while oil slicks covered the bloody coastline; vandalised places where no man-made pollution should even begin to exist.

'John?'

I looked up at her. She was frowning. 'Did *you* see any oil on the beach out by the loch entrance, John?'

I shrugged. It was getting to be a habit. 'No. But obviously there was some.'

'Not necessarily.'

I waved my sodden shoe, pointing it towards her knees where the black patches had ruined her jeans. 'What d'you mean – not necessarily? The evidence is plain, my love. All over your not unattractive legs.'

'I mean we might have picked it up at that last beach. Where I dropped my bag . . . I was kneeling there, remember. And it was too dark to see much.'

'I think you should take your jeans off,' I suggested pointedly. 'And everything else, in case the stain spreads.'

Uncharacteristically she didn't take me up on a proposal that, under normal circumstances, would have had her flaunting brown nudity in two seconds flat.

'I'm being serious,' Fran snapped. She had that look in her eye again – the assessing, newspaper reporter's look. But I didn't have a reporter's mind. Or a lion's courage.

'All right! Then what are you getting at?' I asked placatingly.

'There wasn't any oil out at the sea entrance, John; we'd have seen it if there had been. Yet there's pollution on the beach at the landward end of Fhadaig – up here, beside Laichy.'

'So?'

'So it must have originated from the loch itself; don't you see?'

I couldn't. But I did detect the excitement in her gaze as she watched me almost pleadingly; as if she were willing me to draw a conclusion. I smiled uncertainly.

'No I don't, sweetheart. Unless you're trying to suggest Laichy's got an oil well in its lo . . .'

And then it hit me. Slam!

'Charlie's postcard.'

She nodded, a little white about the lips. '*A well in the loch*, John. Just like Charlie told us. Only he didn't mean a source of water – he meant a source of oil.'

I blinked in perplexity. *Oil*? But what had Charlie been hinting at? O.K., admittedly it was another oddity, but why should it be connected to our mystery?

'A spillage from the harbour?' I hazarded. 'Even a fishing boat, sunk out there in the . . .'

My legs weakened abruptly and I flopped on the bed, staring at her. The way she was watching me I knew we'd both had the same thought at precisely the same moment, but neither of us voiced it. It was too crazy even to contemplate . . . there had to be some less bizarre explanation.

Nevertheless it was a small beginning, if nothing more. Perhaps unwittingly we really had levered the lid of the box containing the secret of my dead father's sextant one tiny fraction more open. One thing for sure – Charlie would know. Out there on bleak Creag Fuar, Charlie Sullivan's ghost would know.

And maybe, at least for tonight, he could afford one fleeting, spectral smile . . .

*

Fiona served us dinner in the quiet downstairs room – thick Atholl brose, and venison so succulent it melted off the fork, all sweet with a red wine sauce.

I took one mouthful and leaned back with eyes closed, entranced.

'Fiona, this is . . . Dear Lord, but it's magnificent. Did your mother really prepare it specially for us?'

She nodded, yet strangely there was no smile. 'She is very fond of you both, Mister Templeton. And she wanted to . . . to . . .'

I eyed Fran quizzically, but she wasn't looking at me; just at Fiona.

'Your mother. She's ill, isn't she, Fiona?' she asked softly.

The daughter of the *Sutherland Arms* blinked confirmation, and it was only then that I noticed her black eyes were glistening with tears. 'This evening; before you returned. My father and the doctor from Durness are upstairs with her now.'

'This isn't an ordinary holiday for you, is it, Fiona?' Fran said quietly. 'British Airways gave you special leave. Because of your mother.'

'She is dying,' Fiona answered simply. 'I want to be here with my father when she does.'

And *I* wanted to stand up there and then and shout, 'Why? Why did you have to lie about Charlie Sullivan when this is happening to you?' But I didn't. I just pushed my suddenly-unappetising venison away and gazed into space. It was an exquisite cut that it had to be Fiona MacFaid herself who tried to comfort me.

'Please eat and enjoy it, Mister Templeton,' she urged, with the smears of unhappiness still wet upon her cheeks. 'My mother will be anxious for you to do that for her.'

We went through to the public bar later. It was something we had to do; to learn as much as we could of the people of Laichy. And there was nothing to keep us in that suddenly chill dining room where there was only the crackle of the fire and the shadowed prints of stiffly posed and long dead kilted soldiers, and our awkward awareness of what was taking place upstairs in the *Sutherland Arms*.

Oh, the bar was full as ever, and the Gaelic mingled freely with the West Coast tongue, but it was a more muted atmosphere that night and only occasionally did a gust of laughter echo round stone walls which had heard the secrets of ten generations of drinking Highland men before. And the dignified sincerity with which they greeted the inevitable. 'Will you have another dram, man, and we will raise our glasses to the courage of the bonnie lady of Donald MacFaid!'

They greeted us too, and made us feel most welcome. As the night grew longer we met Willie McPhee who introduced us to Dougie Buchan, his cousin; who brought in Alex MacNeil, his uncle by second marriage to Mary McKay; and Alex called over Jamie Coull who was the same Mary McKay's second cousin twice removed.

It was our first introduction to the tortuous hereditary interleaving of the Western Highlands of Scotland; and it left us dazed to think that any misery or happiness which took place in any one of the trim granite houses around the heart of the village would spread like ripples across a loch until it washed, however remotely, into the homes of a dozen or more inhabitants. It made us feel uncomfortable too, at first; because the *Sutherland Arms* wasn't simply a hostelry, it was a family reunion every night of the week. But not uncomfortable for long. Not in the company of those hospitable men of Laichy.

We never met Alisdair McLeod the session clerk to St Andrew's Parish Church, who had been skipper of the seine-netter *Morag Jean* before he had retired, and was a very fine man indeed even though a wee bit reticent when it came to the socialising. Oh, and was, of course, uncle of Flora MacLaren who had married MacLaren of Easter Kilry farm down by Barranish, and who was brother to ... but we were left with the inevitable conviction that Alisdair McLeod had to be as upright a witness as any policeman would ever wish to take a statement from.

Only *that* was impossible, too.

And Commander David Scott-Watson, Royal Navy Retired? Now *he* turned out to be someone rather special.

'The Commander?' McPhee had exclaimed when I tentatively raised his name. 'Now there is a fine man indeed. And with a fine son, Mister Templeton, who is carrying on the family tradition as a serving officer in Her Majesty's Royal Navy. You will have noticed their house as you motored down the road. A big white place it is, by the name of Achnashaig.'

'A gentleman,' confirmed Dougie Buchan, his cousin. 'The Scott-Watsons have always been gentlemen; and great benefactors to the community, you know. The wee church hall ... they donated that. And all its furniture, right down to the curtains over the windows.'

'As well as the bus which takes the old people down to Kinlochbervie twice every week in the summer, and is driven by MacRuariaidh my brother-in-law,' supplemented Jamie Coull.

'A fine man,' echoed McPhee, leaving no doubt about the character of Commander David Scott-Watson of Achnashaig House. 'A fine family altogether.'

'They have been the Lairds o' Laichy to all intents for as

long as any man here can remember,' Coull reminisced, looking at his empty glass and then pointedly at Dougie Buchan whose turn it was to buy the next round.

'They're a naval family?' Fran asked. 'It's unusual, isn't it? I've always thought of the local lairds as being military people. The Highland Regiments and so on.'

'Och, Laichy is not an army-minded place,' McPhee announced with a touch of scorn. 'In years past, when there was good herring in the Minch and none of your foreign boats at the fishing, most of the Laichy men were away with the drifters. And to the Royal Navy every time there was a war.'

'Alisdair Wallace went away to the Royal Air Force,' Dougie Buchan pointed out. 'And Donald MacFaid himself was a soldier. In the Argyll and Sutherland Highlanders, no less.'

'Aye, and see what happened to MacFaid,' McPhee countered with devastating logic. 'For was it not when he was an Argyll that the Germans shot the arm off the poor man?'

I glanced at Fran meaningfully. It was the first reference we'd heard in Laichy to the last war. MacFaid had suffered in it. Had there been others? Then I remembered noting the list of names on the tiny war memorial beside the harbour and thinking, even then, how long it seemed for a small Scottish hamlet – and I knew there had been more, much more lost to Laichy than simply the arm of Donald MacFaid.

Not that it meant anything. Certainly not in the context of *Highlander*'s sinking. When that torpedo struck her north of the Minches she had been sailing with a largely Scottish crew as well . . . any grief felt in Laichy for their wartime dead could only have been reflected in the tears of mothers, sons, daughters of my father's slaughtered complement.

'See what happened to Alisdair Wallace,' someone else said pacifically. 'He was gravely injured also. But he was in the R.A.F.'

'Alisdair Wallace was run over by a tramcar in Edinburgh

while he was drunk!' McPhee retorted contemptuously. 'Nothing to do with the war, or the Germans or the uniform he was wearing.'

And so the argument waged. Maybe it was the whisky, maybe the unsettlement of Margaret MacFaid's sickness in the upstairs room, but tempers were fraying in the bar of the *Sutherland Arms*.

'Donald MacFaid lost his arm to the Germans because he was a soldier, are you saying?' came the counter-attack from Dougie Brown. 'Then do I have to remind you, Willie McPhee, that MacFaid also lost his two brothers to the Germans, and that they were Navymen both.'

This time Fran looked at me expressively. It seemed that the war which had killed my father had scarred Laichy with a savage depth that no city dweller could appreciate. It was a sadness multiplied many times through the ancient bonds of kinship.

'They only followed the Captain, Dougie Buchan; as did near enough all the other men from the Laichy drifters when the war came. It was the tradition which killed them, no' the Royal Navy or any other Service.'

'Tradition, Mister McPhee?' Fran inserted quickly. 'You mentioned a Captain, and tradition?'

'Aye, I did. Captain Fergus Scott-Watson of the House of Achnashaig and the father of Commander David. It's aye been the tradition in Laichy for the men of the village to accompany their Laird to the war, Mrs Templeton.'

McPhee broke off as a figure on the far side of the table rose. It was Jamie Coull, and there was a snap to his voice which had never been heard in the conversation before. And a look in his eye that commanded attention.

'Enough of the war, and of dying. You must fill the glasses of our guests, Dougie Buchan, and we shall drink once more to Margaret MacFaid and to the hope of her brave recovery.'

And that was the end of that. Both Fran and I were fully

aware that Jamie Coull who was older and maybe a wee bit more discreet than the rest of those lovely men of Laichy had deliberately called a halt to our talk of tragedies past.

I had the satisfaction of knowing something else though. As we rose and held our glasses to the low-beamed roof above.

'*Slàinte mhath!*'

I had solved another part of Charlie's riddle. And now I believed I knew exactly where to begin our search for the rest of it. First thing in the morning.

*

We left the *Sutherland Arms* early, closing the door quietly for fear of disturbing the MacFaids in their private vigil. Whatever secrets they were privy to, we had no right, and no wish to intrude on the sadness which was to come. I do believe that, could it have halted the cancer which was relentlessly ending the frail life of Margaret MacFaid, both Fran and I would have renounced all efforts to resolve the sextant's enigma. But it wouldn't. And we still had a duty to Charlie.

The storm was much closer as we walked, huddled against the bite of the wind, down the narrow street towards the harbour. The grey dawn light touched no one else and Laichy itself seemed to be empty; silent, as if anticipating some awful thing that had to happen on that cheerless day. But my own sensitivities were blunted by the ferment in my mind, which had kept me staring restlessly through the darkness of the night while Fran slept fitfully in my arms and the sombre tread of Donald MacFaid carried regularly down the hall.

'*The field of St George, yet served by pibroch,*' I breathed as we fought the rising gale. 'That's what Charlie was trying to tell us, Fran. He wasn't referring to an exclusively English battlefield, though -- he meant the White Ensign of the Royal Navy. With the Union Flag in the upper canton, yeah, but mainly the Red Cross of St George on a white field. And *served by pibroch* . . . we discovered last night that most of Laichy's fighting men followed their Laird like a thousand other Scots from a hundred other remote Scottish villages did when war broke out. Only the lads from this parish went into the Navy, and not to their county regiments.'

'But what does it mean?' Fran replied, drawing the whirling hair from her eyes. '*Highlander* was a merchant ship; they wouldn't have been drafted to her, so we still don't have a connection. Unless some of them were in her escort, maybe?'

I shook my head. 'She was a fast independent, sailing out of convoy. She had no escort on that last night.'

'Then what? Where is the link?'

I halted and looked up. 'I don't know. But Charlie must have sensed one; and I believe we're looking at the key to it now. Right here.'

The blank, haunted eyes of the bronze Highland soldier stared fixedly down at us from beneath the steel rim of his helmet while we, in turn, gazed quietly back, and at the beautiful memorial to Laichy's dead sons. Even as we stood there the fresh wreath stirred fretfully as the rising wind took it; and the cold rain fronting the coming storm spattered cold across our upturned faces.

LEST WE FORGET. But we already sensed that the people of this village never would, for something terrible had happened in Laichy on one similar day four decades ago. And, for some still-unfathomable reason, a concerted effort had been made by the people of Laichy to keep the truth of that occurrence from the outside world ever since.

Slowly my eyes travelled down the long list of names. There were twenty-three of them in all, from two World Wars – six from the Great War and . . . Dear Jesus, seventeen from the last! From my father's war. Seventeen men, from one tiny Scottish hamlet.

Then Fran let out an involuntary cry.

'*The dating inscribed of their gallantry* . . .' she breathed tremulously. 'That's it, John – look at the dates. Fourteen of those names . . . they all died in action in the same month!'

I looked, and I digested. And suddenly I knew where – not why, but almost certainly *where* the connection lay between Laichy and the sinking of the Motor Vessel *Highlander* . . .

Captain F. D. Scott-Watson, DSC, Royal Navy. Jan 1941
Petty Officer J. MacFaid, DSM, RN Volunteer Reserve. Jan 1941
Leading Seaman R. MacFaid, RN Volunteer Reserve. Jan 1941
Leading Seaman W. Buchan, RN Volunteer Reserve. Jan 1941
Ordinary Seaman R. MacLaren, RN Volunteer Reserve. Jan 1941
Ordinary Seaman L. Duguid . . .

Twelve names. All killed in action, January 1941.

'January of nineteen forty-one,' I said shakily. 'The month in which my father and his crew were lost.'

Neither of us spoke again for a long time. We stood there before the war memorial, and allowed the biting wind to buffet us unheeded, and stared pensively at the perpetual mourner, and at the bright green wreath below his metal-booted feet with its poppies red as the blood of those who'd died.

Gradually Fran's hand stole into mine and squeezed it lovingly. 'There's a call box on the other side of the harbour. I'll phone the *Northern Citizen* and ask them to look up our war records. We know it must have been a warship; we know the month and the year of its last action, and we know the name of its captain.'

I never lifted my eyes. I was still staring at the recently placed wreath.

'Maybe it was sunk near here. Maybe it was with *Highlander* after all . . .' Her voice trailed away uncertainly. 'What is it, darling?'

'*An excess from Flanders* . . .' I muttered. 'Count the poppies, Fran.'

Her eyes opened wide with abrupt recognition. 'Of course – the poppies. *Flanders* Poppies. In Remembrance.'

'Count them.'

'Thirty-one,' she said a moment later.

'Charlie's *excess from Flanders*,' I speculated with a strange excitement rising within me that I'd never felt before. Swinging to face her I placed my hands on her shoulders, pleading for the ability to comprehend. 'So why only twenty-three names on Laichy's war memorial, Fran? When there are thirty-one poppies on its wreath.'

CHAPTER TWELVE

—— *1941* ——

Jonathan Herschell made the next entry in *Highlander*'s log himself: *1955 GMT . . . Port fwd lifeboat launched by my order, under command of Second Officer Devlin. Capsized immediately, with loss of all 13 hands. No responsibility for this tragedy can be attached to 2/O Devlin nor any member of the crew – their fortitude and gallantry during such a hazardous undertaking added only pride to the tradition of the British Merchant Service. My own under-estimation of the prevailing weather conditions was the sole contributory cause of the accident. Only one body has been recovered; that of Chief Steward Walter Paton. The undernoted crew members are missing, believed killed:*

> *Second Officer Devlin J.*
> *Third Engineer Devine R.*
> *Ship's Carpenter Livie W.*
> *Lamptrimmer Arnott K. . . .*

. . . when he had finished, the Captain signed the individual entry with a steady hand – *Jonathan Herschell: Master* – and then blinked up at the little brass clock above the chart room table. It showed precisely 8.16 – one hour had passed since the Motor Vessel *Highlander* had ceased to be a whole ship. In that time nearly three-quarters of her original forty-three crewmen had died, either as a direct result of the torpedo strike, or during the horror of number one boat.

Thirteen men still survived – if the term 'survival' could be applied to martyrs staked out atop a mound of slowly burning faggots with a powder keg buried within its heart. Such had been the pattern of carnage after the initial hit that a large proportion of *Highlander*'s officers were counted in that ever-diminishing group – Herschell himself; three of his four original Mates; the Chief and Second Engineers; Apprentice Beedie and the chillingly incarcerated Radio Officer Stronach. Only five of her ratings now remained, headed by the redoubtable Bosun McColl; A.B.'s Hotchkiss and Gillan with his mutilated hand, and a resentfully vindicated Jimmie Beattie, who wasnae at a' surprised at the number of officers had saved theirsel's 'cause it wis aye the workin' lads that got the chop first off! If there had been a Communist Party afloat in the British Merchant fleet in 1941, then Jimmie Beattie would've been a founder-bloody-member.

Except he wasnae goin' tae *be* a Communist after this debacle; he wis goin' tae volunteer for bein' a pacifist right away, soon as his feet touched the sacred sod o' Scotland once again.

The thirteenth survivor was Celtic Football Club fancier, Fireman Cullen. He was quite a unique sort of chap, seeing he was the only engine room rating who'd managed to live through the past hour. The only trouble was that the Chief an' Second had made it too, which made it a pretty top-heavy pyramid of command, and Geordie Cullen had a gey uneasy premonition of who wis gaun tae be at the bottom o' the heap when it came tae gi'in' orders. And carryin' them out.

Thirteen men. Balanced on a razor's edge. With the blue touch paper lit on one side, and a suicide jump to the bottom of the North Atlantic on the other.

Carefully, gently, the Captain closed the salt-stained Log Book and placed it safely in the rack alongside his cherished sextant. He would like to have been able to cry a little for the men he believed he had killed, but he couldn't; ship's masters didn't shed tears, they maintained a resolute and dignified exterior. Of all the desperate souls still in *Highlander*, he was the only one denied the luxury of displaying his grief before those in his charge; and more particularly his fear, and the awareness of his own inadequacy.

But the chart room was very private now the need to maintain a watch was suspended, while the Captain was still only an ordinary man.

'Dear God!' he blurted through lips already tightening with anger at his unforgivable self-indulgence. 'Forgive me for the errors I have made . . .'

'Shit!' a level voice growled from behind. 'That's a daft thing tae say and you know it fine, Johnny Herschell.'

Herschell swung round; startled. The Mate was watching him from the wheelhouse door. 'Dae ye want the violins and flowers too, Captain?' McLeod added pointedly.

'Go to hell, Mister McLeod,' the Captain said conversationally.

The older man's mouth eased to a grim smile. 'Is that an order, or a forecast?'

'A forecast. But you'll voyage in good company,' Herschell retorted dryly. 'How's your arm?'

The Mate reached over and awkwardly lifted the torn oilskin coat draped around his injured shoulder. His right arm was splinted tightly to his side with a length of rope. 'Fractured, maybe. The Bosun jury-rigged me . . . said he'd aye fancied tying me up an' throwin' me on a bonfire anyhow.'

'You match the ship; winged an' only able to steam around in bloody circles.'

'Talking about circles – maybe not. The Chief's still down in the tiller flat so it seems there's some prospect of repair yet. McKechnie sent Cullen away tae help. If they get the steering sorted in time at least we can make some attempt to get her back in.'

'Even so it'll be a long haul. Half an engine with a bent shaft? And she'll need full starboard rudder to keep any kind of course even then. There'll not be time, Bill. We've still got two boats left. Only one will be needed. I'll not stand in any man's way if he wants to try to leave.'

The Chief Officer lifted a sardonic eyebrow. 'You'll no' get bowled over in the rush. Och, yon van der Kroon looks like he'd be keen to have a go – he's a guid lad for a foreigner – but there's hardly enough tae make up a boat's crew fit to pull on an oar anyroad. It's all or nothing, Johnny; and the De'il take the hindmost.'

The Captain eyed him for a pensive moment, then shrugged; reaching for his cap. It was funny, the way routine habits ran deep. Like wearing your hat when you were about to blow up. But now they were staying aboard there were other tasks, other priorities. Suddenly Herschell shook off the despondency which had gripped him since Devlin's loss. At least they would go down . . . up? . . . fighting.

'Then while we're waiting for the Chief's report I'll get a fire party together – if there's any pressure in the deck hydrants. What about the Second Sparks?'

What little of McLeod's smile that remained faded abruptly. 'It's going to be a bastard getting the laddie out at all – the Second's got the flame on the snarl of rigging wires now; until they're cleared they can't even get near enough tae have a go at the plates trapping him. They're half-inch steel, Johnny; it could take hours.'

'We could detonate within minutes; he'll not feel it anymore than the rest of us,' Herschell retorted brutally before he could stop himself; but all gentleness had been stripped from their second to white-hot-flash-second existence. Now there was only room for realism.

His Chief Officer didn't move aside as the Captain reached for the door. He just stood there for a moment, looking at his friend.

'I saw you a while ago, mind? In your misery for the lads a'ready lost. You're no' sae hard deep down, Johnny Herschell; no more than I am.'

The Captain blinked at the tough, smoke-blackened features before him.

'You?'

McLeod shuffled awkwardly; embarrassment sat ill on his broad shoulders, showed scarlet under the mahogany weathering of his cheeks. 'A wee tear escaped me too, Johnny. In secret. After the boat went ower.'

There was a long silence broken only by the wail of the storm and the tortured creaks from the wallowing ship. The Mate stared fiercely, defiantly at Herschell.

'Ye'll no' tell anyone. Ever?'

'The only one it matters to already knows,' Herschell volunteered quietly, and with an enormous gratitude. Then he stepped past his friend and into the deserted wheelhouse. The shattered glass crunched under his feet; the silent telegraph still pointed to ENGINES STOPPED.

'Come along, Mister McLeod,' the Captain said. 'I've always wanted to be a fireman.'

*

They didn't fight the fire – not *fight* it in the sense of attempting to extinguish it completely, or even partly. It was too deep-seated on the starboard side of the ship, burning a crackling red well into the tween decks where tons of military stores had been stowed around the Bren-gun carriers in number five. Now they protruded, still finely balanced above the central core of the blaze which was, itself, constantly eroding the heavy wooden hatch boards still sealing the lower hold.

And when *that* happened; when the timber covers as thick as a man's arm *did* finally collapse, then a dead-weight mass of superheated debris would cascade on to the bright brass explosive-charged shell cases carefully ranged below. Whereupon *Highlander* would cease to exist, as a lightning chain of sympathetic detonations blasted through the rest of the ammunition cargo spread within her length.

And that would occur. No one could prevent it happening; Herschell faced that certainty with grim acceptance. So their only prospect for survival – even of living long enough to *attempt* to steam for home – was by preventing the breach of the lower hold covers until Chief Engineer Graham had either restored manoeuvrability to the ship, which might allow them to reach sheltered waters, or admitted defeat and thereby abandoned the last hope of all.

It was like stripping the roof from a sea cave in Hell; looking down from deck level into that savage wound. At the back of the cavern, the starboard side of the hull, the heat slashed in shimmering waves as bales of khaki uniforms, cases of rations, crates of tinder dry bedding, boxes of rifles and small arms, drums of cooking oil, all incinerated together. To port, where the mouth of the cave lay exposed to the sea, there was only the roaring turmoil of water constantly exploding into the void; swirling and crashing, snatching charcoaled and smoking trophies with every roll of the stricken vessel; cataracting and streaming seawards again in polluted falls as she hoisted herself agonisingly towards the jumbling crests of each succeeding range of waves.

The two runaway Bren-gun carriers would – unless checked – prove the weapons which ultimately destroyed the ship; both Herschell and McLeod read the danger signs immediately. Poised as the armoured vehicles were, directly above the vulnerable square of number five lower hold, it only required one more major shock, one excessively violent twist of the hull, and they would topple clear over the edge of the higher deck and straight through the steadily charring wooden covers long before they actually burned away. And the fire would follow that much faster.

Even as they staggered towards the heat barrier – disciplined themselves to brave instant, searing blindness should the fire-lick swoop back across the coaming without warning – *Highlander* plummeted down the slope of yet another

Everest; brought up in the trough with a wrenching crash. The foremost carrier dipped uneasily on its glowing caterpillar tracks, squealed another hand's-breadth forward . . . caught again on saw-toothed plate – and the ship and its thirteen remaining sailormen had come a few moments closer to mushrooming destruction.

They had to secure those heat-buckled juggernauts somehow. But to do that they would have to work on the lip of the Pit itself.

'A cruelty more exquisite than any concept of dead men enduring the fires of Hell,' the Captain thought with a terrible bitterness. 'To demand that my crew should face them even *before* their hearts stop beating . . .'

'Get the mooring wires from the poop, lads,' he said with a casual shrug. 'We're as well to see this job through. While we're waiting for the Chief.'

*

It was from that moment that time ceased to hold meaning for every man aboard *Highlander*.

Except for Radio Officer Stronach, perhaps. Because he was the only one who could do nothing to seek his own salvation; and he had all the leisure in the world to savour the distillation of purgatory, confined as he was in his tailor-made suit of steel.

For the first hour he could only lie and feel the senseless, faltering movement of the crippled ship and wonder if every next lurch could be her last; and watch the flicker of the fire from aft playing crazily across the rounded underside of the mast which had already obliterated his senior and now wedged just above him; and sense the firefly-blue flame of Second Engineer McKechnie's torch as a remote, dancing hope on the periphery of his restricted vision.

In the second hour his panic began to grow as the flame cut closer, because Stronach could see how the torch hissed against metal; exploding in bright cascades of tumbling sparks, and he knew that eventually, before he could be freed, the flame would have to come very close indeed to his own flesh . . . and gradually the slow death of his nightmares became a wonderful prospect in comparison to the imminency of such pain.

Oh, Bosun McColl spoke continuously, encouragingly to him as he worked beside the sweating Second, clawing razor-sharp wire ends away with hands already scarred for life and hurting fit to make him cry himself.

'D'you ever play golf, Sparks?' the Bosun would ask with enormous interest, as if it were the most important piece of information in the world.

'No,' Stronach would answer in a very small voice.

'Neither do I,' McColl retorted. Then there was silence cut only by the splutter and roar of the flame.

'Wot about kids then? You got any kids, Sparks?'

'No,' the incarcerated boy whispered. And then bravely, '. . . but I've got a wife. Julie.'

And then he began sobbing again, because he couldn't bear to think about Julie getting the telegram.

'Ah,' Bosun McColl would say with lofty disregard for the trapped man's misery, even though it was tearing him apart too, deep down. 'I got the kids – seven. I just 'aven't got around to findin' a permanent wife yet, see?'

But it was during the third hour of that dedicated rescue attempt that burrowers and cutters themselves felt the first tingle of a new apprehension. For a curious phenomenon was becoming apparent – the temperature within the confines of the buckled radio room was rising out of all proportion to the thermal output of the torch flame in the Second's hands. And Stronach must have sensed it too, only he was weaker by then and hardly able to speak at all. While perhaps because he'd a lot more time to think, he guessed long before the others why it was happening anyway.

The paint on the after end of the centrecastle deck, closest to the radiated heat from the burning holds, was beginning to blister, as if the spread of the fire to the main accommodation was imminent. And that held, perhaps, the most terrible prospect of all for Radio Officer Stronach.

For the new fires would ignite directly below the steel box in which he lay. He would begin to cook even before he died. In a gigantic frying pan. With the lid on.

*

The duel with the fire until that time had been one of searing danger, with the larger part of *Highlander*'s survivors struggling on a well-deck which – if it weren't for the seas constantly sweeping the distorted steel plating – would have glowed red-hot and carbonised the boot-soles of those who fought to secure the runaway carrier.

Even so they endured the most fiendish extremes – immersed waist-deep in ice-chill water with numbed hands clawing for the safety lines as their legs slammed from under them in one second; being blasted by a physical wall of heat in the next, causing them to stumble back with the moisture boiling in the folds of their oilskins and the hair on heads, eyebrows, the backs of involuntarily raised hands, frizzling to a black stubble. They were cooking too, the tormented men of the afterdeck. Grilling, and then being marinated by the excruciating cold of the North Atlantic in winter . . . and then grilling once more as *Highlander* rolled, and God's hand flung open the oven door yet again.

But still they rigged the hoses as best they could to play within the tween decks where the roaring green water couldn't penetrate unless the ship itself fell over; and they *did* eventually accomplish the most critical task of all by suspending the bight of a mooring wire between two fore and aft situated winches, and after an eternity of frustration managing to haul the wire tight at just the right moment, and snag the tip-tilting nose of the see-saw carrier – thus assuring themselves of living a little longer into that screaming night.

But not indefinitely. For the metal structure of the deck itself was remorselessly being corroded by the fire, and wire grew weak and quickly parted in such volcanic conditions anyway. But nobody lives forever, and even an extra few hours seemed like a good deal when you'd only been measuring the length of your remaining mortal coil in blinks of a red-rimmed eye until then.

They'd never even known whether or not there was any point in their suffering; whether their ship ever would move through the water again and turn her bows, no matter how slowly, for home. Oh, the Chief had stumped up on deck about eleven the previous evening looking like a bad-tempered blob of oil; and muttered incomprehensible invective aimed at quadrant pins which were apparently jammed, an' hydraulic bluidy fluid a' ower the bluidy boat, and by-pass valves that wis completely buggered! And then shambled off back down again without even a cursory glance at the leaping flames or the hysterical fury of the North Atlantic bluidy ocean, leaving no clue in his wake as to whether he could overcome his recalcitrant machinery.

As a source of comfort, Chief Engineer Graham had all the attributes of an undertaker's tape at the bedside of an invalid.

Until one-fifteen the following morning – almost six hours to the minute since *Highlander*'s cancer had first flowered from the slam of the torpedo warhead – when he reappeared again with the ill-humour now obliterated by lines of strain which even he couldn't quite mask.

And said shortly, almost grudgingly, 'Ah can gie you full starboard rudder, Captain. An' maybe ten degrees tae port. But an'm no' promising it'll last if it's treated hard; yon steerin' engine's bluidy near shuggled off've its mountings a'ready.'

The Captain looked at his old adversary, and there was a great swell of appreciation in his heart for the bloody-minded dedication of an ageing, friendless man of the sea. But he didn't dare show it. Chief Engineer Graham would have been wounded beyond measure if he'd shown any thanks.

'I suppose you'll tell me now you'll not guarantee the starboard shaft to survive more than a few turns through the water either, eh? And that I'm limited to four knots even if I can keep her on a straight course?'

'Two!' the ancient mariner growled. 'If ye take mair than two knots out o' yon bit twisted pipe that calls itsel' a propellor shaft, then you're even dafter than ah gied ye credit for. Sir!'

And then the oily mask with the white fluff of hair sticking straight up on top suddenly showed a yellowed, toothy window, and the tip of a pink tongue.

Whereupon Captain Herschell became the second man aboard actually to see Chief Engineer Graham smile.

*

And so the blistered men and the frizzled men, and the frightened men and the injured men wearily prepared to turn their broken ship for home.

They had no illusions; no false sense of hope, for it would take nearly one whole day to claw the spindrift miles to the shore even if the steering did hold, and the shaft did survive the vibration; and they didn't think the ship itself could exist for an eternity like that. Even if she did – if the fire didn't trigger off the holocaust in her belly, nor the sea itself overwhelm her as she presented her vulnerable stern to the running mountains – then she would still raise an anonymous coast in the blindness of winter, where navigation marks were extinguished by the exigencies of war and the breakers would only show under the bow when it was far too late to turn aside even with a proper ship and not a lumbering, wave-propelled coffin.

It was very quiet on *Highlander*'s bridge at one-twenty-five on that black early morning, when Herschell said levelly, 'Slow ahead please, Mister McLeod.'

The Chief Officer swung the telegraphs with his one good arm, and the tinkle of the bells preceded the growing mutter of the engine. Then the deck began to shudder and vibrate, and every loose thing danced a frantic reel as the starboard shaft squealed and screeched into distorted revolution.

'Jesus!' McLeod muttered, feeling sick for what they were doing to the ship.

'Port as far as she can go, Hotchkiss,' the Captain called steadily. 'Don't force the wheel, though. Let her come round herself.'

'Aye, aye, sir,' Hotchkiss returned, and then winked forced cheer through the darkness at the little apprentice beside him. Beedie had stuck to Hotchkiss like a leech ever since the first explosion. 'Wheel's ten . . . twelve tae port, sir.'

'Thank you,' Captain Herschell acknowledged as politely as if they'd been running a summer course down the Clyde instead of attempting to climb a precipice with a broken leg one side and a fractured ankle the other.

But she was turning. *Turning*, by God! Slowly, ever so slowly, the bows were lying slightly further uphill than the stern after the first sighing wave, and a little bit further again after the next . . . and by the next marching crest she was seeming to make way by her own volition; trembling forward in the water, pushing her flared bow deliberately away from the assault of the sea; deflecting its punch instead of wallowing helplessly under its rushing menace.

And as the faint life reborn in her caused tremors through her frame, the men aboard her stared out to where the mountains of Scotland lay so tantalisingly close, yet so unbearably far away. Only the expatriate Third Officer van der Kroon considered them as just a haven in a storm – to the rest of *Highlander*'s wistful complement they represented home, and loved ones, and the peace which comes from Belonging.

*

At one-thirty Second Engineer McKechnie, who hadn't lifted his head from the glare of the torch all the time they were stopped, cut through the last twisted spar blocking access to Stronach. The boy was still inextricably wrapped in his shroud of steel, but at least Bosun McColl could wriggle his way far enough in to stretch through the ever-increasing heat of the radio room, and gently touch the white, slack-jawed face within. It felt cold. Far colder than anything else in there.

'We're goin' home, Johnnie,' the Bosun called with enormous good-humour. Like a benevolent uncle promising a child the most wonderful day at the zoo. 'You'll be gettin' out soon. Get poshed-up an' that. F'r when you see Julie.'

But Stronach didn't answer. In fact, thinking back, Radio Officer Stronach hadn't responded to Bosun McColl's jollifications since just after one o'clock.

Slowly the Bosun eased himself astern until he was clear of the mess. Then he sat on the deck and looked up at Second Engineer McKechnie. He didn't need to say anything; the Second just bit his lip and then twiddled the valve controlling the cutting-torch flame. The blue light sputtered, then died. It seemed appropriate, really.

There was a cardboard box placed carefully out of the way beside the rail. Chief Officer McLeod had brought it up earlier -- as soon as they'd realised why the radio room was getting hotter, and what it would do to Stronach if the fire did flash across to the accommodation below him. Wearily the Bosun picked it up and blinked down at it. He was glad Stronach was dead in a way; so's they never did have to open the box and use what was inside it.

It was an ordinary medical syringe from the first aid box on the bridge, with a large needle. There was nothing in it except air. None of them would have known where to inject it so as to cause a lethal embolism anyway; they didn't teach you how to murder one of your own shipmates in the Merchant Navy.

189

He couldn't help wondering how hard Radio Officer Stronach would have had to scream before one of them could have found the mercy to experiment with it. And which one of them it would have been.

Probably the Captain. He was a grand Captain, Mister Herschell.

At long last a tear squeezed from the corner of the Bosun's leathery eye and trickled slowly down his pug-dog cheek. But it was still only the smoke, dammit! Smoke did a lot o' funny things to a bloke.

*

Even before *Highlander* completed her tortoise-ponderous turn the Captain knew that, without more power, she could never hold the course he'd originally selected – southerly to take her down past the Butt of Lewis and into the comparatively calmer waters where they might abandon under the lee of the Hebrides. The storm was blowing straight from the west now, and its breath shaped the run of the seas which would sweep the ship helplessly onward towards the Scottish mainland itself. And she couldn't steer; even regulating the thrust of her solitary engine all she could do was to stay on a broad heading and submit to the hand of the weather.

The North Atlantic would still be monstrous-crazed within a breeches-buoy length off that jagged Sutherland shore. To survive a beaching there offered as little chance as had a man of leaping from the same cliffs which would almost certainly welcome them. But even that chance was better than no chance at all, as promised by the fire.

'Steady as she goes, Quartermaster Hotchkiss,' Captain Herschell said.

Within a yawing, spiralling thirty degrees or so, anyway.

And she *did* try so hard; the ship. Almost as if she herself knew she was heading for home, and wanted desperately to reach there before she died.

CHAPTER THIRTEEN

Fran seemed to spend ages in the telephone box, talking to the *Northern Citizen*, while I hung around in the lee of it, trying to shield myself from the cutting wind and to make sense out of the poppies. Thirty-one – a seemingly specific number; surely a round thirty would have been logical had it been the choice of whoever had made the wreath?

But even assuming there were deliberate intent, then what possible significance could that hold in relation to *Highlander*? Eight extra flowers . . . yet there had been forty-three men lost when she went down.

Fran was waving frantically from within the booth and eased the door open a crack. She had a piece of paper ready in her hand, but she said, 'A pen. Give me a *pen*, darling, quickly.'

I frowned and offered her my Parker. She grabbed it with a smile and spoke to the receiver. 'O.K., Bert, go ahead if you've got it.' I shut the door again and shivered moodily until she came out. My heart didn't exactly lift when I saw her expression either. It was puzzled. I didn't *need* a puzzled adviser.

'Take a deep breath,' she suggested ruefully. Then she saw my expression and elaborated hurriedly.

'Fergus Scott-Watson was Captain of a British warship, all right. A destroyer – HMS *Kendar*! And the *Kendar* was sunk with appallingly heavy casualties by Stuka dive-bombers; very few survivors were picked up. Bert has no record of names but it seems a pretty fair guess all those Laichy men were among the missing.'

'When?' I snapped. 'What date?'

She glanced at her notes. 'The eighth of January, nineteen forty-one.'

'Which made it . . . five days before *Highlander* was lost. So what the . . .'

'I told you take a deep breath,' she said sombrely. 'It gets even more obscure.'

'I'm breathing.'

'HMS *Kendar* wasn't anywhere near the Minches or *Highlander* when she went down, John. I'm sorry, but she was sunk in the Mediterranean. Off Crete.'

I slammed my fist against the telephone box. Every time, every bloody time we advanced our knowledge we seemed to be two steps further away from a solution. Fran was better able to contain her disappointment, but then she was beter suited for it; her job trained her to evaluate, to gather and assess information and only eventually to see the composite picture. She appeared to read my mind.

'Charlie was a good reporter, John. He had a feeling for the pertinent; an ability to play a hunch. I don't think for one moment that he knew the answer any more than we do now, but he sensed when a seemingly irrelevant detail would eventually prove important to a story. We've got to stay with Charlie, darling; we owe it to him.'

Wearily I hauled the postcard from my pocket and frowned at it. The thumb-marked cows still stared up at me as obstinately blank as ever. I flipped it over.

'*An excess from Flanders* . . .' I repeated heavily. 'All right! So there are eight more poppies than names of Laichy dead. It's got to be that.'

'*A well in the loch*,' she followed. 'That has to be the oil. And it tells us something else as well.'

I lifted an eyebrow. She gave a little shrug. 'That Charlie *was* on at least one beach round Loch Fhadaig. But which one? He couldn't have visited many; he didn't have all that much time.'

'You mean it supports his reference to "*The peaks of the bens – why washed by the sea?*" But we'd already extended St George's Cross and the dating riddle as far as we could. 'D'you really think it has something to do with a cairn, Fran? It seems a hell of a long shot to me.'

'Can you fire one better?' she pressed challengingly.

'No.'

'Then we'll go back to the *Sutherland Arms*, find out how Margaret is and get breakfast – I can always cook it myself to help Fiona – and then go back down to that beach. It's the only place left to go at the moment.'

'Not quite,' I said bleakly. 'I think we should go up to Creag Fuar first, Fran. To where Charlie died. I think it could be important.

She looked at me and I could see the whiteness around her lips at the prospect of being alone on that terrifying mountain. Just her and me, and Charlie.

'Why?'

'Charlie did die from injuries consistent with a fall. Which means he *was* on a cliff. But the police also stated that his climbing gear, his ropes and safety equipment were still in the boot of his car . . . and to me that suggests he was climbing on the spur of the moment. Stupidly, maybe, but nevertheless with a specific reason. Charlie would never have climbed for pleasure without the proper precautions. He must have seen something up high, and tried to investigate.'

I didn't add the rest, because I couldn't face the possibility myself; not now I had got to know the people of Laichy better. Or thought I had. That Charlie Sullivan had died for a much less complicated reason.

After he had been pushed.

*

We found that Margaret MacFaid had rallied slightly when we got back to the *Sutherland Arms*. There was renewed hope in the eyes of both Fiona and the giant man her father. But I think they knew as we did that it was a false optimism, an additional unkindness to wring the last drops of their sorrowful anticipation. Whatever they were hiding, whatever had prompted Fiona to lie as a witness to Charlie's death; then truly the MacFaids of Laichy were being punished far more now than any exposure of the future could bring.

They wouldn't even hear of our preparing our own breakfast. 'You are our guests,' MacFaid insisted with ferocious benevolence, 'and Maggie will have my hide should you be left to your own devices!'

There was something else waiting for us too, though; unsettlingly close to the pattern of our previous visit. A telephone message asking us to call a Glasgow number. An aggravatingly ambiguous message, like everything else that morning.

'The gentleman wouldn't leave a name. He said to tell you that the first time you met, you mistook him for a well-known painter, Mister Templeton,' Fiona said with tart mystification. 'He didn't even appear to know what name you were registered under. He just asked if a gentleman was staying here with a very beautiful lady.'

Fran grinned shamelessly while I glowered. I knew who it was right away – I was getting plenty of practice in wrestling with conundrums. Painter . . . Constable. Constable . . . policeman. Detective Sergeant Donnie McQueen.

I was secretly grateful to him for his discretion, though. A telephone call to a Captain Herschell from the Strathclyde Police would have been embarrassing to say the least.

When I spoke to him, I learned only one small detail, which left me more confused than ever. For it was a detail which made no sense at all.

'He's been having another look over the late McGlashan's statements about the thefts,' I said pensively when I joined Fran at the breakfast table.

'Donnie's nice under that dour exterior. He wasn't happy

about not being able to help us, you know. He didn't have to check again . . . did he find out anything else?'

'Just that McGlashan had sworn – may lightning strike dead every star in the Celtic Football Club if he lied – that he definitely did steal my father's sextant from here. And from St Andrew's Church, at that.'

'And . . .' she encouraged, for she could tell by my expression that there was more to come.

'And that's the funny thing which McQueen felt we should know. You see, McGlashan claimed he only found the sextant by accident. He didn't even know what it was, except it was a "braw wee bit o' brass and maybe good fur a bob or twa". While he was lifting the candlesticks he dropped one which rolled out of sight. It was only when he was hunting for it that he noticed the rosewood box; in fact the way the box seemed to have been hidden was what made him think it might be valuable.'

'Hidden?'

'That's the inexplicable part,' I muttered, stabbing at the thick porridge in its lake of pure yellow cream. 'We know the sextant was cleaned regularly, therefore it was also replaced deliberately in the part of the church where McGlashan found it – under the altar, Fran. Hidden carefully under the altar of Laichy Parish Church.'

*

After breakfast we went back up to our room to change into heavy walking boots and outdoor gear. The wind was slamming at the windows of the *Sutherland Arms* by now, with the rain turning steadily to sleet which slid in long straight runnels down the glass. If we planned to make it to Creag Fuar that day, then we had to go prepared.

Fran slipped the leather coat she'd worn earlier on to a coathanger and rummaged in the pocket. 'I'll give you your pen back now. Before I forget.'

I took it from her and slipped it into my bedside drawer.

'No point in me carrying one as well as you. Or did you have to borrow this because yours has run out?'

She was shrugging into her heavy jersey and I had to wait a moment before her head exploded, flushed, from the tight roll collar. 'I haven't got one with me. I purposely left mine in the flat seeing we were travelling incognito, so to speak – mine's a *Northern Citizen* hand-out; the paper's name stamped all over it. We all use them; they're functional and free.'

'No you didn't,' I retorted. 'Some secret agent you'd make, Francine Templeton. Your pen's still in that elastic super-bag of yours. I know because I dropped it back in there last night after you'd emptied it all over the beach.'

'But you couldn't have,' she persisted doggedly. 'A lipstick or a make-up pencil, yes. But I definitely left my pen at home. I know it.'

I lifted her bag of junk and tipped it upside down on the bed. 'Now I can appreciate McQueen's problem with all the swearin'-tae-God McGlashans . . . see?'

She picked it up blankly. 'But I *know* I left it. I remember thinking what a fine reporter I'd be without a pen. I even hunted through the desk for a plain one to bring instead.'

I was beginning to get irritated; we'd enough to puzzle us without Fran getting all obscure. 'Well no one else from the *Northern Citizen* is likely to have been on a remote beach like that . . .'

We both blurted it at the same time.

'CHARLIE!'

And suddenly we also knew which beach Charlie Sullivan had been investigating. I must have found his pen by sheer chance as I was fumbling blindly in the cracks of the rocks, and included it in the recovered articles of Fran's. But how had he come to lose it in the first place? Charlie was a tidy man; he would have kept it clipped firmly in a safe pocket. I picked it up and examined it with an eerie feeling of anticipation. The metal clip was twisted; bent out at right angles. It had required a deliberate pull to do a thing like that,

Or a wrenching impact. Like, say, falling from a height.

Such as a cliff; just as the Highland Police had claimed. Only now we had a new dimension to consider – that while we'd always assumed there had been something odd in Charlie's death it had never occurred to either of us before then that it had taken place anywhere other than on Creag Fuar.

Not until now.

Until the jigsaw suddenly began to fit together with a frightening inference.

*

We stood on the highest point of the cliff where it overhung the little cove. To our left, the seaward hand, it fell sharply into the diagonal track leading to loch level; on our right it sloped much more gradually until it merged with the breakwater of Laichy harbour and the first houses of the village itself, less than half a mile away. Gazing again to seaward, the black forbidding silhouette of Sròine Riabach reared stark against an exploding backcloth of Atlantic fury. Between these two opposing heads of the entrance to Fhadaig the seas were creaming in with awesome bulk; every serrated wave a good thirty feet from trough to crest and the unleashed power of the devil carrying a horror to any small vessel crazed enough to venture out.

I shivered; it was a sight no seaman could find easy to look upon. Not that it was better to stare downwards instead; that long vertical drop to the beach where the child-spawn of the greater waves finally crashed and curdled and gurgled as if desperate to reach the base of the rock face itself, and very nearly succeeding. Only a narrow strip of foreshore now remained clear of the sea, and a wider rock plateau hissing with spray where the ground began to rise up into the path.

I turned back to face Fran. She was the most beautiful

creature I had ever seen, and I hated myself for what I was doing to her – the anxiety I was forcing upon her. For a long moment we stood there with the wind howling a macabre lament and the sleet stinging fierce on every inch of exposed skin, and neither of us said anything because it wasn't a time for words. Words were not a necessary thing anyway, when all we had to do was gaze into each other's eyes to understand the message of love.

I hitched the bowline in the rope from Fran's car tighter under my arms, and swung to face the edge. If I didn't go then I would have lost the courage; and if I lost the courage, then I would have lost any chance for Charlie's ghost finally to lie to rest.

'No slack,' I shouted, gesturing to the turns already prepared around the well-seated rock behind us. 'Pay out steady as I go.'

'Be careful, darling. Please.'

I looked up at her wide-eyed apprehension one last time before I tentatively eased myself over and felt for my first foothold on the seemingly sheer rock below.

'That,' I assured her, 'is the most unnecessary request of the bloody year!'

It could only have been my nerve-strung imagination, but I could have sworn the elements increased their violence a hundred times in that first moment of descent. I was scared almost to the point of paralysis before I began; once my head sank below the level of the clifftop I was terrified out of my mind. The wind battered my splayed body, snatching and shrieking and buffeting me with a malice which caused my eyes to close in involuntary prayer. Within seconds I had frozen there with the sleet a spiteful tattoo on my face, my back, my clutching hands already numbed with the desperation of panic.

It was then that the weirdest thing happened to me; fear-sick as I cringed upon that awful face. I found myself listening to the sadness of the wind, and perceiving it was a direct descendant of that dreadful storm which had pounded this same beach forty years ago; the great, great grandchild a thousand times removed of the violence which had overwhelmed *Highlander* on the night of her U-boat. And realising, too, that not only had my father's crew faced that hazard with grim and professional resolution, but had done so in the expectation that they would be bombed or mined or torpedoed as the Battle of the Atlantic rolled remorselessly over them; not just perched on a rock with a nice safe rope linking them to their loved ones.

I had a sudden memory of old Arthur Davidson and the way he'd looked at me back in the Company office that time when he was reminiscing of those men from a war long past. 'They used to come into the office,' he'd said with a wonderment I hadn't fully understood, 'and they'd ask if we had another ship ready for them seeing their last one had been blown from under them . . . yet they were still red-eyed and sometimes even shiny-black engrained with fuel oil. But they had a terrible anger about them, Captain. A fear and a sadness and that driving anger all at the same time.'

And then I thought of forty-three of that same breed of seamen, and of the inscrutable veil which still persisted to obscure their connection with Laichy . . . and I *did* understand the terrible anger, then. For I had become an angry man too.

Slowly I began my descent. I knew precisely what I was looking for, and as the dripping rocks rose steadily above me I fumbled and tugged at every outcrop within reach. And then I found it.

A strata of crumbling, corroded stone roughly a third of the way down. I didn't even need to probe to confirm what had really happened to Charlie – suddenly a great chunk of it broke away from beneath my feet and I remember squealing with renewed terror as I felt the tenuous link with Fran cut agonisingly under my arms, hanging there for an eternity of horror until my scrabbling boots finally regained another toe-hold. Breathing stertorously I crushed my face uncaringly to the bitter, calcified vein of Judas rock and peered along, the sleet now screaming nearly horizontal in its fury and stinging my half-closed eyes.

It was there, though – the scar marking the point from which Charlie fell. Maybe ten feet to my right and virtually unnoticeable to anyone looking from the beach below. Only my point-blank view of the torn clumps of moss and the darker shades of recently displaced earth was enough to convince me that Charlie Sullivan had been there at the penultimate moment of his life. I felt conscious of a great sense of relief, because just as I was certain now that Charlie had fallen here, and not on Creag Fuar, I was also satisfied that he had been the victim of his own rashness. In tolerable weather, and from an experienced climber's viewpoint, it was probably an undemanding face. Too deceptively inviting for a rock pundit with the excitement of the hunt in his eyes – like Charlie.

Yet it still didn't answer the biggest mystery of all. Why then, had some person or persons in Laichy felt it so vital to conceal the place of his death; and for distinguished religious officers – and, indeed, Flora MacFaid who surely had enough to bear already – to feel compelled to give the lie substance?

There could only be one answer – that this storm-battered cove held the key to the real end of *Highlander*. I stirred and began to ease myself lower, still searching, but this time for something the nature of which I couldn't even begin to conceive. One thing was pretty sure from what I'd already learned – there would be no sudden flash of revelation; whatever had happened in Laichy could only be finally unearthed in Fran's professional manner, by dogged perseverance. It seemed equally certain that, as Charlie's body had almost certainly been transposed to Creag Fuar, then whatever had caused his fatal interest would also have been removed. But I had to look. I was halfway up the bloody cliff; I didn't have any choice.

I didn't even notice anything when I actually reached the ledge I'd observed from the beach the previous night. It was just . . . well . . . a ledge. Still twenty-odd feet up the cliff face and perched on an overhang which explained why Charlie Sullivan, with his contempt for heights, probably found it more tempting to climb down than to struggle up from below. I'd even frowned along it and mentally shrugged dismissal when I absently licked my nerve-dried lips . . . and tasted salt. It was only then that I became aware of the fine spray mixing with the steady sleet, and of the fact that the misting rumble of the breakers was being carried by the wind, high as I still was.

'. . . *washed by the sea*.'

I stared along the ledge again. Hard. And caught sight of the alien, rounded stones for the first time.

Grimly I eased myself sideways, stretching precariously until I'd scrabbled a few of them towards me. There were eight altogether . . . eight rounded boulders which had undoubtedly been placed there from the beach itself at some time in the distant past; easily recognisable by the manner in which the action of the water had smoothed every rock to a gentle convection while nothing else on that exposed ledge revealed any quality other than the angular erosion of wind. Then it struck me as odd that some of the stones were clean on their top face, while others were green with the slime of moss. Carefully I flipped a clean one over . . . whereupon it, too, revealed a vegetable patina of age. Only very recently had they been displaced. As though dismantling something which had stood for many years.

Like a cairn. Fran's cairn.

Composed of eight separate stones. Eight. Precisely the same number of excess poppies placed so reverently on the war memorial to Laichy's dead.

She came racing down the track to the beach as soon as she'd felt the rope finally slacken, and had peered apprehensively over to see me waving from the bottom. Until she'd actually made it, and thrown herself into my arms with a squeal of relief, I'd been even more frightened for her than she'd been for me. One slip on that steep, crazy-scree pathway and she'd have finished up like . . . Charlie.

Eight poppies. Eight stones in a cairn. A sextant which should have been lying fifty fathoms down among the bones of a long-dead ship . . . and oil.

I knew then what had happened. At least to the Motor Vessel *Highlander* in 1941, if not to her crew.

Fran watched doubtfully as I walked to the edge of the creaming, gurgling water. Even now, despite the breakers and the flying spray I could detect the sluggish, emulsified patches which washed in constantly. Kneeling I captured an elusive globule, rubbing it between my fingers. It was thick; much thicker than the light gas oil used to fuel any inshore fishing boat.

Fran came and stood beside me as I stood erect, staring distantly out towards the rearing, white-cold centre of the sea loch of Fhadaig. I knew she had duplicated my own conclusion when she said softly, tremulously, 'How long would it take, John? For a sunken ship's fuel tanks to corrode and rupture?'

I couldn't have answered a question like that an hour before. But I could now – the visual aid to my education was sticky on my fingers; black and sticky, like congealed blood.

'It takes forty years,' I muttered. 'Precisely.'

*

We had been in St Andrew's Church for nearly an hour before we were finally interrupted. The kirk door was standing open as it had been when a Glasgow small-time thief called McGlashan had once chanced to pass, and hesitate a while.

We'd deliberately avoided calling at the manse. I knew both what I had come for and where I would find it, and I hadn't needed the Reverend Hamish Watt Stewart to guide me on the last leg of my search. I specifically hadn't wanted him to for that matter; not right away. There were still questions, many questions, but I knew that first hour would be a time for pain, and a hushed and personal reverence, and I only wished for Fran to share it with me.

So it was only when it had grown too dark to read within the silent interior of Laichy's tiny kirk, and after Fran had switched the lights on, that he finally appeared at the door in cautious attitude. But by then I had learned almost all the answers to the questions which had plagued my sleepless nights.

To all except one. That still remained as the most baffling, inexplicable riddle of all.

Why?

'Mister and Mrs Templeton – John. Francine. Then it *is* you?' he confirmed uncertainly, his boyish face revealing polite mystification. 'I saw the lights go on from the manse . . .'

He stepped forward hesitantly and then wavered. 'Look, of course you are always welcome; this *is* the House of God and always kept open to His children, but . . . ?'

We could detect his inner conflict; his anxiety not to intrude upon genuine worship struggling with a sceptical perception that such was not our true reason for being there.

Gently I closed the book lying on the pew before me. His eyes fell to it and I got the feeling that he already anticipated what I was going to say before I did so.

'My name isn't Templeton, Minister – it's Herschell. Captain John Herschell.'

Fran came over beside me and slipped her hand into mine while we watched the Reverend Stewart of Laichy Church. Yet strangely there was very little reaction to observe; certainly no shock, no display of guilt. Only a calm surprise, almost the acceptance of a religious man at the many ways in which God evinced His will.

Or perhaps he wasn't really surprised at all. Perhaps he'd been expecting this thing to happen one day, particularly after the sextant had been stolen and the secret of its continuing existence compromised. Or maybe Hamish Stewart had been anticipating my arrival for even longer than that. For six years, in fact ... ever since he had inherited the custody of the village's sad secret from the previous incumbent of St Andrew's; the Reverend William McKail.

Who, in his turn, had first undertaken to keep that awful trust from the original witness to a certain event. From a loving man called Crombie; spiritual guardian of Laichy Parish during the period which had included the evening of January 14th, 1941 ...

When the shattered, listing hulk that had once been the Motor Vessel *Highlander* finally clawed for refuge in the sea loch of Fhadaig.

CHAPTER FOURTEEN

—— *1941* ——

Dawn never did really break over the labouring *Highlander* on that last day of her life; it passed without notice, and with only the slightest lessening of the gloom to mark its impotence.

The sky was still lowering; the North Atlantic still hurling black with only the coffee-cream streamers of foam to show it possessed any presence outside the immediate vicinity of the ship. Even the spray hanging almost continuously above her running counter would be lost to the keenest eye aboard any searching warship unless their respective courses virtually closed, for there was an opacity to the day which blurred vision; created ghosts where crisp outline should have claimed attention . . . she was passaging through a secret world as if already consigned to Limbo; already denied to the sight of man.

'It's as though we've ceased to be,' the Captain reflected. 'Even I cannot be sure if we still exist. Not even I could point my finger on the chart, and say with certainty – "There is *Highlander*. There is the place where twelve men and a ship sail in company . . ." '

They had no way of telling how far or how fast they had travelled. Any log streamed from her taffrail would have been immediately flung forward into her paraplegic rudder, its line severed, its bright brass-finned rotator only a momentary flash in the boiling water before vanishing for ever.

They had no way even of assessing in which direction they had ultimately moved. The steering compass had become a hysterical whirligig; spinning constantly as the ship yawed and skidded when each successive wave overtook her, passed under her, continued to roar ahead of her while her bows sighed down and down and down to be left behind as if she were almost steaming astern. And no navigator could have expressed any opinion more accurate than that they were definitely making good a mean course to the east. Or more or less to the east, anyway.

Probably.

Oh, Jonathan Herschell had lifted his sextant from its polished wooden box just before theoretical dawn broke according to the prediction of the *Nautical Almanac* for the year 1941. Carefully he had carried it out to the wing of *Highlander*'s bridge, as had both Third Officer van der Kroon and Fourth Officer Findlay, where they had waited with the silence of the exhausted in the hope of obtaining a dawn sight, while Mister McLeod stumped in one-armed frustration beside the chart room chronometer.

But of course the dawn never had really come. And the sun itself had ceased to be. Just as – or so it seemed to the Captain – had the Motor Vessel *Highlander*.

*

By mid-day the fire had burned whatever cargo had been combustible in the upper parts of five and six; now only tons of ash remained, glowing red and occasionally exploding in vicious spurts of revitalised flame. But there was a terrible heat buried within that sullen clinker and they all knew it was corroding, chewing its lethal downward advance through the hatch boards of the lower holds; still determined to destroy its prize before the North Atlantic – or now, perhaps, the soaring crags presented by the west coast of Scotland – could claim her for themselves.

The Bren-gun carriers still held precedence as the most likely trigger. By three in the afternoon they had eased their buckled, armoured corpses further and further over the lip of the tween deck until the first in line was suspended only by the thrum-taut counterbalance of the hastily rigged wires. There was no way now to replace those constantly weakening lifelines, no matter how savagely the tracks of the machines sawed and crushed and chafed at the stranded steel with every lurch of the ship, for since she had turned her stern to hobble before the storm the after welldeck had become a seething welter of green water in which no seaman could move.

No man aboard would have been prepared to try, for that matter. There comes a time when fatalism overtakes determination; and that time had come to *Highlander*'s survivors. There was an additional and more practical reason too – that when and if they should make their landfall, they would need all the strength they could retain to overcome what promised to be the most hazardous time of all as their helpless vessel flung herself upon the coast, and them upon God's mercy.

Because when it came to track records it *did* seem that the Lord had been a little sparing in compassion this trip out. They had all looked upon the charcoaled monkey-corpses in the greasers' mess deck; and had watched the tumbling boat of Second Officer Devlin. And listened to the fading sobs from the trapped Operator Stronach. So there wasn't one among them who didn't plan to rely more on his own animal strength and his Board of Trade lifejacket than any divine aid, when it finally came to paying off the ship.

Just after four o'clock in the afternoon it became night again. Though it didn't make a lot of difference because there hadn't been a daytime to miss. But still, it *had* to herald the last evening at sea. One way or another.

And so the dark grey turned to black about *Highlander*.

While her twelve remaining complement turned to whatever secret introspection a man does cherish when he's frightened and very much alone.

*

By 6.15 p.m. the motion of the ship had begun to change imperceptibly. Both the Captain and Chief Officer McLeod sensed it together; she was staggering more, wrenching her stern more violently now as each following sea caught her and threw her forward.

Staring aft from the bridge wing, hunched like old men against the freezing crack of the wind, they could detect that the wave forms were undergoing subtle change; becoming shorter, steeper; breaking and smothering at the crests with even more viciousness than before.

'Shallowing,' McLeod confirmed expressionlessly. 'We'll not have long to wait.'

'Then we'd better get ready,' Herschell retorted. 'There won't be a lot of time to decide how to play it, once we get a sight of what's ahead.'

He leaned over and peered along the boat deck; most of the off-watch men had huddled there since early afternoon, just waiting. No one had shown any desire to seek shelter in the accommodation; none of them fancied ending like Stronach, imprisoned inside a steel box, if she did blow. Only the Chief and Second Engineers and Fireman Cullen were still below decks because that was both their natural environment and their place of duty – until either the bridge rang down *Finished with Engines* or the already tortured starboard shaft finally fractured, and they ceased to have a useful function in the process of survival.

'Mister van der Kroon?'

'*Kapitein*?'

Herschell heard McLeod sniff disapproval beside him and smiled wanly. It didn't matter what language they spoke – when action was needed, then seamanship and steady nerves were the only qualities which would count. And Jan van der Kroon had proved himself a most capable young officer.

'Stand-by number three boat, Mister, if you please. As soon as you judge we are in calmer water, then lower it to embarkation level and wait for us to join you . . .' He hesitated; he didn't think that would be the situation they found themselves in at the end. 'But if I order "Abandon", then don't wait for anyone else – neither myself and the bridge party nor the engineers. Simply leave as best you can and make for the shore. Understand?'

'*Ja, Kapitein!*'

It was the Dutchman's turn to hesitate, frowning up through the darkness. 'The number tree boat . . . it is not a Disney boat, *ja*?'

The gust of laughter which swept through the group was immediately savaged by the wind. But it didn't matter. Even the tiniest of smiles was worth an extra lifebuoy at a time like that.

*

At ten minutes to seven Herschell and McLeod took a last careful glance at the chart. They knew they had to be somewhere south of Wrath and the Pentland Firth; *Highlander* had certainly made no northing under the prevailing wind and sea conditions. But how far south? At what point on that scarred and jagged coastline would she arrive?

'Between Handa Island and Cape Wrath,' Herschell stabbed his finger without any real certainty. 'No further down, Bill. Otherwise we'd have benefited from the lee of the Hebrides long ago.'

Which left them only hope of raising one of the remote Sutherland sea lochs in search of sheltered water. 'Laxford; Inchard . . . ?' the Mate muttered speculatively. 'Get her inside the heads o' either an' we've a good chance. Maybe even of saving her by flooding her stern below water.'

'Or there's Fhadaig?' the Captain added. And looked bleak.

McLeod followed his eye. 'Man, yon entrance is so narrow ye couldnae steer a Glasgae Corporation bus intae it wi' a following sea.'

The ship hurled herself forward out of control as if to underline his words, then fell back as the roller raced ahead of her. Both men felt her yawing drunkenly to port, and heard the indefatigable Hotchkiss cursing from the wheelhouse. It was a bad twist, that one. Neither mentioned the levitated carrier in number five, but both thought hard about how many more shocks its sorely-tried suspension could take.

'We'll maybe not have a choice,' Jonathan Herschell said calmly. 'If I see one break in that bloody cliff-line I'm going to take her into it or bust, Mister McLeod. Laxford, Inchard, even Fhadaig – they're all better than a vertical rock face in this weather.'

'I'll better away out tae the wing again,' McLeod grunted. 'There's only our eyes and our ears now to warn us. D'you want a fo'c'sle look-out posted?'

'No. Keep every spare man on the boat deck; she could hit full tilt before they could escape aft, and they'll not see much more than we can from the bridge anyway. Not in this . . . and put your lifejacket on before you go out again. You're not exactly rigged for swimming, you know.'

Chief Officer William McLeod grinned wolfishly. 'You get me intae one o' they sea lochs, Johnny, and ah'll be away off this bluidy firecracker like a wee speedboat. You'll see pure poetry in motion, man; arm or no arm.'

The Captain's answering smile faded as soon as McLeod left on a scrunching tread of broken glass. He had things to do now, in these closing minutes of the voyage home, and he much doubted if there would be time or opportunity when the last battle of all had ended.

There was a yellow oilskin bag in the seat locker. Quickly he opened it and stuffed a spare lifejacket into the bottom – at least it should float, even if he didn't. Then he returned to the chart table and opened the Log. Neatly, methodically, he began to make his final entry as master of the Motor Vessel *Highlander*:

1900 GMT . . . Standing-by to abandon by lifeboat should conditions prove favourable. In the event of my own loss during the trial to come, let this record stand as a tribute to the endurance of this ship, and of the steadfastness and courage of her crew.

. . . he wanted to write more; include some profound wish that those who came after them might learn from the deliberately-inflicted agony of *Highlander*, a casualty of total war, and reflect upon it during the uneasy days of peace which must surely follow. And maybe even benefit a little. But he knew they wouldn't. Just as he accepted that, when the war was finally over, his name, and the names of his dead crew, would simply be inscribed upon some obscure memorial – and then forgotten. Along with all the other bloodied lessons of sacrifice and terror.

Perhaps the most he could hope for was that his own son, John, wouldn't completely forget him. Oh, not for himself and the inadequate father he'd proved to be. No. Simply for what he represented – for the tradition and the bloody-minded dedication of those who sailed, and would continue to sail under the Red Ensign of the British Merchant Fleet despite everything rapacious owners and faithless politicians and the sea itself could do to deter them.

So he didn't add anything more to the last testament of *Highlander*. He simply signed it *Jonathan Herschell: Master*. And placed it sadly in the yellow oilskin bag.

Reaching against the roll of the ship he brought his old sextant box down from the shelf and packed that, too, above the Log. Then he doubled the neck of the bag before whipping it securely with a length of small stuff . . . and it was ready. Waterproof; buoyant – if any part of *Highlander* was to be cast ashore, then at least the true story of her martyrdom would be revealed while maybe, as a bonus, young Johnny Herschell might still receive his sextant.

It was only when the Captain stepped on to the bridge

wing; before his eyes had become accustomed once again to the velvet darkness, that he first heard the distant rumble from ahead.

And sensed that the end was very near indeed.

*

The steady roar from forward was noticed at the same time by the five men on the boat deck. Gradually at first, interspersed with the shriek of the storm, but then more strongly as if it were the constant beating of some Wagnerian drum.

Able Seaman Gillan and converted-pacifist Jimmie Beattie hurried to look, conditioned to anticipating disaster with every minute which passed. The two junior deck officers and Bosun McColl deliberately completed their preparations in number three boat, and only then walked forward, each with stiff casualness in his gait; each with a tiny voice within him screaming 'Run! Runnnnn and seeeeee!'

It was only when the five of them had formed a white-faced line gripping the teak rail, mis-shapen and awkward in their hunchback lifejackets, that there *was* anything to see; and only then as a vague impression against the blackness at first; some macabre trick of the night spawned from crucified imagination. Surely no reality could be attached to the flickering, misting curtain which appeared to materialise across their path.

Even Bosun McColl, who believed he'd already seen every beauty and every awfulness the oceans could devise to bewitch a shellback sailorman – even *he* frowned in disbelief at first, and half-turned away to dismiss it as a mischief of the elements; an optical cruelty reflecting, perhaps, the snow-capped mountains of a Scotland still many miles ahead and well below a horizon which couldn't possibly be *that* close anyway.

Then he realised that without light there could be no reflection, while the hanging, flinging curtain really *was* less than a mile ahead. And that it wasn't an illusion at all because it did exist.

And the Bosun blurted 'Mary Holy Mother save us . . .' as the towering cliffs of Sutherland slammed into stark and undisputed vision, with the great Atlantic rollers smashing into skying sheets of spray higher than the funnel of the ship herself while stretching from side to side as far as his rheumy eye could see . . .

. . . it was precisely sixteen minutes past seven on the evening of January 14th, 1941. Twenty-four hours to the second since the Motor Vessel *Highlander* had been struck by a torpedo while going about her war. And had subsequently been presumed sunk, without trace.

*

From the bridge Herschell could only gape during those first paralysing moments when the visibility lifted to reveal that nightmare spume blocking the sea ahead.

But the ship didn't even hesitate; the ship kept driving and running under the chase of the storm, lifting and streaming forward, closing with lemming determination as if too far stressed in her burning agony to tolerate living when the means of her own destruction lay but a few more turns of her weary screw away. Or was she being kind by her juggernaut cruelty? For she must have sensed that no mere man could have brought himself to approach that maelstrom given the slightest option to abort; not even with the knowledge that to turn and claw again to windward was also to die.

Perhaps it was thus that *Highlander* supported her Captain, in that when his resolution briefly faltered then she herself pressed him onward. And thereby offered him and his helpless complement the only chance of survival they would get that night. Jonathan Herschell took strength from his ship in a way which only a mariner would understand, and became again a seaman and the Master.

Wedged against the rail he lifted his binoculars, coldly scanning for a mark, some guide on which to base his crippled approach. An abrupt movement beside him, the nudge of kapok, and he knew his Chief Officer was there too.

Then he stiffened, ignoring the iced spray flailing raw cheeks. 'D'you see it?' he shouted. 'To port, Mister. Two points on the bow . . . a darker line.'

McLeod gazed fiercely for what seemed a long time, and then he nodded. Turned. There was a burning intensity in his eyes which told Herschell he had been right.

'Less spray,' the Mate roared back. 'No breakers, like the sea's running clear through the cliffs.'

'Then we must take it,' the Captain was already stumbling back towards the wheelhouse. 'Come to port, Hotchkiss. Hard as you can pull her to port, man.'

McLeod followed him briefly, shouldering the splintered door for balance. 'It's gey narrow . . .'

'D'you see a wider gap? Do you then?'

The wheel was already over; Hotchkiss straining, mouthing, 'Ten o' port wheel, sir, an' ah cannae get a spoke mair fae the bastard.'

'She'll not come up,' Mister McLeod predicted matter-of-factly. 'She'll no' run wi' her quarter to this sea, Captain. Not to port.'

Herschell snatched the engine room telephone from its hook. It was lifted below immediately. Maybe the Chief himself didn't have all that much to live for, but it seemed he cared more than his ill-humour suggested for the others.

'I want thrust on the starboard screw, Mister Graham. As much as you can give within reason. For maybe five minutes . . .'

'Aye, aye, sir,' the Chief called, and Herschell could only stare blankly at the phone in his hand for almost as long as it had taken him to understand the horror ahead.

'What's wrong?' McLeod snapped tensely. 'What the hell's wrong down there, Johnny man?'

'He said "Aye, aye",' the Captain muttered disbelievingly. 'He's actually goin' to do it, Bill. Without an argument!'

'Shit!' Chief Officer McLeod raged as he shot back out to the wing. 'The auld bastard's used up a' the miracles we're due for in the one go.'

Steadily the revolutions climbed, and the deck shuddered and vibrated frenetically. Herschell felt the ship coming round to port and struggling for the thin black gap in the white wall now dead ahead. But she couldn't run much longer.

'. . . You still there, Chief?' he queried to the phone.

'Aye,' Graham's distant voice answered flatly.

'I'm trying for an entry into what seems a narrow loch. There's no way of telling how far it runs inland, or if she'll pile up on her way through.'

'Then ah'll send Cullen up tae the boat deck now,' the Chief shouted. 'Me an' the Second can handle what needs tae be done fine on our own.'

'Affirmative . . . and, Mister Graham.'

'Aye?'

'If we hit – get out. If the shaft goes – get out. Don't wait for orders; just get McKechnie and yourself out. Fast!'

There was a pregnant silence. And then it came. 'Och, dammit tae hell, man. Ye'll still need the generators; lights . . .'

Herschell replaced the receiver gently, smiling for perhaps the last time. But it was good, reassuring somehow – to hear Chief Engineer Graham arguing again. As he turned towards the door he noticed the Apprentice's eyes fixed wide upon him. He kept the smile up, just for Beedie.

'Would you do something for me, Mister Beedie? Very important?'

'Sir?' More of a squeak than an acknowledgement.

'Would you go and assist Mister van der Kroon and the

Fourth Officer with number three lifeboat, please? They need as many good chaps as they can get, you know.'

A great swell of pride smothered the previous fear of the boy, while only his loyalty to Hotchkiss made him hesitate from the most important task he'd ever been given.

'Aye, you away an' help, Mister Beedie,' Hotchkiss said with enormous solemnity. 'If I ken there's a proper sailor standin' by the boat, then ah'll feel an awfy lot easier about leaving when it's due.'

So Apprentice Beedie hurried from the bridge, being possibly the happiest seafarer ever about to abandon his ship. But then again, you don't think about dying or anything as extreme as that when you're only fifteen years of age. Not really think about it actually happening to you . . .

The Captain performed one more task before they entered the dementia which he was now practically certain formed the entrance to that small loch shown on the chart as Fhadaig.

He carried the weighted bag of confidential books to the end of the port wing and dropped them over. They were swallowed by the sea immediately. It was his last defiant act of war, and one which he carried out simply to protect other seamen on other ships more fortunate than his. Because there were too many secrets in that canvas bag which could compromise their own safe passages, and Jonathan Herschell didn't think he could look after it with any certainty. Not any longer.

Carefully he placed the other bag – the yellow oilskin bag – beside the head of the ladder leading to the boat deck. And then stepped forward to stand alongside Mister McLeod, binoculars already raised and ready.

*

They heard the crack and buzz-saw whine of wire parting under strain even as young Beedie joined the group waiting tensely beside the readied boat.

Fourth Officer Findlay echoed their mutual fear first; before he followed the already running Bosun to the after end of the boat deck.

'Christ, it's the carrier in five . . .'

And it WAS!

At the very moment in which *Highlander* nosed into the gap and towards refuge the leading armoured vehicle – a shapeless smoking hulk by now, with scaly evil snout and blackened plate – began to slide forward . . . hesitated . . . rumbled forward again and slowly tilted nose down . . .

'NOOOOOO!' Findlay pleaded. 'Please, no!'

The rear end of the carrier lifted . . . caught jarringly under the front suspension of its runaway follower, and stopped again.

The superheated ash concealing the now wafer-thin lower hold boards directly beneath glowed briefly in urgent encouragement.

*

With only one engine and half a rudder she was simply a sliver in a boiling kettle once she entered between the heads of Sròine Riabach. High on either side of her the great black cliffs towered, yet even above *them* flung the spectral pallid claws of the North Atlantic storm. It was an insanity of the elements; a force a million times greater than the resolution of any ship, even one so valiant as *Highlander*.

And so she yawed despite the skill of Captain Herschell and the sweat of Quartermaster Hotchkiss on the failing helm. As the seas followed her into Fhadaig in rolling pursuit; colliding and rearing together in frustration at the unthinkable prospect of her escape, so they took her smoke-obscene stern and flung it spitefully to starboard; tearing her practically beam-to the mutilated troughs, broaching her savagely across the too-narrow span of safe passage.

Jonathan Herschell heard her scream her apology as she smashed into the base of Riabach, and perhaps he cried his grief for her anguish in chorus. If he did, no one heard his lonely voice, for suddenly there was only the thunder of fragmenting water and the harpy-shrill of the gale across the peaks, and the constant skirl and screech of lacerating steel.

Second Engineer McKechnie actually *saw* the jagged green rock exploding into the engine room and tearing aft towards him with the roar of an express train, with the black freezing sea jetting and thundering in its wake. He heard the starboard propellor shaft disintegrate as the huge bronze screw struck granite bottom – yet he'd only scrabbled six rungs up the shiny escape ladder before the whole complex web of catwalks and platforms and pipes and valves disintegrated above him and carried him in a hideous cage to meet the sea and the rock, and the end of all his fear.

And Chief Engineer Graham? He never even tried to leave his post at the controls. He simply stood there and watched as the water rose to engulf him; and reflected how much better it was to enjoy ten seconds longer as a ship's engineer than live ten more years as a friendless, shore-bound relic. And then he died too, in the most contented moment of his life.

While *Highlander* continued to shudder and roll her grindstone way into the calmer waters of Loch Fhadaig. She was already sinking before Captain Herschell had dragged himself erect from where the collision had flung him; far less staggered to the after end of the bridge to see Fourth Officer Findlay running to meet him, and the boat already swinging free in the davits; anonymous shapes fumbling and piling into it with McColl and van der Kroon struggling to ease the falls.

'The carriers,' Findlay screamed. 'They've fallen! We got fire in the hold, sir; runnin' like liquid. Clean through the boards!'

Suddenly they were gliding peacefully through waves a mere twenty feet high. On either side they could make out the snow-scattered mountains of their very own Scotland, and low down to starboard – on the edge of the loch itself – there were flickering lanterns and the promise of kindness and the safety they had fought so hard to attain.

Only it was too late now, because the first detonations were already flashing from the after well deck, and there were too many shells and bombs packed too close together . . .

They were too bloody *late*!

But he still carried out his last duty of all, Captain Jonathan Herschell. When he cupped his hands around his mouth and roared in a strong and steady voice, 'ABANDONNNNN SHIP!'

And then calmly picked up the yellow oilskin bag. And followed Chief Officer William McLeod and Quartermaster Hotchkiss to the lifeboat.

CHAPTER FIFTEEN

The old book before me was yellowed and stained by many things; smoke; sea-spray; fear-sweat . . . blood. But it was still legible, and I could still remember the bold hand of my father which I had seen on many letters, and was now seeing again in this last, desperate cry from the grave . . .

Scotia Steamship Company

DECK LOG; M.V. *HIGHLANDER*. VOYAGE 12

Hamish Stewart moved uncertainly along the aisle until he stood beside Fran, looking down.

'How did you know it would be here, John?'

'My father must have struggled to bring his sextant ashore; he was a seaman and it was part of him. But he was also the master of a ship, with a master's responsibility. I knew that if he had time to save the sextant, he would certainly have saved *Highlander*'s Log. And that you would have kept it, too, for whatever reasons you had.'

'It was kept in reverence, and in the holiest place of all. It is important for you to understand that.'

I looked at him, but I didn't feel hate; only sadness.

'I understand many things already, Reverend. Charlie Sullivan's body, for instance . . . it was moved from the beach by the harbour up to Creag Fuar to ensure the police wouldn't notice the oil, wasn't it? Because if the pollution people were brought in, then maybe too many questions would be asked; too much official interest in why the Laichy people didn't even know there was a ten thousand ton coffin on their doorstep . . .'

He was surprised then; genuinely shocked. 'That poor climber? He was a friend of yours?'

It was Fran who answered, barely in a whisper. 'It's an inadequate description, just a friend.'

Stewart's head bowed momentarily. 'It will also be inadequate if I tell you Mister Sullivan's remains were transferred with the deepest respect and decorum.'

I shrugged. 'And unnecessary. We saw the cairn; the wreath. We know you – the church and its officers – acted only in what you believed were the interests of the Laichy people. But why Fiona MacFaid? Why did Fiona, young and obviously unconcerned with whatever happened forty years ago, feel compelled to commit perjury over Charlie's accidental death?'

He gazed at me steadily. 'Because Margaret MacFaid is dying, John; you know that yourself . . . and Fiona will do anything to prevent, certainly to delay, the truth being revealed before that unhappy event takes place. She offered to immediately, you know. To support Alisdair McLeod and the Commander in bearing false witness . . . but not in the eyes of God; they bear no guilt for that.'

'The Commander – Scott-Watson of Achnashaig. The sinking of HMS *Kendar* did have something to do with what happened here in 'forty-one didn't it? And am I right to presume that Donald MacFaid, Fiona's father, was also involved in what happened on that beach after *Highlander* foundered?'

'They call it Aileach, John. *The rocky place.* There were many fathers in Laichy involved in that terrible event. And mothers. May God have forgiven them, but even the women of the village were there. Waiting . . .'

'Eight poppies,' Fran said quietly. 'Eight stones in the cairn on the ledge above Aileach. Did only eight of *Highlander*'s crew reach the shore, Hamish? *Eight* . . . out of forty-three?'

'Shocked; burned; oil-covered; terrified; already punished beyond endurance,' I heard myself intone with the sickness of coming horror already certain in my throat. 'Yet at least they found themselves cast ashore to meet the bereaved mothers of another British ship's lost crew. Mothers who *must* have felt compassion, surely . . . so why, Hamish? *Why*?'

'Because something else was waiting for your father and his pitiful companions on Aileach that day, John.'

I slammed my hand uncaringly on the time-ravaged Log of the M.V. *Highlander*. The moment for riddles was past forever.

'Why?'

'Another presence,' the Reverend Hamish Watt Stewart persisted, and his ashen face echoed the disillusion which six years of custodianship had etched into his young soul. Six years of doubt in his faith; perhaps even in the power of his Church to triumph over Evil.

'For the Antichrist himself was also waiting for your father and his men at Aileach, John. The archangel ruined . . . the Devil Incarnate!'

* * *

FINAL CHAPTER

The great storm had been buffeting Laichy for three whole days before the policeman came on his motor bicycle, all the way from Kinlochbervie; goggled helmet drawn well down against the cruel sleet, and the double front of his leather cycle-coat plastered stiff with the snow which had thrashed him as he came over the track by Creag Fuar. It had been a brave thing for him to do, and a dangerous thing to risk that exposed and desolate ride where, had some accident befallen him, he might well have lain covered without help from man nor beast until the winter had gone from Sutherland. But the policeman from Kinlochbervie was a conscientious man, and had accepted it as his duty when the sub-postmistress contacted him, to go in haste to Laichy hamlet.

And so he skidded and puttered in low gear down the treacherous cobbled street, scattering McMhuir's sheep in galloping confusion as they huddled in the lee of the cottages and disturbing even the widow Mac an Leister's sorry ducks from their cosy beds. As he passed, so every curtain in every window moved aside and eyes peered suspiciously out before growing wide with surprise, for there had never been such a strange contrivance as a motor bicycle passing down the only street of the hamlet. Come to that, only the one motor car before then, other than the bright red Post Office van which called every fortnight with the letters. It was the Scott-Watson's vehicle from Achnashaig House, and even that had never turned hardly a wheel since the Captain had taken the young men into the Navy.

Not a soul was actually on the street to see the policeman

pass, for the wind had risen to near-hurricane force coming out of the west, and neither the fishing boats from Laichy nor any other harbours lining the Minches – not even the bigger steam drifters down in Oban – would be foolish enough to venture to the grounds before the gale was spent. The weather had succeeded where all the German aeroplanes and U-boats had failed. Meanwhile Laichy had withdrawn even further into its geographical seclusion and would remain in poverty-stricken introspection while the rest of the world carried on with the war.

Certainly it had stayed a long way from Laichy, the war; noticeable only by the wistful faces of the mothers and young wives who had waved their boys goodbye in the previous year, and by the empty spaces in the boats as a reminder that those same young family fishers now manned Oerlikon and torpedo tube in the warship of the Captain instead of creel and net.

But still a distant war; a war which affected only the big towns and the cities. Until the policeman came on his motor bicycle from Kinlochbervie, anyway; and stopped outside St Andrew's manse. And brought that war to Laichy.

He'd eased himself stiffly from the saddle and hesitated a while as if summoning courage. Then grimly, very deliberately, he strode through the white-shrouded graveyard of the kirk and knocked upon the manse door. Had any man been watching closely he would have seen the nervous way in which the policeman from Kinlochbervie fingered the satchel at his side.

It was the Minister Crombie himself who answered, smiling initially in avuncular query. Then he registered the policeman's pinched, grey expression and he guessed, long before the officer spoke, that he would be needed a great deal in the black hours which promised to follow. While he couldn't have known it then, the Reverend Dougal Crombie became a man who would never smile again without a haunted sadness coming to his eyes; not until the day he died.

'Meenister?' the policeman muttered uncertainly, for Crombie had eased his cleric's collar and slipped gratefully into carpet slippers while out of the ken of his critical flock, and wore only patched trousers and a faded jacket of tweed.

'Aye.'

There had been a hint of prayer in the Reverend's answer even then; a plea to God that it might not really be happening.

'The Inspector thought we should contact you first, sir. That you should be asked to help, seein' there are . . . there are . . .'

Crombie's eyes fell to the envelopes the policeman was drawing nervously from his satchel. Buff envelopes. Post Office Telegram envelopes. And there had never been one of those delivered to Laichy since . . . the last Great War.

'So *many*?' the Minister whispered.

'Fourteen, Reverend. I am terrible sorry, but there's fourteen a'thegether.'

'Dear Lord have mercy upon them,' Crombie gasped faintly, clutching at the doorframe. For the Reverend Crombie was not a young man, and not a very brave man either; and suddenly the manse itself seemed cold.

The policeman realised his duty was done, and was thankful for that knowledge. Turning away with an awkward salute, he began to walk uncomfortably back towards his bike.

The minister gathered himself and called querulously, 'Please? You must be gey chilled . . . can I offer you tea, laddie? A hot drink to see you on your road?'

The policeman halted without looking back. 'I'll not put you to trouble, Meenister; you'll be sair enough pushed to giving all the comfort you can on this sorry day.'

Only then did he turn and blurt out what had been in his mind all that long and bitter ride from Kinlochbervie.

'The Lord's infinite wisdom, Meenister Crombie? Or just a bluidy waste?'

But the Reverend Dougal Crombie was already gone, forcing himself to reach for his Bible and his winter cloak. And the great grieving was about to begin in Laichy.

*

He had gone up to break the news to the big House of Achnashaig first; not thinking they might already have been informed, because they had a telephone and Fergus Scott-Watson had been a four-ringed Captain, Royal Navy. There were those in high places in the Admiralty in London who wished to treat the kin of their peer a little more kindly than a bureaucratically terse buff paper would allow.

Regret to inform you your son 0433827 LDNG S/MAN MCPHEE J killed ... And DORWARD. And MACFAID. And MCLAREN. And ...

... he had only got half way up the slope, with the storm screeching maniacally around his ears and the big black cloak whipping and snapping at the stick clutched in his trembling old hand, when he met young Lieutenant David walking slowly down towards him. When the pink-cheeked naval officer and new Laird of Laichy saw the minister approaching, he immediately snapped into a determined stride, while only his liquid gaze betrayed his emotion when they finally joined.

'You've been told then, Reverend? We've not long had the call from the War Office. I'd ... hoped to break the news to you myself.'

The minister of Laichy placed his hand gently on the erect boy's shoulder and stared long into his eyes. Aye, there were tears there, but only private ones to match Dougal Crombie's own. No one else in the village would be permitted to see them.

'Your mother, David. Is she taking it hard?'

'She's taking it . . . bravely. I think she guessed it was Father, and *Kendar*, as soon as the phone rang. Perhaps my being on leave just now has helped a little, too.'

The minister stared back down the mountain at the huddled wee cottages round the surf-white head of Fhadaig. 'I am so sorry. Just as I am heart-sick for all those poor people, not yet aware of this terrible thing.'

'Fourteen from here, including Father,' the Lieutenant said distantly. 'Fourteen families to come to terms with their bereavement.'

'Not only fourteen, David – many, many more. In nearly every one of those homes someone will have lost someone they loved. It is the sadness of the Highlands.'

'She fought for twenty minutes before they took her, you know,' the young man muttered and there was fierce pride there. 'The Stukas must've paid a bloody price for *Kendar* and the Laichy men.'

'Aye, they would have fought very hard. Laichy has always fought hard against the violence of the sea and their country's enemies; English or German.'

'I bet they gave 'em hell!'

So they turned with heavy hearts, the old man of God and the young man of the Navy, and walked slowly together back down the track into Laichy. Things could never be the same for the village once they had completed the duty before them; they knew that already. It was the end of an era.

But neither of them could have guessed that it was also the beginning of . . . a nightmare.

*

By the time they had hammered upon thirteen doors, and looked upon the bloodless, suddenly-stricken faces of thirteen families, the storm itself seemed to have reached a new intensity of violence. As the dreadful news spread throughout Laichy, and the first wails of cruelly-dawning understanding rose from the pinched grey lips of old mothers

227

and young, fresh-married widows alike, so did the shriek of the wind pluck the chorus of their wretchedness and amplify it; hurl it high to the streaking clouds obscuring the jagged peak of Creag Fuar and mutilate that sorrow, until even those sounds of women's anguish had turned to the laughter-scream of cacodemons celebrating at the bloodied altar of War.

The older men of Laichy did not cry. Not openly. For they were Highlandmen and borne by the same fierce pride as Lieutenant David. They were near all men of the sea as well, and that was a savage living for anyone, which bred an uneasy kinship with the ever-hovering company of Death. They were quiet men of mahogany skin and labour-honed muscle, their sinews strong as the lines with which they fished the waters off Fhadaig. Maybe they were poor men, but they carried their threadbare dignity as had their fathers before them, and not one among them would have bared his secret desolation; not even to the womenfolk of his own grieving house.

Least of all, perhaps, to his own womenfolk.

So it was that by the time the Reverend Crombie's first ordeal had muted to one of merely reiterating feeble consolation, and young Lieutenant Scott-Watson had returned to sit with his mother the Captain's widow up at Achnashaig; and while the black curtains of mourning were still being drawn across near every tiny window in the hamlet; so it was that the doors cracked open, and figures were seen for the first time in the street, all hunched and clutching faded coats against the stab of the gale as the men of Laichy converged upon the one place where a woman would never be seen to go, and where a grieving could be shared with those of equal status; maybe even eased a mite by the curative properties of the *uisge beatha* – the mellow water of life itself.

There was a great deal of whisky being taken by four on the

clock of that terrible afternoon in Laichy. In the crowded wee bar of the *Sutherland Arms*.

*

It was not lost on those already bitter men that the sadness of that day should have touched the very refuge of their own lament. The tragedy of the community had been visited, not once but twice on the *Sutherland Arms* itself; for the hurt which numbed others had been doubly inflicted upon the family of the innkeeper, the staunch Neil MacFaid.

When the *Luftwaffe* Stukas had finally swooped from a brassy Cretan sky some three days before, and ripped the vitals from the turning, twisting, spitting HMS *Kendar* like the gut of a herring gouged by a trawlerman's thumb, not one but two of the beloved MacFaid brothers had been trapped with those other Laichy sons within her capsizing hulk.

Which meant that only one sweet pride now remained to continue the line of Neil MacFaid, and his name was Donald. But already he, too, had suffered a savage martyrdom in the service of his country and his King. For the young MacFaid still wore the uniform of a corporal in the Argyll and Sutherland Highlanders at the time of the *Kendar*'s sinking, but in a very short while he would be plain Mister MacFaid again because his presence in Laichy was that of a convalescent . . . he was a part man now, and no more use for the fighting. His good left arm had been torn clean from his shoulder by a shell from a German gun many months before. On a frantic strip of beach remembered as Dunkirk.

And so one further ingredient was added to fuel the fire of Laichy's growing anger, for the wounded Donald MacFaid, still a gallant and impressive figure in his kilt and puttees and high-necked shiny-brass-buttoned khaki with its empty left sleeve pinned neatly across his chest – his very presence there, by virtue of his still-visible pain and resentment, was adding a new dimension to the brooding reflections of his fellow parishioners.

It was Hate that the quiet rage of Donald MacFaid introduced into the Laichy men. Hate, and maybe even a hint of fear of the Germans.

Because there had never *been* Hate before in Laichy, not even during the Great War when the news of bereavements had come on separate occasions and their impact absorbed by the spread of time. Certainly not a proper Hate; the kind that Donald MacFaid had learned; the kind which heats the blood and brings the desire to smite thine enemies as a varnish to a man's lowering brow. Until that day the hate of the village had been as distant as its involvement in the new war; a detached disapproval of the evil ambitions of a foreign man called Hitler as alleged by the almost as foreign English voice of the BBC – to those few of them who even *had* a radio. The only real reminder of the threat from the Godless Hun came in the blackout regulations passed from Kinlochbervie. 'Och man, that German bombing aeroplanes should ever wish to explode a wee, inoffensive place like Laichy?' And, of course, to the fishermen themselves warned of the constant if seldom evinced threat of submarine and mine should they venture beyond the Minch. But they never spoke of that concern to their women. Yon was not a thing a woman's mind could encompass.

Still not a proper hate, though. Not until those few hours had passed since the coming of the telegrams; and many a glass had been taken – maybe a few too many glasses had been taken to salute the memory of their kinsmen never to return into the shadows of Creag Fuar. And then more glasses out of respect for the late Captain, Fergus Scott-Watson of the House of Achnashaig. And even more to do honour to the newest Laird o' Laichy: now Lieutenant David, his son.

Slowly the Hate fomented, and was honed to a keen frustration every time they looked upon the mutilated Donald MacFaid standing firm beside the bowed figure of his stricken father in the *Sutherland Arms*. Every man's thoughts became focused on what the German savages had done to Laichy village; and a desperate wish that he could strike back.

It was seven o'clock in the evening of the 14th January, 1941.

Precisely the time when the glaring red eyes of Mammon himself were first seen to rise from the monstrous seas outside the entrance to Loch Fhadaig.

*

It was McPhee who saw the approach of the Antichrist first; McPhee who was just the third hand on the *Bonnie Lass*, and who should never have spent his pitiful few shillings so quick to drown his sorrow for the poor brother *he* had lost to the bottom of the Mediterranean sea. Because McPhee was a simple-minded soul even when sober, and often spoke wildly about demons and ghoulies and things which went splash in the sea loch of a night.

He always staggered down to the loch when he had partaken too handsomely of the *uisge beatha*, for then McPhee was aye sick to his stomach, which was not to be tolerated in the street outside the *Sutherland Arms* where the true Highlandmen could hold their drink and still walk steady up the hill even whiles their eyes bore the glaze of anaesthesia.

That was why the tattered, spindly figure of McPhee was down there at the harbour wall despite the mourning still being celebrated in the tavern; and while the muffled sobs of women still were heard from behind the closed doors and hooded windows of each cottage as he'd staggered by.

It was only then, after his belly had ceased to heave and all the hard-earned money he'd spent had finally died to a trickle of vomit falling between his splay-bent knees, that he managed to raise his aching, spinning head . . .

. . . to see an unbelievable scene taking place before him – for the eyes of the very Devil himself were coming towards McPhee from out of the Stygian, spray-frantic gloom.

Maybe merely to say that he *saw* it would be an oversimplification. A man doesn't just *see* something of such appalling import – he stares at it. Gapes! Through fear-dulled eyes, widening more and more as the evil thing approaches; snaps into hideous focus . . . explodes upon his brain to leave the imprint of terror.

They were just the eyes at first, mind; flickering and red as the brimstone of hell. Low down and sometimes blinking as a rearing Atlantic roller flung itself high between the heads of Sròine Riabach . . . but the eyes always reappeared, closing remorselessly upon McPhee and fixing him with their malevolence; steadily rising from the black depths of that storm-maddened ocean.

He began to stumble backwards; with his thin white lips working soundlessly and his ashen face a pinched horror at what was coming to fall upon the village. Even though his sole-flapping shoes kept catching in the flakes of net, and every so often his heels would trip unheeded over creels and pots and coils of rope, McPhee kept retreating without once taking his eyes off the coming of the Demon to Laichy.

At last he could make out the hideous bulk of it. Shapeless. Awful in its very anonymity; flickering and seemingly rolling against the blackest night of all black nights. Och, dear God, but it was of a terrible big size. So huge, in fact, that its infernal mass appeared to fill the gap between the heads of Loch Fhadaig; towering almost to the lofty crest of Sròine Riabach itself.

It was then that McPhee first heard Belial's roar. A vast sea; much greater than any he had seen before, came rushing and hissing with such violence that he could detect its approach even a mile away at the other end of the loch . . . and then it exploded against the base of Riabach and flung a hundred feet clear into the storm-ripped night, whereupon the shrieking gale snatched it and crushed it, and flung it down towards McPhee in whirling clouds of spray. But it was the colour of that spray which finally converted McPhee's terror into action – for it was red. Blood red! Red as the Inferno itself from the reflected glare of the Devil's eyes.

And that was when the Antichrist roared. As that great Atlantic sea took the gigantic form of him and swung him with a contempt that told McPhee that surely the Good Lord had maybe come to help at last. Until he saw the monster strike agonisingly into the very rocks of Riabach and shudder, yet continue to enter, even as the scream of a thousand nightmares rent the maelstrom of Fhadaig.

McPhee screamed too. Stood there and screamed for the Meenister Crombie tae come quick, and for a' they God-fearin' souls of Laichy to kneel in prayer because the terrible vengeance of Auld Clootie would surely be visited upon them now.

The wailing from the women's houses faltered, while the angry mutter of the men's voices stilled for a moment from the doorway of the *Sutherland Arms*; for McPhee's shrill plea for deliverance had keened higher than the cry of the wind, and more cutting than the sleet which battered at the rough slate roofs. Then Asmodeus wallowing in from the sea roared again in growing rage as the Lord flung him once more upon the rocks of Sròine Riabach, and thus did smite him with all the Power of His Glory.

Suddenly there was a stunning flash from the eyes of Asmodeus which lit up the whole loch and the very mountainside of Creag Fuar; and he breathed fire and smoke from his nostrils while the boom of his demoniacal fury scattered a million cowering wavelets across the bigger waves of Fhadaig; and the terrible fingers of that same rage went spinning and trailing orange smoke high, high, higher into the racing, storm-black sky . . .

. . . whereupon the undernourished jelly that was McPhee of the *Bonnie Lass* collapsed in a dead faint of whisky-induced hysteria as the ten thousand ton carcass of his devil fell over and began to sink below the waters of Fhadaig.

It was twenty minutes before eight o'clock.

. . . and the real possession of Laichy by the Arch-fiend Lucifer was only just begun.

*

As the rumble of the cataclysm clattered doors and rattled windows and echoed through every room in the hamlet, so people lifted their heads with the shock of it. In the *Sutherland Arms* each angry man blinked speechlessly at his neighbour for a full half minute of fuddled disbelief; and there were many there who debated in their clouded minds the possibility that maybe the world was ending for more than those fine laddies already taken, and this truly was the crack o' doom as forewarned in the Guid Book of the Lord.

For a full half minute. And then there was a concerted rush towards the door which saw the most sober falling into the street first with even the most euphoric but ten seconds after him.

The Reverend Crombie heard it as he was sitting helplessly with the widow Mac an Leister; helplessly, because the knowledge that she was grandmother to Margaret – not only the bonniest lass without dispute in Laichy, but also betrothed to the most eligible boy in the village, the grand Corporal Donald MacFaid of the Argyll and Sutherland Highlanders and a wounded hero to boot – was poor comfort to an old woman on the night she was crying for two male grandchildren, now bloated corpses drifting eerily within the sunken 'Y' gun turret of HMS *Kendar*. Yet even that sorry soul raised her haggard face in agitation at the distant tumult.

Young Lieutenant David heard it up at Achnashaig and immediately recognised the roar for what it was; because the new Laird of Laichy had served as a junior officer in the *Warspite* during the second battle of Narvik Fiord the year previously, and had grown familiar with such violence then.

But the snow was settling deep on the higher ground between Achnashaig and the village by that time, and even though Scott-Watson set out for the loch at once it would take him a long, hard struggle to reach the water's edge. Too long a struggle.

By twenty minutes before eight every soul in Laichy had started for the street in panic. Even the most desperately stricken of all that populace – the recently-wed girls who had learned of their fresh-faced young husbands being torn from them even while their love was still in the first bloom of promise – even those poor lassies rose fearfully in their black dresses and hastened to join the shadowed throng hurrying towards the harbour and a view of Loch Fhadaig.

There they gathered, all those people plucked so unkindly from their mourning, while the wind howled a madness and the snow-sleet an awful scourge; and the torches and the lanterns reflected stunned eyes gazing blankly to see what awfulness had descended upon them. In those first moments there were many more than just McPhee who imagined they might be witnesses to Armageddon.

For indeed it could well have been the sky to roof the bottomless abyss of Pandemonium. What with the constant rumble beating from the hurtling clouds, and the great red and green flashes leaving a pain etched in every staring retina, and the whistling shrieks of Tophet-fire catherine-wheeling in a splay of crazed hysteria from the centre of the loch, while the flickering glare rebounded from the slopes of Creag Fuar to turn even the virgin white snows to a macabre-tinted grue . . .

'The people that walked in darkness have seen a great light . . .'

Minister Crombie was kneeling now with many round about, with tightly closed eyes and careless of the frozen ground which cut frail knees in the agonies of Calvary. The Reverend was not a brave man and had no idea of what was happening to them, but the words of Isaiah came keenly to his mind and at least they formed a prayer most appropriate.

'. . . they that dwell in the land of the shadow of death, upon *them* hath the light shined . . .'

A girl began sobbing, while a ripple of terror ran through the watching crowd. The drink in the men and the sadness in the women already confused them enough without this added trauma. They were ill-educated people; good people raised in earnest belief of God's infinite compassion, yet simultaneously thundered at from the pulpit of the kirk each Sunday with the promise of eternal damnation to any who strayed from the prescribed path of the Lord.

And so the panic grew substance. For if any man had ever gazed upon a diversion guiding him straight to Hell, then surely he was seeing it in Loch Fhadaig on that night of sorrow and fear. And you would not be shown the signpost unless you were expecting to travel down the road?

'The Wicked One is coming!'

'Auld Horny . . . out o' Fhadaig! Tae punish us . . .'

''Tis the Apocalypse!'

'Run! Run for your lives fae the Cloven Hoof!'

It was young Donald MacFaid who arrested their incipient flight. MacFaid the corporal in the Argylls, stood staunch before them with his one remaining arm protectively around the shoulders of his Margaret. Donald MacFaid, whose severed stump proved intimacy with the violence of man-made bomb and shell and bullet, and who had already suffered the true knowledge of what hellfire and damnation really is.

'Is it all of you taken leave of your senses?' he cried. 'Those are only explosions out there. That is a *ship* in the loch . . . a great ship in from the sea.'

But even a ship? In Fhadaig? Man, there had never been such a ship ever seen by most in Laichy; only the men who went out into the Minches after the herring had viewed a real ship before, and even then mainly the steam ferries which plied the harbours of the long Hebridean islands to the west. Never had any vessel larger than a drifter ventured into Fhadaig, for while it was a true sea loch and twenty-seven fathoms deep in its middle no captain would dare risk the broiling narrow gap off Sròine Riabach merely to bring his command to Laichy. There had never been a reason for such folly before.

Yet there was one in it now! As their eyes were guided by the understanding that it was created by men and not by their own fear, they could detect her long black silhouette, with the mast and the high rounded stern which seemed to rise even higher as they gazed in awe; and the vast funnel canting forward and sideways; and her navigating bridge falling over monstrously to meet the foam-swept surface . . . and the glaring eyes of her which had never been the Devil's eyes at all but the fires which raged against her centrecastle and in her afterhold from where the explosions had erupted – gradually those fires were being extinguished as the near-freezing sea poured leaping and raging and thundering in its remorseless occupancy. As the flames were overwhelmed, so clouds of steam began to pour upwards from Fhadaig instead, and enormous gouts of boiling water jetted high into the sky.

It was ironic that those open-mouthed parishioners of Laichy, while not even realising it was an ordinary ship out there at first, were still better informed than the rest of the world on that occasion. They still provided the only audience there ever would be. To the otherwise secret dying of Captain Herschell's *Highlander*. In the sea loch of Fhadaig.

*

No one person initiated it; it was a movement of the mass, but suddenly they began to drift towards the nearest point to where the great ship was foundering. 'Aileach,' the cry went up. 'Take yourselves to the wee stony beach at Aileach.'

The Reverend Crombie, still kneeling in prayer – though for what and for whom he was no longer certain – opened his eyes to see the tail of his flock streaming away from him in straggling disarray. It made no difference that he creaked to his feet and uttered a plea for calm . . . there was a strange relief from sadness into madness striking Laichy in that moment; and not even his appeal to remember their own fresh dead was enough to halt that growing stampede.

So the whole village hastened along the narrow, storm-swept path above the rising cliffs. In the dying fires from the loch and the flickering, swinging glow from lanterns raised high to pierce the blackness you would have seen a disordered line of running, stumbling souls headed now by the grim-faced Donald MacFaid striding hugely in his Highland uniform; and with the men in their good suits soaked shiny black by the sleet, and the young women and the old women with their loose funereal mourning billowing and whirling uncaringly as they hurried . . . and the panting, growing excitement constantly snatched to unintelligible vowels by the skirl of the giant west wind; and the very old women merely able to gasp as their children harried them to greater effort.

It was just as the very last and slowest of them – Minister Crombie himself – had skittered to the bottom of the steep path down to Aileach that the final explosion came: a detonation which stopped every man and woman dead with the clattering trickles of displaced scree still tumbling down behind them. Then, as they stared across the convulsing waters of Fhadaig, they saw the denser shadow of the Motor Vessel *Highlander* lie wearily, belatedly on to its side and begin to slide faster and faster into the snatching waves. And as it went the funnel – which was bigger than any cottage in the whole of Laichy – began to break away and tumble forward too; and the aftermast collapsed and pressurising ventilators began to screech, and the steam jetted whiter than the pure spindrift . . . before there was a second convulsion; from under the water this time – a giant boiling which reared and gouted spears of foam to shield the disappearing stern.

And when that had died, and the surface of Fhadaig had returned to being an ordinary nightmare of frantic water, there *was* no ship; there was nothing. Except for the blackest blackness of all, and the wind. And a new tension.

Because abruptly the excitement faltered. Maybe it was aggravated by the misery of the weather; maybe by the fact that the funereal gloom blanketing the once more empty loch had jolted them too savagely back to awareness of their own collective bereavement. Whatever it was, their brief diversion from hard reality was ended, and the return of it struck even more bitter than before.

Together they huddled on exposed Aileach and gazed dully into the future, without even summoning the effort to retreat. All the time the breakers smashed thunderously against the rocks and the sea spray itself formed a white wall constantly curving above them as the force of the Atlantic blasts ripped it in a sigh against the looming cliffs behind. A young lass began to cry again, and then another . . . the grief of Laichy had reached its most acute.

MacFaid still stared over the loch, the one arm the Germans had left to him clasping the shoulders of his beautiful Margaret. Had any man had time for anything but his own sair reflection, then he would have seen that Donald MacFaid was listening; and not just to the shriek of the wind.

Abruptly the corporal tensed; stiffened alert with keen grey eyes ignoring the scourge of sleet to probe the walls of advancing water. Before he swung round anxiously; his sharp command carrying across the distraught sobs of women.

'*Listen*! Each and every one of you . . . listen!'

Even the Reverend Crombie moving wearily through his

flock with his ineffectual love for them, and his inability to be of comfort to them in this time when he should have been the greatest help, even he felt compelled to turn and obey the voice of Donald MacFaid.

Until everything was silence other than the steady roar of the sea.

And then they heard the men.

Or what surely must have been men, out there in the raging water; because the sounds which carried to them at first were recognisable only by the aroma of human fear that accompanied them. And the nature of those sounds struck a chill into hearts already numbed with misery . . . desperate, terrified sounds. The retching, choking gurgles of men with lungs already filling; the racking coughs from burning, swallowed fuel oil; the cries of the tormented and the nearly-drowned; of agony distilled and endurance already over-killed.

The pitiful hopelessness of the shocked, burned, baby-weak survivors from *Highlander*, who had struggled valiantly to within a spit of safety only to have been cast upon the cruel waters of Fhadaig.

Slowly, the first of them to reach the firm ground of Aileach staggered from the surf. Somehow he sensed the people waiting for he stopped and opened his arms imploringly, etched before them against the hanging backcloth of the spray; a blackened, oil-saturated silhouette in the attitude of the Crucifixion . . .

A horrified murmur rose as men, women, even wee children moved to aid him. Until . . .

'. . . *Zorg voor me als't je belieft!*' the hideous man-wrack bubbled.

Whereupon those who had moved forward to embrace a soul infinitely more distressed than even they themselves, stopped dead. And stared. While the import of that alien tongue struck deep into every listening ear.

'Zorg voor me als't JE BELIEFT . . .' the object retched again. 'Please look after me . . .'

But the unfamiliar English words never reached the slack mouth of Third Officer van der Kroon, because he had never been able to speak his adopted language very well even when fit, while now he was exhausted and past any thought at all. But no one watching could ever have imagined a situation like that . . . not finding a Dutchman on Aileach. From a British ship!

'Yon is a German speaking . . .' a voice muttered nervously from the crowd. 'Yon's a bluidy German!'

And that was an equally excusable mistake; because if you were a Laichy man and had never been south of Kinlochbervie in your life, then you would detect little difference between the Dutch and the teutonic languages; maybe even Chinese, for that matter. And this was a time in the war when not only those in remote Scottish villages were falling prey to fanciful rumours; there were many in the cities and even in the great houses of the land who were quick to seize upon the outrageous and accept it without question – mysterious signals were being flashed from the schoolhouse roof; 'Nazi paratroopers are being dropped in the disguise of country vicars . . .' or, even more excitingly, '. . . as *nuns*! With their Schmeisser machine-pistols concealed under the flowing lines of their habits!'

Was it surprising, then, that the confused and credulous minds of the naive inhabitants of Laichy were quick to seize upon, and compound, that first hysterical assumption? Suddenly an ugly stir ran through the good people gazing upon the unrecognisable creature that was Third Officer Jan van der Kroon of the Motor Vessel *Highlander*. The compassion which had met him as he'd floundered from Fhadaig evaporated; only the unreasoning rage of their bereavement was left to flood the cavity in each of those ill-informed souls.

Even MacFaid himself felt the anger. But then MacFaid's reason was impaired because not only had he lost his good right arm but also, now, his brothers; and MacFaid already possessed the Hate. The Germans had taught him that themselves on the beaches of Dunkirk.

But nobody actually *did* anything. Not even then.

Van der Kroon stumbled another step and turned, blindly listening to the raspings of his drowning shipmates in their struggle for Aileach. Blindly, because Third Officer van der Kroon was sightless; his eyes burned cruelly with the thick fuel oil exploded from *Highlander*'s after tanks.

'*Min oogen doen pign* . . .' he appealed. 'My eyes are hurting me . . .'

'They killed my Jamie,' a girl shrieked suddenly. 'The Germans; they killed my darling Jamie!'

The storm squealed a fresh excitement while the waves pounded a new peak of dreadfulness upon the beach; rushing and gurgling and snatching around van der Kroon's reeling, bloodied legs as if trying even harder to reclaim him. Suddenly there were MORE men attempting to crawl from the boiling surf; vomiting, pleading mutely, quite past saving themselves . . . it truly was the Devil's time at last.

'My bonnie David,' a whisky-maudlin father crooned distraughtly. 'Yon Nazis kilt him too wi' their bombs!'

'And my fair-haired Charlie. And Alisdair McGeoch who was barely married on to Shona afore they plucked him fae her . . .'

'The evil ones. The German ones!'

'*Zorg voor me als't je belieft* . . . !' Third Officer van der Kroon of the Motor Vessel *Highlander* screamed beseechingly, conscious then of a terror far greater than he had known even when his ship blew up beneath him. '*ZORG VOOR MEEEE* . . .'

It was the distracted widow Mac an Leister who struck the first blow. Only a tiny one; a denunciatory gesture of grief lapped out by an old woman without the strength to hurt. But it was still enough . . . and the Devil had squeezed the trigger of Laichy's mourning.

Even while the horrified Minister Crombie was opening his lips to implore them to reason the crowd surged forward, pushing him aside. Their harpy-shrieks swamped his disbelieving cries as the next fist struck towards the pathetic focus of their Hate. And then the next. And the next . . . until the mutilated thing that had once been Third Officer van der Kroon was hideously lifted; plucked aloft by frenzied clawing hands, and cast back into the bloody waters of Fhadaig.

A chilling cackle went up and was ripped by the gale. 'The Germans! Kill the Germans!'

'An eye for an eye . . . revenge for our braw drowned laddies!'

Not one of the glaring, snarling suddenly-possessed of Laichy paid heed to the shouts from the cliff top where the newly arrived Laird David stood, transfixed by revulsion at their maniac work. It truly was a scene from the Inferno of the Damned – with young and old all ghastly under the flickering light from the lanterns; the berserk men, the poor widowed lassies wailing their deprived malevolence, the venerable elderly of Laichy who now appeared only as demented hags with their twisted, obscene masks and their whirling black-witch rags.

The next uncomprehending victim was dragged savagely from the surf; hauled dully unprotesting across serrated spurs of rock, for when the fall of the Bren-gun carrier *had* finally detonated the fireball within *Highlander*'s belly, number three lifeboat had barely managed to pull the length of a heaving line away from her towering sides. The explosion had spat a lick of searing flame across that inadequate gap to shock and maim all but two of its occupants; because Able Seaman Gillan and Fireman Cullen were neither shocked nor maimed in that initial holocaust but simply decapitated by a great scything steel plate which skip-stoned across the heaving waters and across them. And then there were only eight survivors from the Motor Vessel *Highlander* still striving for the shore through the red-lick whirlpool of her going.

Bosun McColl was that second arrival. Even then he had maintained his courage – even when the boat itself capsized as it slewed beam-on to the pounding surf of Aileach he had continued to roar giant encouragement despite the upper parts of his body being roasted from the flash. Until, that was, the snatching hands of Laichy pulled the flesh like the cooked meat it was from the bones of his arms as they clawed him through the rock, whereupon even Bosun McColl lost the power to use his native tongue and could only whimper in the international language of excruciating pain as the good people killed him in the mania of their possession.

Third they despatched the resolute Chief Officer William McLeod, who was fortunate and never knew what his fellow men were doing to him, because his right leg had been blown off at the knee and he was already unconscious when Jimmie Beattie of all unlikely heroes dragged him ashore. Jimmie himself never had time to enjoy being a hero though, or to suffer the ultimate terror of the others, for he was too busy kneeling and kissing the ground of his beloved terra firma and promising that fae now on he wis definitely gaun tae be a *soldier* f'r the rest o' the war, because sodgers never had tae go on bluidy boats – when his turn came, and a massive rock wielded by a once-kind Highlandman caved in the back of his frizzled skull.

Fourth Officer Findlay only discovered that there were worse things than the power of the North Atlantic when it was far too late. In fact he was still trying to smile his dumb gratitude through a grisly hood of scorched and peeling skin at the moment of his death. Quartermaster Hotchkiss just didn't believe what was happening to him after all the effort he'd made to ensure that little Apprentice Beedie at least managed to reach the shore – only to discover the two of them immediately forced back and held under water until the sea did finally complete its self-appointed task.

Stare-eyed little Beedie believed it, though, and that was perhaps the most awful thing of all, because he had been so proud to be a British seaman and thus felt the disillusionment more keenly than any other murdered man from *Highlander*. Except that he couldn't have explained to anybody that what they were doing to him wasn't really fair, even if they hadn't been drowning him at the time, because his child-pink lungs were already too far corroded and black as the Pit with the diesel slime which choked him.

Apprentice Beedie was the seventh pathetic flotsam creature to be smashed back into the freezing clasp of Fhadaig by the Hate even while Scott-Watson was still driving himself down the scree path in bellowing appeal. The only remaining soul of sanity by then was the shock-eyed Reverend Crombie; but even he had ceased to pluck unavailingly at the backs of his rabid flock and bowed helplessly, mouthing a prayer as inadequate as he himself had proved in the end.

'Forgive Thy children, Merciful Father, for they know not what they do!'

And so the last spectre of all emerged from Fhadaig to stumble haltingly through the surf of Aileach. This final man was perhaps the most dreadfully injured of any, with his gaping wounds already oozing red through the grue of foulness shrouding him. Yet incredibly he still clung to a bright yellow oilskin bag; and just for a moment the slackly vacant faces parted before his grim approach. He must have sensed that something abominable had already occurred – the animal stench of that terrible happening hung more culpably than any words – yet he seemed to drag himself erect, and stare fearlessly about him through bleach-white eyes in a black shining mask . . . and cast upon them all an awful condemnation.

Too late did the wild MacFaid detect the four dulled rings of gold upon the last man's cuff; gleaming barely through the fuel oil mulch. And recognise the diamond shape within and understand it for what it signified – because the captain of the gallant ship which had once saved him from a beach called Dunkirk had borne such rings; only *he* was standing firm on the bridge of a British merchantman!

Even as that final valiant man was overwhelmed by the grieving-hate of Laichy, and clawed and pummelled into broken obscenity with the yellow bag flung carelessly aside on Aileach, McFaid was already raving for them to stop . . . to *hold*!

. . . only it was too late by then. Far, far too late.

To preserve the life of Captain Jonathan Herschell; the last of those wartime merchant sailors who had struggled to bring *Highlander* into the haven of Loch Fhadaig. And some of whom had survived every hazard the Devil had cast before them.

Except for the good people themselves. Of a quiet wee village called Laichy.

EPILOGUE

I sat for a long time after Hamish Stewart had completed his history; just sitting in the quiet of that tiny kirk with the Log Book of *Highlander*'s last voyage open before me and only Fran's gentle sadness to break the silence.

I finally had discovered the secret of the sextant. It was a secret I would have been better never to have pried into. I only had to glance at the harrowed eyes of Laichy's present minister to understand that he, too, had borne his awful trust only after an agony of heart-searching and a martyrdom of recurring doubt. But the Reverend Stewart was merely a custodian; nothing more. And his duty had been to protect his charges, not to crucify them.

Mine wasn't.

Yet I fully realised what it would do, should the truth ever be broadcast. Laichy's collective bereavement had also been my own. But in their case had followed Laichy's hideous guilt and ultimately – for I never questioned that it *did* still continue – Laichy's forty years of community punishment through the strain of their fears for each other. The sins of the elders . . .

Hamish Stewart stirred as though reading my mind. His voice was quiet and resigned.

'*Delicta maiorum immeritus lues*, Captain. Typically instanced in young Fiona MacFaid's case . . . "Though guiltless, you must expiate your father's sins!" Had any action – *were* any action to be taken against those implicated who remain alive today, and there are still many, then it would strike to the heart of the whole village; as much now as did the deaths of those boys when *Kendar* was lost. We are one family, John; and what hurts one of us is, by definition, a cruel blow to us all.'

'It was a cruel blow to my mother,' I said dully. 'And to seven other families of *Highlander*'s crew who died unnecessarily.'

'Would they feel better for knowing? Would anything be gained by punishing a whole community now; when the majority of them weren't even born when it happened? They weren't wicked people, you know, the last generation of this village. They were kindly souls who faltered. I quote again – *Indignor quandoque bonus dormitat Homerus*. "But if Homer, who is good, nods for a moment I think it a shame!"'

'Anger is a brief madness,' Fran whispered miserably.

The young minister looked at her in surprise. 'Then you've read Horace too, Francine?'

'A long time ago,' she replied. She was watching me by then and I knew what she was willing me to say. But I felt sick; too sick for forgiveness.

'What happened to . . . the bodies?' I asked.

'They were brought here, to this church, when the awfulness of what they had done dawned on those tormented people. For two days, John, until the storm had gone, they kept constant vigil over your father and his crew. The whole village watched over them, the old and the young . . . in a way they shared their grief for their own blood with *Highlander*'s crew. Your father *was* mourned, believe me. They were all mourned as one; all those gallant men of the sea.'

'And then what?'

'*Highlander*'s dead were taken down to the harbour on the third night; and they say the street was lined with bowed heads and the crying of women . . . and they were placed aboard the *Morag Jean*.'

'Alisdair McLeod's boat? Your present Session Clerk?'

'His father's craft then. It was forty years ago, mind? But

248

his son has carried the memory of it ever since. And protected it. Even as an old man himself.'

'Which was why he, too, concealed the real place of Charlie's accident,' Fran echoed. 'And Lieutenant Scott-Watson . . . his was the same reason. Only he's a retired commander now, and an elderly man as well. God, but he must have suffered – the knowledge which he held yet never reported; not even as a serving Naval officer.'

'He's also the Laird,' Hamish said quietly. 'He and I, we have a common responsibility.'

'So my father *was* buried at sea after all,' I muttered.

'With all the dignity and care of the Church, John. In the middle of that night and even then with the possibility of the U-boat which had torpedoed *Highlander* herself still being in the area . . . but they held on until well off the entrance to Fhadaig; the old and the young McLeods, Scott-Watson, Donald MacFaid.'

'MacFaid?'

'He had demanded to go. Even as a wounded soldier and not a true man of the sea he still insisted on paying a last sad homage . . . and so they were interred, with the Reverend Crombie to perform the last rites. They did everything they could, John. With reverence and love.'

'Does Donald have any idea that we know, Hamish?' Fran asked. 'Has he guessed why we came at all?'

Stewart's face was grave. 'No. But he has another concern now. I don't believe he will care one way or another what happens to him after Margaret has gone.'

My fingers gripped the Log with savage resentment. I couldn't forgive; not even when fully aware of the misery it would resurrect I couldn't forgive Laichy for what it had done!

'I can understand the cairn at Aileach now, and the eight extra poppies. I even accept that they are sincere memorials and maintained with that reverence you speak of . . . but they are anonymous. And the oil from what few unruptured tanks *Highlander* must still hold after all this time – that'll dissipate soon, too; and then there will be nothing to betray her existence. So why did they keep the sextant? And this Log? Presumably they were found in the oilskin bag my father carried ashore. Yet they – Crombie, MacFaid, Scott-Watson . . . the whole village – must have realised they were relics which could bring everything to public knowledge at any time. Why jeopardise the secret unnecessarily?'

'Because no man or woman in the whole of Laichy could bring themselves to destroy them, John. It's as simple as that. They knew the agonies your father must have suffered in his struggle to swim ashore while burdened with that heavy bag. And they sensed the importance of them to him. Oh, the Log Book may have been his master's duty in part, yes. But the sextant? That was something he loved so much he even risked his life to try to save.'

'And so it's been part of the altar of St Andrew's Church ever since,' Fran breathed, with the tears sparkling afresh in her lovely eyes.

I stood up and took her hand. Stewart must have guessed we were leaving Laichy and watched expressionlessly as I lifted *Highlander*'s Log and led her to the door. It was only then he called after me, and I could hear the compassion in his young voice.

'John?'

I stopped; turned. 'Reverend?'

'Please . . . Would you delay telling the authorities? Just for a while?'

'How long a while?'

'Until Margaret MacFaid is . . . in the keeping of the Lord. It would be a kindness beyond any other you could show, John. And not required for very long now.'

I felt Fran's hand squeeze mine, and suddenly I knew what love really was. And sadness. And how closely they were linked, not only with us but also in the hearts of Donald and Fiona MacFaid.

'I have a four month voyage due,' I said. 'I'll do nothing. Until then.'

The last thing I saw as we left Laichy on that dreich November day was the tall white column of the war memorial before the little harbour. And its fresh green wreath of remembrance.

With the eight extra Flanders poppies. As red as the blood in my veins.

*

It was early April before we returned to Laichy. I had another seemingly endless voyage behind me, and an eternity of lying awake in my berth and staring sightlessly up at the deckhead as I'd listened once again to the ghosts of that crew of long dead sailormen.

And to the voice of a very special spirit as well. For Charlie would always symbolise a ninth red poppy in that wreath; even though he hadn't fought in any war other than my own.

We stopped Fran's car outside the church and walked slowly towards the door of the manse. It was the same door that a policeman had approached with heavy heart over four decades before. Hamish Stewart opened it, and I noted his apprehension immediately he recognised us.

'Well, John?' was all he said, though.

I held out the tattered Log of the Motor Vessel *Highlander*, and the old rosewood box engraved with the legend JONATHAN HERSCHELL. I'd already cleaned the sextant within. And blinked a little as I did so.

'Look after them,' I said quietly, 'and pass them into the keeping of your successor, Hamish. Because they belong to Laichy now. With all my forgiveness, and my love.'

We were staying at the *Sutherland Arms* – and for a whole two weeks this time. Donald MacFaid's soft voice had been delighted and welcoming when I made the booking on the phone. We knew we had a true friend, whenever we passed by.

We stopped for a moment of reflection at the mossy grave of the Reverend Crombie; but we had another pilgrimage to make, and it didn't lie far beyond.

To Our Beloved Wife and Mother

MARGARET MACFAID

In God's Eternal Mercy

We stared at it silently for a long time, and then Fran suddenly caught her breath.

'Look, John!' she called.

It was a tiny green plant, just peeping through the grass beside the grave.

'*Primula scotica!*' she said. And began to cry.

Her tears didn't last long, though. Because I kissed them away, right there and then in the little churchyard of Laichy, in Sutherland.

Just as the sun peeped over the great slope of Creag Fuar and a billion tiny wavelets sparkled in the sea loch of Fhadaig.

And the happy time came back for Fran and I.

Brian Callison

'There can be no better adventure writer in the country today.' *Alistair MacLean*

'One of the best writers of modern sea stories.' *Daily Telegraph*

FONTANA PAPERBACKS

Fontana Paperbacks

Fontana is a leading paperback publisher of fiction and non-fiction, with authors ranging from Alistair MacLean, Agatha Christie and Desmond Bagley to Solzhenitsyn and Pasternak, from Gerald Durrell and Joy Adamson to the famous Modern Masters series.

In addition to a wide-ranging collection of internationally popular writers of fiction, Fontana also has an outstanding reputation for history, natural history, military history, psychology, psychiatry, politics, economics, religion and the social sciences.

All Fontana books are available at your bookshop or newsagent; or can be ordered direct. Just fill in the form and list the titles you want.

FONTANA BOOKS, Cash Sales Department, G.P.O. Box 29, Douglas, Isle of Man, British Isles. Please send purchase price, plus 8p per book. Customers outside the U.K. send purchase price, plus 10p per book. Cheque, postal or money order. No currency.

NAME (Block letters) _____

ADDRESS _____

_____

_____
